# Deadly Diamonds

Also by John F. Dobbyn

Neon Dragon
Frame-Up
Black Diamond

# Deadly Diamonds

A Novel

# John F. Dobbyn

Oceanview Publishing
Longboat Key, Florida

Dobbyn,
John

ISBN: 978-1-60809-092-1

Published in the United States of America by Oceanview Publishing,
Longboat Key, Florida
www.oceanviewpub.com

10 9 8 7 6 5 4 3 2 1

PRINTED IN THE UNITED STATES OF AMERICA

I can't help wondering if this book or any of the others would ever have been written if it had not been for the joy and inspiration and faith and love I see in the eyes of the one who gives everything in my life real meaning. She is my first reader of every word and the one I want to please more than anyone on earth. I love her more than I thought possible. My bride and adventure mate and title-writer and very closest pal. I thank God for My Lois.

# PART ONE

# CHAPTER ONE

October 2012

It was two a.m. when I pried my fingers off the keys of the piano at Big Daddy Hightower's Boston Jazz Club. I groped my way through the darkness around tables of die-hard listeners toward the anticipated smack of crisp autumn air outside. On the way out, I owed a quick wave of gratitude to Sonny, one of Boston's top ten bartenders, for the evening's flow of Famous Grouse Scotch.

As I leaned over the bar to catch Sonny's eye, I felt an arm around my shoulder the size of a wrestler's leg. I thought it was Daddy Hightower, owner of the club and legendary jazz bassist, saying, as he always did, "See you next Monday, Mickey." Only Daddy could make "Mickey" an acceptable nickname for "Michael."

It was a jolt to look back into blue eyes under flaming red hair on a six-foot six-inch titan who could only be a descendant of ancestors from the Emerald Isle. The grin on his face was, at first, comforting. The point of the blade just below my ribcage less so.

The accent was unmistakably South Boston Irish.

"No unfriendliness intended, Mr. Knight. Consider this a gentlemanly invitation. Unless, of course, you've a mind to decline."

I was frozen to the spot. I could feel the blade penetrating two layers of clothing and working through one layer of skin.

"I'm inclined to accept. Could I ask what 'gentleman' sends the invitation?"

"I think not. If he wanted you to know, he'd deliver it in person now wouldn't he? Shall we be on our way?"

The arm on my shoulder turned me away from the bar in the direction of the door. I braced in that position for a second and showed him my empty hands. "Let me just do this."

I reached slowly into my pocket and pulled out a twenty dollar bill between two fingers. I waved it at Sonny down the bar and tossed it in his direction. "Good night, Sonny. Tell Daddy it was cool. Especially, the Cole Porter."

I could feel the blade begin to make more serious inroads. It was now through at least a second layer of skin.

"To be clear, Mr. Knight, I'm under instructions to deliver you in one piece. I could improvise on that if you get cute. Are we on the same page?"

"I'm not being cute. I tip Sonny every week. He'd be offended if I didn't. Make sense?"

His only answer was to usher me in lockstep toward the door. I slowed our movement as much as I dared. The darkness of the club made it impossible to make out anything but moving silhouettes. I knew if we cleared the door, I was down the rabbit hole and no way back. I also knew that if that knife went in much farther, I'd be beyond caring.

In the slowest steps I could manage, we reached the door. I could visualize the sign, "Abandon hope all ye who—"

In that instant of incipient panic before the final step through the door, I felt the arm fly off my shoulder. I tumbled off balance onto the floor. My first instinct was to roll as far from the door as I could get, but I found myself frozen against a still form that was massive enough to block any movement. My second instinct was to scramble to my feet and grab the nearest chair for support.

Before I could do either, the lights came up, and I saw my six-foot-eight-inch guardian angel, Big Daddy Hightower, standing over the unconscious form of my Irish escort.

"I'll never understand your taste in friends, Mickey. Who's your buddy?"

It took a few seconds to get my voice out of soprano. "Thank you, Daddy. You were quick on the uptake. You got my message."

I wanted to thank Sonny too. He and I had an agreement for a lobster dinner at Durgin-Park twice a year on me in lieu of weekly tips. When I threw him the twenty, he knew something was off. He must have gotten the word about the bozo with his arm around me to Big Daddy, who remembered that the only Cole Porter we'd played all night was, "I've Got You Under My Skin." Daddy apparently put it together as I prayed.

I propped up against the end of the bar and took a minute of breath catching. "Let's let him catch a nap, Daddy. Would you check him for weapons? He's got at least one knife with a wet blade."

Daddy did a quick body search and tossed me his billfold. His driver's license showed a South Boston address and the name of Paddy O'Toole.

I speed-dialed the number of a particular security service that I could literally trust with my life. In the two years that I'd partnered with the redoubtable lion of the criminal bar, Lex Devlin, to give legal defense to some strange clients in some strange walks of life, I'd had more than one occasion to do just that. In spite of the hour, Tom Burns caught it on the first ring.

"What's up, Mike?"

"Sorry to break your sleep, Tom. I need a good man, not without artillery, *post-haste*."

"I never sleep, Mike. You know that. Where?"

"Daddy's. How soon?"

"I just sent the message. Do you want him seen or unseen?"

"Seen. Tell him to come in. I'll wait."

"You won't wait long. He's almost there. He was in the neighborhood."

"You're golden, Tom. What's his name?"

"Depends on what he has to do to get you out of the fine mess you've gotten yourself into this time. Probably best you didn't know. Call him 'Charlie.' He likes that name."

I turned around and the open door was filled with the form of yet another giant. Charlie had arrived. At my mere six foot one, I was beginning to feel like the runt of the litter.

"Charlie, can you bring this bozo back to consciousness?"

I had sorted through the options that seemed obvious. First and most desirable—get the hell out of Dodge. Not actually the best choice. Whatever and whoever put Paddy O'Toole's arm around my back in the first place would still be out there, and as a criminal trial lawyer, I'd be readily accessible to a second try.

The second option, less desirable, but safest in the long run, was to accept the invitation of whoever sent him—but on my terms. Charlie scooped up the now-groggy disarmed body of my escort and propped him against the bar.

I asked Sonny for a straight shot of Jameson's Irish Whiskey and waved it under his nose. It speeded the process. When he was back to consciousness, I handed him the shot. He eyed it with suspicion, but the familiar scent led him to down it in one gulp.

"Good morning, Paddy. Now that you've had breakfast, let's finish your mission. It's not the most gracious invitation I've ever had, but I'm going to accept it. Let's go."

Paddy was the dictionary picture of ambivalence. The obvious question that stood out on his furrowed brow was whether or not to lead me to his undisclosed principal under the reversal of circumstances. I had to get him off dead center.

I handed him his cell phone, which was among the items Daddy found in his pockets.

"Call the man. Tell him I'm willing to come. It's his play."

He hit a speed-dial number and mumbled into the phone. Based on the flow of Gaelic invectives that must have strained the cell phone's little earpiece, his principal did not suffer the turn of events gladly.

I grabbed the phone out of his hand. "This is Michael Knight."

Abrupt silence. I continued. "I don't know who you are, but, apparently, you know me, and we seem to have business. I don't do command performances. On the other hand, if you want to meet and talk nice, I'll be all ears. What'll it be?"

More silence. I gave him a minute to get a grip on the change of procedure.

"Mr. Knight, I'll apologize for the inappropriate beginning. I'm used to dealing with a more crude element. And time is definitely of the essence."

I could sense a distinct elevation in the level of intelligence. There was a calm in the voice that encouraged a second beginning. In a public place.

"How immediate is the problem? How about breakfast tomorrow morning?"

"No, Mr. Knight. I think not."

"Then where and when?"

"Are you familiar with South Boston?"

"Are you familiar with Beacon Hill?" I was still not comfortable with the idea of meeting on his playing field.

"Won't do, Mr. Knight. There's something you should see. Understand, this is in the nature of a professional engagement. You'll be paid. Extravagantly."

That gave me more jitters than O'Toole's arm around my shoulder. "I think you better understand. I'm a lawyer. Maybe not the type you're used to. I intend to keep my bar membership intact. I think this conversation is coming to a close."

"A moment, Mr. Knight. I know your reputation. I'm asking nothing that will, shall we say, tarnish it. That said, I think you'll find this one of the more interesting meetings of your career."

Now he had me. What I may lack in physical dominance, I, unfortunately, make up in raw curiosity. More than once, it's driven me into what the Chinese curse refers to as "an interesting life."

"Then where?"

"Please put Mr. O'Toole back on the line. He'll be a more courteous escort in the future."

Before handing the phone over, there was one more question burning a hole in the curiosity lobe of my brain.

"And just to prepare me for the meeting, your name is?"

"All in good time, Mr. Knight."

# CHAPTER TWO

It was past three a.m. when our little convoy pulled up outside the Slainte Pub on L Street in South Boston. It appeared closed, as the law required at that hour. Paddy led me and my adopted shadow, Charlie, to a side entrance. We climbed a set of well-worn steps to a second floor office. Paddy rapped once. A voice I recognized from the phone conversation gave a brusque, "Get in here, Paddy."

A seriously subdued Paddy led the way. I followed quickly enough to catch the daggered look toward Paddy from the sixtyish, white-haired individual rising to stand behind the desk. From a physical perspective, Paddy could clearly have bounced his five-foot, roundish body across the floor like a basketball. Equally clearly, that one look sent Paddy hulking to the side of the room like a cowed pup.

I was next in. The hand extended across the desk bode a warmer welcome than that given to my thuggish escort, Paddy. On the other hand, when my other escort, Charlie, came through the door behind me, the look froze and the hand retracted, leaving no doubt that Charlie was not only uninvited, but unwelcome.

"Mr. Knight, you and I have business. It's private. I thought I implied that. Who's this?"

We stood facing each other, Charlie behind me with his hands in his overcoat pockets, clutching heaven-knows-what form of artillery and giving me a sense of well-being that I didn't fancy doing without.

"Call him 'Charlie.' He likes that name. Given the tone of your invitation—" I glanced over at Paddy, who had gone from cowering to sulking. "—you can consider Charlie a permanent attachment. If that doesn't work for you, I say we part friends. Your choice."

The reddening of his complexion from the collar up indicated that he was more used to giving the choices—probably to those without options. Whatever caused him to think he needed me apparently put the lid on his natural instincts. A hand shot across the desk. I nearly jumped into Charlie's arms until I realized it was the offer of a handshake.

"Mr. Knight, we're off to a bad start. Let's begin again. Have a seat, please."

Based on the fact that the hand did not hold a gun, I accepted the courtesy. Before sitting, however, I needed some ground rules. I remained standing.

"Mr. Knight, I give you my word, you're in no danger. My man here—" Another withering glance at Paddy, for whom I was developing unexplainable sympathy "—lacks the gentility to convey the tone I intended. I have a simple favor to ask. Again, you'll be paid handsomely."

"I'd be more convinced if I knew your name."

A smile cracked the previously rigid features as he rose from the chair and approached Paddy. "I'm surprised you need to ask, Mr. Knight. However—"

He took Paddy by the elbow and led him to the door. "Paddy, be a good man. Take Charlie here downstairs to the bar. Anything he'd like. And Paddy, please, like a gentleman."

He looked back at me to see how the plan went down. It was a gamble, but again curiosity trumped fear. I nodded to Charlie, who showed clear hesitation. He was under orders from Tom Burns, not me, and most certainly not our host.

"It's all right, Charlie. This is why we came. I'll be down shortly." To emphasize it, I accepted the offer of a seat.

Reluctantly, Charlie followed Paddy down the stairs. I'd have bet my Bruins season tickets that nothing liquid passed his lips while he waited.

My host closed the door. He came back and leaned his backside on the desk in front of me. There were deep lines forming in his forehead above the white eyebrows that I couldn't quite figure, given the relative strengths of our positions.

Our proximity let him lower the tone to just above a whisper. "Do you have children, Mr. Knight?"

"Never married. And, again, this would be easier if I knew your name."

He nodded and walked around to sit behind the desk. "You're obviously not from South Boston. Can you tell me the name Frank O'Byrne means nothing to you?"

The words, "Oh, crap," bubbled up in my throat but never made it to the vocal chords. For the ten years I'd taken an interest in any part of the *Boston Globe* that didn't concern the Bruins or Red Sox, the name, Frank O'Byrne, was constantly linked with the word "allegedly," as in "allegedly the boss of all criminal activity in the Irish communities of South Boston, Charlestown, and Dorchester."

The expression on my face made playing dumb a nonoption. "Your reputation precedes you, Mr. O'Byrne."

"Good. That saves needless explanation. I won't bother telling you that much of what you've heard or read served more to sell newspapers than to expose the truth. I hope you've lived long enough to assume that."

"That said, Mr. O'Byrne, I have trouble imagining what I can do for you that an army of thugs couldn't do better. No offense."

I caught the faint crack of a smile. "You're a piece of work, Mr. Knight. I see we can speak frankly to each other. That'll make it easier. Let's get down to business."

"Let's not, Mr. O'Byrne. Not yet. A couple of preliminaries. Are you asking for legal advice?" I was thinking of the promise my senior partner, Lex Devlin, and I made to each other never to take on representation of anyone who made murder a tool of the trade.

He rubbed his hand across the lines that were back on his forehead. "I could dance around the definition of legal advice, or we could just get to the matter at hand."

"There's a reason for asking. I can't represent you."

He looked at me for the length of a deep breath before speaking. "I'm not going to ask why. I'll just say that it's not me. It's someone else I'm concerned about. Now can we stop the chess match?"

"Again, no. Whom are we talking about?"

Another deep breath. "My son, Kevin. And it's not a court matter. Not yet. It could be."

That was a horse of a different hue. The newspaper articles I was trying to pull back seemed to concede that the criminal life stopped with the father. The son was ensconced behind a Chinese wall, so to speak. He was, if memory served, a junior at Northeastern University.

"In that case, if you please, one dollar. Cash, check, or stamps. No credit cards."

He looked puzzled.

"Mr. O'Byrne, I don't want to have to go to jail for not answering a prosecutor's questions about whatever you're about to tell me. You and your family are magnets for grand juries. Let me have a dollar, and for the moment—understand, *for the moment*—I'm retained counsel for you and your son. That means attorney-client privilege."

The furrows were gone, but so was the smile. He pointed a disconcerting finger in my direction.

"Let there be no misunderstanding on that score, Mr. Knight. If you were to disclose anything said in this room to anyone, prison would be the least of your worries."

I had no answer. The cards were on the table, especially the ugly ones. My heart, soul, and mind reached a unanimous conclusion: *Get Charlie the hell up here and hit the street.* If I had fifty cents for every time in the next two weeks that I regretted not following that conclusion to the letter, I could retire to Bimini.

"I'll take the dollar now, Mr. O'Byrne."

He shrugged and reached into his pocket for a bill.

Without another word, he led the way down the back set of stairs and turned left into an alleyway. I'd have valued Charlie's company, but Mr. O'Byrne and I were both alone.

Fifty feet into the alley, a bulb over a doorway picked up the gleam of a Cadillac, Black Diamond Edition, high end. I could make out the drooping figure of what looked like a boy in his late teens, head in his hands, sitting on the stoop beside it.

"Kevin, come over here."

The boy looked up and squinted at us, silhouetted against the backlight from the street. The voice brought him to his feet. He was closer to my height than his father's five-foot something. He looked lean and athletic with a confident way of moving, but even in that light I could see red rims around his eyes.

"Kevin, this is Mr. Knight."

His hand came up automatically, but no sound.

"Tell him, Kevin."

He looked at his father like a child actor being pushed on stage by his mother.

"Tell him. He can help. I know how these things work."

He looked up at me from a slouch. I could hardly hear the words.

"I was with two other kids. We . . . I never did anything like this. One thing led to another. It was like a dare. Dad, I don't want—"

A fist shot out of the father's side that caught him in the ribs and straightened him up. The voice that went with it even straightened me up. "Speak like a man! You get into a man's trouble, you act like a man."

The boy was looking me eye-to-eye now. The stammer was gone. He seemed to want to get it all out in one breath.

"We saw a man leave the keys in the car. They dared me to drive it around the block. They thought because of my father I'd dare to do it. The man came back when I was driving off. He ran down the street screaming. I panicked. I drove here."

"Where was the car when you took it?"

"In front of Patrini's Restaurant."

"Oh, crap in spades. Tell me you don't mean Patrini's in the North End."

He just nodded. I looked over at his father who clearly understood the reason for the question.

"I don't suppose you'd know, but did anyone follow you here?"

"I don't think so. I was gone before they could catch up. It was dark, about midnight."

"Who were these kids? Are they from the North End?"

"No. They're just kids from South Boston. Classmates."

"Not to be indelicately racial, but are any of them Italian?"

"No. Irish."

"All right. Any race other than Italian'll do at the moment. Do you know why I'm asking, Kevin?"

"Yes. But I was just going to drive around the block."

"In a car that was undoubtedly owned by a made man in that little social club, *La Cosa Nostra*. You hit the jackpot."

I turned to his father. "Out of overwhelming curiosity, why did you call me?"

His father took me by the arm and walked me ten steps away from his son. "Word gets around. You and your partner, Devlin, handled a case for the son of Don Dominic Santangelo. I hear they go back. This thing needs to be brokered."

I just shook my head at the inappropriateness of me in all of this.

"Listen, Mr. Knight. I think you're more savvy than you let on. There are, shall we say, territorial disputes between them and us."

"You mean the Italian Mafia and the Irish whatever-the-hell you call yourselves."

He caught the disdain and stifled a small eruption of what could be an Irish temper.

"The disputes I mention are mostly under the control of cooler heads, but at the moment—" He moved his hand in a way that said "dicey." "This matter needs an intermediary with influence, but not aligned with either side. You and your partner come to mind."

"How fortunate for us. And when the damned bullets start flying, guess who's in the middle? Hear this. Mrs. Knight's little boy, Michael, is not that mentally challenged. Hasta la vista."

I thought it, and have frequently wished that I'd said it. Instead, I provided a logical solution.

"Look, Mr. O'Byrne, to hell with the brokering and all the complications. Let's go with the KISS principle. From what your son said, they probably don't have any idea who took the car. Simple solution. Have someone drive it and park it a few blocks from Patrini's Restaurant. Make an anonymous call to Patrini's and tell the maître d' where the car is. The odds are he'll know who owns it. He gets the car back in one piece, and life goes on. For everyone."

I started to turn and walk. He caught my arm.

"And yet, Mr. Knight, do you suppose I need you to belabor the obvious?"

"I wondered the same. And yet, as you say, here I am."

He nodded. "There's a minor complication."

He crooked his come-over-here finger and walked to the back of the car. It was a simple move, but it neutralized every soothing effect of the evening-long's seriatim sips of the Famous Grouse scotch. He waited until I was standing directly in front of the Cadillac's trunk and hit the release button. The light from the trunk was perfectly adequate to illuminate every feature of the very dead body of a man curled into the same fetal position in which he began life.

I've seen dead bodies. You can't be even partially Irish without chalking up more wakes than weddings, but this one had unique features. The knife in the back was the origin of a seepage of blood that surrounded the body like a backdrop. The noose around his neck underscored the labeling of the deceased as a traitor. The final touch was the wad of ten dollar bills stuffed into his mouth like the dressing in a turkey. Without an exact count, I'd have bet that there were thirty bills—the thirty pieces of silver paid to Judas to betray our Lord. A bit heavy on symbolism, but the point was made.

My mind was spinning. O'Byrne was right. This was a complication. The thugs in the North End were unlikely to let this go as boys-will-be-boys. The Cadillac could clearly be traced to the owner, and the state of its current occupant could mean a life sentence for the killer if the boy who took the car went to the police. And, frankly, if I thought along their lines, I'd be inclined to play it safe and assume that he might.

All things considered, Mr. O'Byrne was right. It looked like the start of an "interesting" day.

# CHAPTER THREE

"Did you touch the body?"

That was aimed at both O'Byrnes. The elder, being more vocal, shot out a quick, "Of course not." The son just fell in line with a head shake.

That was a test. One of them failed it, but which one? There was a small gap between the line of congealed blood and the body in the trunk. Someone had moved the body after it had been in the trunk for some time. I was inclined to believe the father's word. He seemed to have enough sense of his own power to handle any situation without resorting to lies. The son, on the other hand—

I walked over to the stoop where young Kevin was back sitting with a hangdog, woe-is-me look on his downcast face. I sat down beside him. I put my arm around his shoulder and smiled a compassionate smile. That was for the benefit of the father, still peering into the trunk, but keeping an eye on me as well.

"Rough night, eh, Kevin?"

He looked into my understanding face and nodded.

"Any idea whose car this is?"

The head shook.

"How about the guy in the trunk? Any idea who he is?"

Another shake.

"What were you and your friends doing in the North End?"

"Pizza."

Aha! I had a conversationalist on my hands at last.

"You kids go over there much?"

Another shake, followed by "Never."

"Uh-huh. I'll need the names and addresses of the other boys with you."

He looked stunned by this unexpected request. I kept smiling.

"Just to get this in context, Kevin, do you have the foggiest idea of how much trouble you're in?"

A blank, juvenile look appeared to go with the turned-backward baseball cap. "I didn't do anything. I just borrowed the car. They'll get it back."

I edged closer and kept smiling. "See, here's the thing. No, they won't. That baggage in the trunk is what's called a dead body. It has to be turned over to the police—car and all. The boys in the North End will never see the car or the body again. I figure that'll be like a cherry bomb in a wasps' nest."

He looked like the sudden victim of shock and awe. He was looking at me, but I noticed he kept a sideways view of his father.

"Get a good grip, Kevin, because I'm going to tell you why I think you're in ten times as much trouble as you seem to let on."

I noticed that he shifted into a calm alertness that shucked off the appearance of little-boy panic. I kept the beneficent smile and locked eyes with him.

"You see, I think your father is just what he appears to be with no pretenses. But I think you're a lying, sleazy piece of crap. Keep looking at me. I don't think you want your father in on this."

His eyes narrowed to slits. A coolness set in that had me convinced that I was looking at someone ten years older in savvy than the clueless kid in the turned backward cap.

"Figure this, Kevin. Unless you've got mind rot, the son of the Irish South Boston mob boss doesn't just cruise into enemy territory for pizza. There are pizza shops in South Boston."

He started to get up. I put pressure on the arm I had around his shoulder.

"Sit there. Second, you'd have to be brain dead not to know that a top-of-the-line Cadillac in front of Patrini's belongs to someone you don't want to mess with on a juvenile dare. Third, if it happened the way you said it did, why in hell would you open the trunk rather than just ditching the car on the first dark street? And given all of that, just how sappy do you think I'd have to be to buy your little juvenile prank story?"

About then, I caught sight of Mr. O'Byrne coming within hearing. I figured the fewer the complications, the sooner I could kiss this whole unpleasant episode adios. I stood up to include the father in our little chat.

"Here's where we're at, gentlemen. Like it or not, I'm in it. I've seen the murder victim and it has to be reported."

"The hell it will, Knight!"

"The hell it won't! Think about it. This kid is your son. How do you know they don't know that in the North End? What happened to that guy in the trunk could be a mercy killing compared to what they'll do to your son if they get him."

That produced silent thought.

"We need to do two things, Mr. O'Byrne. We need to get this car and body into the hands of the police, and we need to get your son someplace safe until I get a chance to try to make a deal with whoever owns the car. Isn't that what you called me for in the first place?"

He gave it some silent thought and sat down next to his son. Kevin looked over at him with a fully restored "I'm-sorry-I-was-a-bad-boy-Daddy" look. Mr. O'Byrne looked up at me.

"I'll take care of Kevin myself. I can take him to—"

"Whoa! Hold it there. I don't want to know. If I'm asked, and I will be, I want to say I don't know where he is without blinking."

"Alright. What about the car?"

I was improvising on tired brain cells, but leaving it outside what was apparently the office of the Irish mob boss could invite a shooting war. On the other hand, I had to take a story to the police that involved a minimum of tampering with the evidence.

"Get one of your men to drive it. Do it now. Gloves on. Have him park it close to police headquarters facing Tremont Street in Roxbury. You can use the community college lot. Tell him to give me a call at this number when it's there, and then tell him to get the hell out of Roxbury. I'll call it in to the police station before the car gets stolen again. Make sense?"

Apparently, no better plan occurred to him. "And you'll start making the contacts, right?"

"As soon as the sun comes up."

He looked at his son who had nothing to contribute. He looked back at me.

"Do what you can, Knight. I'll pay the bill."

I caught another knowing look from the slippery son behind the father's back. I thought to myself, *You sure will. And I'll bet my fee'll be the smallest part of it.*

Thank God, my senior and only partner, Lex Devlin, forty-year veteran of countless wars in the Boston criminal courts, was of that peculiar gene structure known as a morning person. I was waiting in my office in our suite at 77 Franklin Street at six thirty when I heard the ding of the elevator.

His surprise at having me walk him to his office at that hour was minor compared with the shock of what I was about to suggest. I started with the good news. "We have a new client." And it went straight downhill from there.

"Michael, how the hell do you get us into these things?"

"I take it you know O'Byrne."

He laughed one of those laughs that does not imply humor. "Oh, yeah. For more years than you've been alive. There's not much that can make me ashamed of being Irish, but your new acquaintance is at the top of the list."

"In answer to your question about involvement, not my choice."

I filled in the details, including the fact that I got a call around four a.m. from a thuggish sounding South Boston voice that said the car was "you-know-where." The reporting situation was now in my court. It required delicacy, and there was no one awake at the hour of four a.m. with whom I could be delicate. I therefore took the least complicated course of simply making an anonymous call from a pay

phone to Boston Police Headquarters and telling a Sergeant Wis-
nowski where he could find a hot Cadillac with an interesting passenger. He undoubtedly knew the neighborhood well enough to get
someone on it while it still had enough unstripped parts to identify
it as a Cadillac.

Mr. D. was half reclined in a desk chair that strained under his
square-built, six-foot bulk, fingers locked over his chin, eyes closed—
in other words, the position in which he had listened to enough of
my bizarre tales over the three years of our association to strain the
heart of a lesser man. Fortunately, there was affection in his quiet,
almost fatalistic response. "Michael, I repeat myself. How the hell
do you get us into these things?"

I assumed that he was referring to the fact that we were now, so
to speak, the fragile pin in a grenade that could ignite the most in-
cendiary mob war since the era of Whitey Bulger.

"It's a gift. More to the point, how do we put out the fire? Since
the next play seems to be ours, may I make a suggestion?"

"I'm all ears."


It was nine thirty when we pulled up to the curb outside of the Sacred Heart Church in the heart of what was still an Irish blue-collar
section of Charlestown. I wondered if my stomach grumblings were
the result of memories of a previous adventure that began in the
hushed, candlelit shadows inside that monumental stone sanctuary
or anticipation of the meeting that Mr. D. had called into being that
morning at my suggestion.

Monsignor Matt Ryan was at the side entrance holding the door.
As before, he and Mr. D. greeted each other with the warm embrace
of unrelated brothers whose ties began in their early teens. The greet-
ings were jovial, but the air hung heavy with the seriousness of the
business at hand.

"He's in my office, Lex. Come in, Michael. We seem to meet
under the strangest circumstances."

I couldn't debate that one. Monsignor Ryan led us in silence
through the empty body of the church behind the altar to his office.

A much smaller man of roughly the same age as Mr. Devlin and the monsignor rose from his seat with a smile and two open arms that received Mr. D. in an embrace that also bespoke decades of brother-like ties. In spite of the hour, Monsignor Ryan brought three glasses of red wine to sanctify the rekindling of the brotherhood, and one for the young interloper who had called them together.

These three were as unlikely a match as any that could be cast in Hollywood. Two had survived the teenage street fights of a tough Charlestown neighborhood of Irish immigrants. One of those two had become a highly ranked boxer before being called by God to fight for souls in the uniform of the Church. The other took his passion for battle to the arena of the courtroom.

And then there was the third, Dominic Santangelo, the kid from the North End of Boston, the third musketeer who had shared the "one for all, and all for one" code during Matt Ryan's rise through the ranks of boxing, until life's crossroads forced a decision on Mr. Santangelo that splintered the brotherhood. Mr. Santangelo had chosen the path of a different brotherhood and had risen to be the former reigning don of the Boston family of *La Cosa Nostra*.

There had, in fact, been a forty-year moratorium on the bonds among the men in that room, until, as Monsignor Ryan liked to put it, God produced a crisis in Mr. Santangelo's life that brought them together in an embrace that was cheered in Heaven. That was one year ago. Once again now, the embraces were rekindled, the toasts were made, and the business at hand was faced. I sat to the side and let Mr. Devlin broach the question.

"Dominic, the last time we sat in these chairs, you made a decision. You vowed to pull out of the business you'd followed those forty years. As far as I know, you've kept that vow."

"Do you need to ask, Lex?"

"No, I don't. I trust you the way I trusted that scrawny little Italian kid who barreled into a fight on the side of me and Matt, how many, fifty years ago, give or take? And that makes this difficult."

Monsignor Ryan knew what was coming, but Mr. Santangelo leaned in with concern in his eyes. He raised his open hands.

"There's nothing you can't ask me, Lex."

"I hope that's true, Dominic, because I'm going to ask you to go back to the people you knew in that life and help me make peace."

There was no hint of retraction of the offer of help, but there were lines of concern at the suggestion of recrossing bridges that must have been burned in his withdrawal from another life. Mr. Devlin laid out all that I had brought to him that morning, including the discovery of the body and its condition. Nothing was held back.

"The boy says he made a mistake, Dominic. A stupid mistake, but didn't we at that age? I don't speak for his father. His father's troubles are of his own making. I leave him where I find him."

I watched the face of Mr. Santangelo and tried to read what was behind those eyes. If I saw more to the story than young O'Byrne was disclosing, what must a man who had lived the life of mob treachery have been reading into it?

"The car is gone, Dominic. That's in the hands of the police, but that's just a matter of money. The father'll make up the financial loss."

Mr. Santangelo stood and walked a few steps in thought. When he turned back, he seemed to be fighting something inside.

"Lex, we just drank wine to a new day of trust between us. It's a trust that has cost me more dearly than even you could know."

"If you have regrets, Dominic—"

"Hear me, Lex. I won't dishonor the toast we just drank." His eyes were now burning into those of Mr. Devlin. "And I'll demand the same of you."

Mr. Devlin was on his feet. "I don't understand."

"You don't, Lex? You don't? Then let me say it clearly. There's nothing you can't ask me as a brother. But you don't ask as a brother. You give me this story that I don't think you believe yourself. This poor little eighteen-year-old boy with his little juvenile pranks. This is the son of a man who would have killed me in a breath if I had let my guard down over the last forty years."

"I said I don't ask for the father."

"That's not the point!"

They were within a foot of each other. The heat and the volume were rising, and the priest was on the verge of coming between them.

"Stay there, Matt. This is a boil between Lex and myself. It has to be lanced. I need to know that Lex didn't come here to play me for a fool."

I could see the wounding in Mr. Devlin's eyes.

"Dominic, I say before this priest we both love, in God's church, that was not my intention. I meant no deception. I heard this story not two hours ago from Michael. He was dragged into it against his will in the early hours of the morning. I have one concern and one only. It's not for O'Byrne. He's not worth the trouble. It's not even for his son, whom I've never met. We're not in kindergarten. I see the inconsistencies as clearly as you do."

"Then why do you ask me to go back to that life? I've cut ties. Who in that Irish mob are you trying to protect?"

"None of them. They're a blight on my race."

"Then what?"

"The peace, Dominic. The peace. Dear God, if you can't see it, who can? They're tinderboxes. My Charlestown and South Boston and your North End. If I know that, you know it better. If a shooting war breaks out over this, it's not just O'Byrne who'll suffer. The whole city will suffer. Innocent blood along with the guilty."

They stood together for what seemed like an age. No words passed between them. Monsignor Ryan and I were totally rigid awaiting an outcome that could have gone in ten different directions, most of them bad.

Dominic Santangelo was the first to lower his eyes. His tone was softer, and he was looking at Monsignor Ryan.

"Father Ryan, I look to you not as my old friend, but as the priest. Give me your absolution. I doubted my friend. The years have made me a suspicious, untrusting old man. Tell him I was a fool. Lex Devlin has never done a deceitful thing in his life. Ask his forgiveness for me."

I saw Mr. Devlin walk over and turn Mr. Santangelo toward him.

"You're asking me to forgive you for being human, Dominic. I'm more human than you are."

Mr. Santangelo patted the hand on his shoulder and sat down. The crisis of confidence had passed, but the concern was still written on his face.

"What you're asking, Lex, I'm not sure I'm in a position any longer to make the peace. Some bridges have been burned beyond repair. What might have been done years ago as a matter of power—" He held up his hands. "I no longer have the power."

"But you have the will, Dominic, and you know the players. I think you know where the hot spots are on your side. It's worth trying."

"That much I can do. Where's the boy now?"

Mr. Devlin looked at me.

"I honestly don't know." I thanked God I could say that with a straight face.

Mr. Santangelo smiled a knowing smile and nodded. "I'm sure you don't. My old nemesis, O'Byrne, hasn't lost a step."

Mr. Santangelo rose and shook hands all around, mine last of all. He held my hand and looked into my eyes while he said, "You're a smart young man, Michael. Be careful of whom you trust. We have an old Italian saying, 'If the devil were sick, the devil an angel would be.'"

# CHAPTER FOUR

I'd done what I agreed to do. Beyond getting Mr. Santangelo to intercede, it was pretty much out of my hands. With that blissful, foolishly optimistic thought, I was back in my office by ten.

My indispensable secretary since my early days with my former law firm, Julie, whom I would never demean by sending her out for coffee, had a steaming cup of Starbucks' best at my desk with the *Globe* open to the Sports section.

I was savoring the glow of Rick Santee's report of the three-goal shutout our Bruins had handed the Toronto Maple Leafs the night before when Julie buzzed.

"Michael, there is one creepy guy on your line. I don't think you should take this one."

"Julie, if I didn't take calls from creepy guys, we'd lose half our clients."

"No. Michael. Your clients are weird. This guy is creepy. I think I'll just tell him you're out and hang up."

"Thank you for the coffee, Julie. It's delicious. Put him through."

"And when this turns out badly, and I say I told you so—"

"Just put him through, Julie. I have one mother. That's the quota."

Not that I'd tell Julie or she'd screen out some of our most lucrative clients, but her instincts have always been right on. Those first words over the phone in an acutely Irish brogue, "Mr. Knight, I have a message from Kevin O'Byrne," sent an icicle straight up my spine.

"And whom might I be talking to?"

"You're talking to someone who's telling you that Kevin is not available to tell you himself. I'll give you the message."

"Just for the sake of credibility, what does 'not available' mean?"

"It means that the young Mr. O'Byrne wants to meet with you, you being his lawyer and all. You can ask him yourself."

No lawyer could have framed an answer giving less information. The tone suggested that there was no water in that well.

"Where does he want to meet?"

"He'll be at the benches across from Kelly's Roast Beef on Revere Beach Parkway at midnight. Do you know the place?"

"I do."

"Then I'll say good morning to you with one last word. He has something rather delicate to say to you. Be alone."

I was tempted to ask, "And will he be alone?" but nothing in the conversation so far suggested that I'd get the truth.

I spent the rest of the afternoon asking myself why in the name of sanity I'd get more involved in this thing. The extent of my representation of the highly questionable Kevin O'Byrne ended with our laying his problem in the lap of Dominic Santangelo. The answer to my question came around four that afternoon when Mr. Devlin called me down to his office.

He was on the phone when I walked in. He nodded me into my usual chair facing his desk and hit the speaker button. I recognized the cantankerous voice of the predominant source of professionalism in Boston's District Attorney's Office. Billy Coyne was of Mr. Devlin's vintage. Their frequent jousts on the field of honorable combat, i.e., the criminal justice court, had bred an unusual bond of respect—even affection—that showed through their constant exchanges of verbal jibes.

"Michael's here, Billy. I'll let you break the news. You're on speaker."

"Hello, kid."

If I live to be a hundred and win appointment to the United States Supreme Court, I'll never outgrow Mr. Coyne's epithet, "kid."

"Hello, Mr. Coyne. What news?"

"I understand you represent Kevin O'Byrne."

I held my hands up in mock shock to Mr. Devlin. I was unaware of any representation, or desire for representation, beyond what I'd done. Nevertheless—

"And if that's true, Mr. Coyne?"

"Lex, is your boy getting cagey here?"

"He's not my boy, Billy. He's my partner. He can speak for himself."

"Then speak, kid. Do you represent him or not?"

There was no point in hedging. He had me curious.

"Yes, I suppose I do."

"Then I'll give you the courtesy of a heads-up. Your client's just been indicted."

"Interesting. For what?"

"For murder. Salvatore Barone. His body was found in the trunk of his own car in Roxbury early this morning."

Mr. D. and I exchanged quizzical looks. He took the lead.

"Are you going for a record here, Billy? You usually let the body cool before you go to the grand jury."

"This one has legs in a lot of different directions, Lex. Kid, you're on notice. You're welcome for the courtesy, in case you were about to thank me."

Mr. D. jumped in. "Billy, the last time you did a gratuitous favor, Nixon was in office. What do you really want?"

"This is for you, kid. There's a bench warrant out for young O'Byrne's arrest. Needless to say, if he came in on his own, it could work in his favor."

"In other words, Mr. Coyne, you don't have the foggiest notion of where to look for him, and your life would improve if you could talk me into bringing him in."

I heard a sigh over the phone. "Lex, you've turned the kid into the same kind of cynical pain in the rump I've been dealing with since we met. Now I've got two of you."

I caught Mr. D.'s grin. I picked it up.

"Thank you, Mr. Coyne. That's high praise. I'm curious. What possible evidence could you base an indictment on?"

"The body was found in its own blood in the trunk of his own car. There were fingerprints in the blood under the body. Guess whose? We had his prints on file from a DUI incident a few years ago."

*Kevin, you devious, lying little punk. Now we know who moved the body.*

"That's interesting. Anything else?"

"Tell you what, kid. Why don't I leave my office open tonight? You can drop by and rifle through the file. Short of that, given the unprecedented generosity of this office, shall we agree on when you can have young Mr. O'Byrne here in custody?"

"Much as I'd like to return the favor, I have absolutely no idea where he is." And thank God I foresaw that someone might ask.

There was a pause. "You wouldn't set yourself up for an obstruction of justice charge, would you, kid?"

"Not a chance in the world."

I enjoyed seeing the catbird grin on Mr. D.'s face. His prosecutorial counterpart was seldom snookered into an unbalanced exchange of information. On the other hand, I knew the grin would evaporate if he knew where his junior partner would be at midnight.

The flow of normal humanity that packs the sidewalk in front of Kelly's Roast Beef on Revere Beach Boulevard was gone for the day. Only the nightly column of Harley-Davidsons remained, stacked in rows as props and seats for another breed of humanity, tattooed and pierced in every conceivable piece of corpulent flesh that showed around the cutoffs that carried gang colors. The midnight air off the ocean carried a chill that magnified my biting pangs of "what the hell am I doing here?" That thought alternated in waves with the question, "Is the O'Byrne kid worth the shivers?"

And, still, I took a seat on one of the benches across the street from Kelly's. The guttural rumble of the occasional Harley coming to life drowned out any sound that wasn't covered by the rhythmic ocean surf. That explains why the first inkling I had of company was something cold and steely at the back of my neck.

My inclination to spin around was chilled by that same Irish voice from the phone call.

"Sit still, Knight."

"Good evening to you too."

The steel thing bumped the back of my head.

"I have little time for a smart-ass, Knight. This can be brief or it can be unpleasant. For you. I'll have one piece of information and be on my way."

I knew to a certainty what was coming, but I asked anyway. "What do you want to know?"

"I have business with your client, O'Byrne. Where is he?"

"I have no idea."

The steely thing rammed into my neck with more force.

"Now, that's not the way to conclude our little meeting. Shall we try just one more time?"

"What business?"

"What?"

"What's your business with the O'Byrne kid?"

This time the crack on the back of my skull brought stars and the start of a sickening headache. The next one could do some real damage. I thought I'd try the truthful approach.

"Listen to me, whoever the hell you are. I was retained by his father. He put the kid in deep hiding after a certain incident that you probably know about. He was afraid I'd have to turn him in if I knew where he is. He wouldn't tell me. I can't give you what I haven't got."

I braced for another rap that could put me under the bench. It didn't come. I could hear the raspy breathing beside my ear. "Shall we put that to the test? But not here. Get up and look straight ahead."

The steel thing was pushing into the back of my skull with a pressure that commanded obedience. I got up slowly. A grip on my arm led me around the bench and out toward the sidewalk. He was so close behind, I could feel his hot breath piercing the chill.

We walked in slow lockstep across the sidewalk and stepped off between the Harleys. My head was in a frozen position straight ahead.

We drew little or no attention from the boozed and drugged-out apes and apettes around the bikes.

Then, in one flash of God-given inspiration, I suddenly fell in love with every hairy one of them.

The only things I could move were my legs, but that was enough. With every ounce of spastic force I could gather, I side-kicked the bike on my left. In the next instant, I gave a hip-check to the one on my right.

It was gorgeous. Like a line of giant metallic dominoes, Harleys on both sides smashed into each other. Headlights shattered. Fenders crumpled. Mirrors scraped gas tanks before ripping off their moorings and splashing glass in every direction. There was a din you could hear in Chelsea.

The Irishman was frozen where he was. I dropped flat on the pavement. The only thing that muscled mass of biker humanity saw when they looked up from the pile of twisted chrome, scraped paint, and broken glass was my least favorite Irishman. They assumed what I hoped they'd assume, and they came at him like a herd of buffalo. He backed off, waving that steely thing—a gun of sizeable caliber—in a semicircle to hold them at bay.

In the din and distraction, I crawled back to the bench area, over the wall, and landed on the beach in pitch darkness. I overcame the desire to sprint full tilt along the beach in either direction. Instead, I propped myself up to a level where I could follow the action.

I got a good look at the Irishman, tall and athletic with a chiseled cold face, the type you see in prison on conscienceless stone killers.

He was still holding the pack at bay. They apparently recognized the automatic weapon he was waving and knew he could spray pain and death at most of them before they could get in the first blow.

I was stunned by his unflustered coolness. He just eased his way out of the circle of suddenly sobered goons. No question, he was in firm control, in spite of the odds. When he'd backed across the street, he fired one stuttering spray just over their heads. The bikers dove for the ground.

By the time they looked up he was out of sight—theirs, not mine. I had worked my way down the beach and crossed the street ahead of the Irishman. I was in a darkened driveway when he ran past on the side street beside Kelly's. Fortunately, he had parked his car only two blocks away or I'd never have been able to keep up.

I was in another dark driveway when his car sped past. One well-located streetlight enabled me to read the license plate.

I got on the cell phone. Again, Tom Burns picked up on the first ring in spite of the hour.

"Michael, can't you get a day job?"

"I'm working on it. I've got a license plate number. Can you check it out?"

"You mean 'will I?' Mikey. You know I can."

"I mean can you now, when most sane people you could contact are in bed?"

"I seldom deal with sane people. What's the number?"

I gave it, and he put me on hold. It took about seventy seconds.

"It's a rental, Mikey. Came from the airport. The passport he showed says he's from Dublin, Ireland. It shows the name of Seamus Burke. Based on the way you ask, it's probably a phony passport, so you know where that leaves us."

"Did he give an address in this country?"

"Yep. Could be phony too."

"Just in case, what is it?"

"Forty-two Park Street. Appropriately, there's an Irish pub just around the block. Molly Malone's. You know Dorchester?"

"Not too well."

"Then it comes with some friendly advice. Unless you're just in and out for a pint, stay the hell out of there. You have a way of asking questions that ticks people off. Don't do it with this crowd."

"To be more specific?"

"A lot of IRA sympathizers down there. From the bad old days. Don't mess with them, Mikey."

"You know me, Tom. A born coward."

"Oh crap, Mikey. That's what you said the last time."

# CHAPTER FIVE

This was getting out of hand. While it may be in the elusive Kevin's favor to be off my radar, it was beginning to cause me unacceptable grief. It was time to go back to the source.

It was nine thirty the next morning when I pulled up in front of the Slainte Pub on L Street in Southie. This time I used the front door. With the exception of a couple of barflies having a liquid breakfast, and two husky laborer-looking types at a table at the far end of the room, I had the bartender's attention all to myself.

When I asked him to ring Mr. O'Byrne for me, he leaned over the bar and got cozy and whispery. "Is he expectin' ya?"

I leaned over and mimicked his whisper, like there was anyone sober within hearing. "On the scale of people he's expecting, I'm about minus one. My name's Michael Knight."

That put him off. I could see the wall go up. He put on an official tone.

"And what business might you have with Mr. O'Byrne?"

"And your name is?"

He gave me a cautious, "Ron."

"Look at it this way, Ron, if I tell you the business I have with Mr. O'Byrne, I wouldn't bet a dime on your chances of living past lunch."

His face froze in a frown. I pointed to the phone behind the bar. "Shall we get on with it?"

It strained his decision-making powers at that hour, but he picked up the phone and punched in two numbers. This time he whispered into the phone. Whatever came back seemed to take the stress out of his wrinkled forehead. He hung up and just pointed to the stairs at the back of the pub. He also gave some kind of hand signal to the soldiers at the table in the back. I assumed that signal allowed me passage with both legs unbroken.

Mr. O'Byrne was at the door to the office at the top of the stairs. He was not unfriendly, but I wasn't sure I was his first choice of a morning companion either. He offered me a chair and sat facing me in the same position as the previous night.

On the theory that if you give, you'll get, I filled him in on our meeting with Dominic Santangelo. That was the easy part. The news of the indictment of his son for murder didn't go over so well. He was on his feet and pacing like a caged tiger.

"How the hell do they indict Kevin? The kid's as clean as you are."

"Maybe so. You'd know better than I would, since you haven't chosen to share a lot of information about my client."

That stopped the pacing. The tone got seriously edgy. "What the hell do you mean by that? Kevin's a college junior. He's going to be premed. He has nothing to do with anything. You hear me?"

"What I hear is a lot of self-serving crap. That sweet kid of yours is up to his ears in something rotten. It's got me in the sights of one D.A. and at least one Irish thug that I know of. My life's on the line for that little punk, and it's about time you tell me where the hell I can find him."

That little oration, delivered eye-to-eye and at ten decibels louder than my normal tone, satisfying as it might have been, would undoubtedly have landed me in the Lopez & Gonzales Funeral Home in Jamaica Plain, with my Puerto Rican mother and twenty-three assorted relatives embroidering my good qualities in doleful Spanish. Thank God, it never passed my lips.

What I actually said was, "What I mean, Mr. O'Byrne, is that if you still want me to represent Kevin, I need some basic information. The most basic being where he is. I need to talk with him."

That kept me alive and cooled the atmosphere.

"What about the indictment? What's that about?"

"The guy in the trunk. They're charging Kevin with his murder."

That put him in orbit again. "How the hell can they do that? They got no evidence. He just borrowed the car."

"Nevertheless, he is indicted. If I'm still his lawyer, this is when we've got to get busy. How do I reach him?"

He slammed the back of his chair and set it spinning. I thanked God for office furniture. The only other thing in the room to hit was me.

He walked to the window and looked down at L Street for what seemed like a full minute. I thought he was trying to reach a decision about sharing the whereabouts of the evasive Kevin with me. I found out I was wrong. When he turned around, it wasn't anger, and it wasn't temper written on his face. It was pure fear. His voice had a calm that was more disturbing than the previous outbursts.

"I don't know."

"You don't know what, Mr. O'Byrne?"

"I don't know where he is. I took him to a place we have in New Hampshire. I figured he'd be safe."

"And?"

"We had a signal. He'd only answer the phone there if he knew it was me. I called all day and all night. Nothing."

"He could have gone out."

"Not without letting me know. I sent a man up there this morning. The place was ransacked. Kevin was gone."

I walked out of the pub and sat in my Corvette with my fingers on the key. The image of the Irishman from the night before filled my mind, and I froze over a simple decision—to start the car or not. The mental connection between Irish thugs and car bombs kept my fingers from moving.

Damn it! This was not acceptable. Two decisions clicked into place like tumblers unlocking a safe. The first was simple. I gave the key a sharp twist. Either the car would start or, in the words of Longfellow, "The cares that infested the day would have folded their tents like the Arabs, and been blown the hell right out of my mind." That's a paraphrase.

Since I heard the Corvette's sweet, low rumbling engine sound, I assumed it was the former. The second decision took more conscious thought.

At 7:42 p.m., most of the area around 42 Park Street in Dorchester was in darkness. I'd been there, fighting off the chill and nerves since five o'clock by rationing out a double order of McDonald's fries, one every three minutes.

I watched the Irishman's rental car pull into a space by the sidewalk. Seamus Burke's every movement getting out of the car and walking up the steps to the large front porch told me that in any physical contest, I'd be a sorry loser.

Burke seemed relaxed, as if on temporarily safe turf. I sensed that his guard was down as he slipped a key into the front door. I had a moment that I'd never have again. From the deep darkness of the porch behind him, I seized the moment.

"Burke! Freeze! Keep your hand on that key and look at the door."

He had to be shocked, but you'd never know it on the surface. Not a muscle flinched.

I stayed in the dark and reenforced the command. "One look either way and your blood'll be on that door."

"You mean you'll shoot me, Knight."

"Bingo. Boy, you're quick."

There was a grin at the corner of his mouth. He slowly turned and looked in my direction. "Turn back around, Burke! Hands on the door!"

Nothing. He was not only not obeying my command, he was slowly walking toward me.

"Take one more step, and so help me, I'll—"

"No, you won't, Knight."

Now, I was the one in shock. I had no gun to back up the bluff and nothing to even throw at him. He came within three steps of me. Just as I was about to call on my jellied legs for whatever distance I could get out of them, he pulled up a chair and sat down. I found myself breathing as if I'd run ten blocks.

"Sit down, lawyer. Let's talk."

Sitting was one way to get back control of my bodily functions. With no better options, I sat.

"Damn, lawyer. You are pitiful at this gangster stuff. It's a good thing you've got a day job."

When I had control of my vocal chords, I asked, "How did you know I didn't have a gun?"

He stretched his long legs out against the railing and leaned back. We were like a couple of old farmers in rockers after the chores. Not the scene I had imagined.

"First of all, if you had a gun, you'd have had it in my face, full cocked, so I could see it. No chance of a misunderstanding. Second, a gun gives you confidence. You'd have barked out the orders like a drill sergeant, not like a tenor in a boys' choir. You've got a solid set of stones on you, Knight. But no gun."

He lit up a cigarette while I took it in.

"So what brings you here?"

"We have unfinished business, Burke. I'm not going to look over my shoulder for the rest of my life. I'm here to tell you one more time. I have no idea where Kevin O'Byrne is. You can either—"

"I know that."

"What? Then why did you scare the crap out of me last night?"

"I didn't know it then. I do now. No sane man would brace me on my own porch to tell me a lie. So your client's gone missing, eh?"

"He seems to have eluded both of us. You apparently want him as much as I do."

He laughed softly. "You gathered that, did you?"

"Why do you want him?"

"No, lawyer. We're not on the same side yet."

"Maybe we are. In a way. They say the enemy of my enemy is my friend. Maybe if we share information, we both come out ahead. Finding Kevin is not going to be as easy as you might think."

"Why not?"

"Aha. Maybe you can use my help."

"What makes you think I'd play fair with you?"

"I don't know. My instinct tells me you would. I'll go with that."

"So what have you got for me?"

"Kevin was hidden out by his father someplace in New Hampshire. I don't know where. Anyway, it looks like he's been taken by someone. He's not there, and the place has been tossed. I thought it might have been you, but apparently not."

Burke took a deep draw on the cigarette.

"Your turn, Burke. Who do you think has him, and while we're at it, what's your interest in this?"

"If I answered your last question, it'd be the last thing you'd hear on this earth."

"Then let's skip that one. How about the first question?"

He thought while he took another deep drag. "The dead man in the trunk. His name was Sal Barone. He was a lieutenant under the current Boston Godfather, as you people like to call him. Antonio Pesta."

"That much I know."

"Barone's right-hand man is a goon by the name of Pasqual Salviti. They call him 'Packy.' You want a name? That's a place to start. One thing."

"What?"

"Don't pull a stunt like this on him."

"I don't plan to. Why not?"

"He's a loose cannon. Not wired right upstairs. You understand? He'd have blasted you from here to Sicily before you said two words."

"I'll remember that." On the basis of probably never having another chance, I pushed it one final inch. "You still have me curious. What does an Irishman from Dublin have to do with a mid-level Boston Italian hood?"

He just shook his head, not to the question, but to the gall of my asking it.

"On your way, lawyer, while you can still thank God you can walk down those steps."

# CHAPTER SIX

Since his wife's passing, Lex Devlin's comfort zone had come to include his two-bedroom condo overlooking the Charles River, his Franklin Street office, the state and federal courthouses, and a small cluster of restaurants of which he could recite the menus from memory. Anything that pulled him out of that zone awakened the furies of irascibility that had led junior associates at his previous firm to interpret his initials, A.D., as "Angel of Death."

The young priest to whom it now fell to lead Lex down seemingly endless corridors was already feeling the heat of those furies. A band of perspiration had lubricated his Roman collar by the time he reached the ornate door. He knocked softly and opened it to announce the presence of Mr. Devlin to the red-robed figure behind an Olympic-size mahogany desk. That function performed, he beat a grateful retreat.

The two figures left in the spacious office could have been carved from similar massive blocks of granite. The silver-haired one in a red robe came around the desk to offer a handshake.

"Mr. Devlin. Thanks for coming. Given the conversation we're about to have, suppose I call you 'Lex.'"

He gestured Lex into a seat by a fireplace and sat opposite. Lex sat, but his rigid discomfort was hard to miss.

"And what do I call you? I'm not much on gratuitous titles."

That brought a smile. "Neither am I. I cringe when they call me 'Your Excellency.' I take it I won't have that problem with you."

"So what's the alternative?"

"How about the only title I ever wanted. Father Peter Ferrigan."

"Done. So why am I here, Father Peter Ferrigan?"

The man opposite settled back, but looked Lex dead in the eye. "Because in about two sentences you've confirmed that you're the man I need for the job."

"I doubt that."

"Really. On what basis without knowing the job?"

Lex leaned back with an eye on the cardinal in a look-before-leaping moment. Based on what he saw, he took the direct approach. "I'll give you two. You can take your pick."

The cardinal raised his hands in a "bring it on" sign.

"First, I don't respond well to summonses. Second—do you mind a blunt answer? No padding?"

"Do you give any other kind?"

"No."

"Then?"

Lex paused and shifted his weight. He knew the answer. It was the words that had to be chosen. "All right, here it is. I know you've been in that chair less than a week. You've got no track record with me. But there's nothing I've read about your predecessor's handling of certain problems that makes me want to line up on the side of this office. At my time of life, I get to make the choice."

The cardinal's smile met neither Lex's anticipation nor his desire for a quick out.

"I'll be equally direct, Lex. Given what you've said, you couldn't fill my expectations more if you'd been sent from central casting."

There was a soft knock before the door opened. The same young priest stood with a tray and two cups in the doorway.

"Come in, Daniel. Come in. He won't bite."

The priest walked with a rapid step to hold out a steaming cup of coffee to each of the men. Lex accepted it and took one sip. It only deepened the scowl.

"Not to your taste, Lex?"

Lex looked his opposite in the eye.

"Too much so. Black, two sugars. Why the hell have you been checking up on me?"

"You can go, Daniel. Thank you. No interruptions now, please."

"Yes, Your Excellency."

The cardinal sighed. "I can't break him of that. You see why you're a breath of fresh air, Lex."

"Actually, no. If what you want is an opinion straight from the hip, read Mike Loftus's column in the *Globe*. I'm not your man."

The smile was gone. "You are, though. And in five minutes, you'll take the job. Not because I'm asking you. Because you wouldn't have it any other way."

Lex was silent, but his attention was now totally focused.

"I was sent here from the Chicago archdiocese a week ago. No secret. I'm here to shake things up. Top to bottom. You don't know it yet, but I'm as tough as you are. You and I came from the same kind of blue-collar Irish neighborhood. You know the kind of steel that puts in your guts. But that said, it doesn't mean I don't get the shiverin' fits when I think of what's ahead."

The cardinal leaned forward. "I could easily lose my way, Lex. These scandals are unchartered ground. I need a compass to keep me on course. I need someone to tell me to go to hell if I'm out of line."

Lex sat farther back in the chair. The scowl softened, but remained.

"Look, Cardinal."

"Father Peter. At least in this office."

"Right. I'm just an old criminal trial lawyer. This dog's too old to change traces."

"I don't want you to."

"Then, what?"

"Right now I want you to hear me out. Then do what you wish. You will anyway. I'll only apologize ahead of time for the pain I'm going to cause you in the next two minutes. I can't avoid it."

The two were eye-to-eye. The cardinal let his last words sink in to prepare the soil before he spoke.

"Lex, there's an infection that's been festering in the Church for years now. If you've been on the planet, you know what it is. We're talking about abuse of children. We've had some rotten apples in the

clergy. Not many, but one is too many. Some of them have been unfortunately allowed to stay. I was sent here because I'm supposed to
be a hardnose. And I am. Zero tolerance is almost too much tolerance
in this mess."

The cardinal paused for a deep breath and a rub of the forehead.

"Lex, I got a complaint yesterday. It came to me directly. A young
man about twenty-six. He's married, has a young daughter about
seven. He's had an alcohol problem since his teens. He's only worked
as a day laborer, and that's getting more infrequent."

"I'm beginning to see where this is going."

"I'll get to the point. He says as a boy he was sexually abused by
his parish priest. Repeatedly over several years. It's a hell of a story.
Turn your stomach."

"They all do."

"True. This one's particularly vicious. I've talked to this poor
man. I have no reason to doubt him. I'm going to do what I was
brought here to do. There'll be no fooling around with some in-
Church investigating committee. I'm going to the district attorney
for possible criminal prosecution of the priest. The press will eat it
up, but to hell with them."

"It sounds like the decision is made. Why am I here?"

"I've talked to the priest too. He denies everything. I have no reason to doubt him either. I think he's a good man. I want you to handle his defense."

"That's more in my line. But, that's not a 'yes,' yet. Let's be clear.
Would I be hired by the Church or the priest? Which one's the
client?"

"So there's no confusion and no conflict of interest, you'll represent only the priest."

"That seems more simple."

"It's not, Lex. It's a damn mess."

"Why so?"

"The priest is your friend Monsignor Matt Ryan."

# CHAPTER SEVEN

Lex Devlin had done some boxing in his youth. A time or two he'd been hit so hard just below the ribs that every speck of air had been driven out of his lungs till he thought he could never get it back. He felt that same sensation, sitting in that chair, gripping the arms like a vise. There wasn't room in his mind for the fears that fought for predominance.

Two primary thoughts continued to dominate in alternate waves. First, that Matt could not possibly have done what he was accused of. Second, that the truth would be irrelevant. Even a "not guilty" verdict of twelve jurors would not wipe the poisonous lingering suspicion out of the minds of the people in Matt's home parish. The old "where there's smoke, there's fire" adage has long legs.

When he reached the street, Lex drove with the windows down to let the chilled air take the heat out of his throbbing head. He drove through the very streets of Charlestown where three boys—Matt Ryan, Dominic Santangelo, and Lex Devlin—had run like brothers in the youthful assurance that they owned the world. They lived and breathed as one through every moment of Matt's ascendancy through the rankings of professional light heavyweight boxers. The memories of those days seemed to rise like mist from the streets. They made the mission Lex was on almost unbearably bitter.

Lex pulled up in front of a gym in one of the old sections of Charlestown whose character had not been bulldozed by urbanization. The gym had always looked to him like an enduring symbol of Matt's fighting spirit. Now it looked tired. Lex noticed the cracked paint and sagging door for the first time. It stood, but it showed the scars of decades in a hard-times neighborhood.

In the ring in the center of the gym, Lex saw two scrawny, wiry boys with oversized gloves dancing around each other like a couple of tentative pit bulls. A large man in sweats was leaning on the ropes, yelling alternate jibes and encouragement.

"Timmy, do you think you're on *Dancing with the Stars*? What the hell are you doin'? For the love of the saints, will you plant yourself? This is not a road race. Kevin, when I said a moving target, I didn't mean a fifty-yard dash. That's the stuff, Timmy, now jab! Kevin, get those gloves up! Protect that pretty face or your mother'll have my scalp."

Lex came up behind him and put a hand on his shoulder. "Let's talk, Matt."

Matt called the match and sent the boys to the showers after extracting a promise of two miles at a fast jog. He accepted Lex's invitation for a beer and a sandwich at the pub around the corner.

When they walked through the crowd of noon customers, it was "Hi, Father." "What's up, Father?" "Can I buy you one, Father?" down the entire length of the pub. On another day, Lex would have basked in the reverence and affection for his pal. Today each word bit like a scorpion, knowing that when the word got out, the tide would turn viciously.

They took a table at the rear of the pub where their words would be drowned out by the buzz of voices.

Lex hardly knew how to start. Matt saved him the agony.

"I can see by that sour puss on you you've heard the word from the cardinal." Matt grabbed Lex's shoulders and straightened his slouch into a straight-up position. He used the same tone he had used on his teenage boxers. "Would you look at you, you old grouch? Are we going to have a good lunch or attend my wake?"

Lex forced a smile. Matt leaned closer, but the tone was the same. "Let's get this over with before the beers come so I can enjoy your good company. I'll write the scene. First you say, 'Matt, my old friend of forty some years, or should I say Right Reverend Monsignor Ryan, by any chance did you commit the worst and most disgusting and vile breach of the confidence these good people have placed in you?

And did you do it over and over again to a boy who you picked up off the streets and treated like a son when his own father was too deep in the sauce to care about him? And if you did, how could you keep such a despicable secret all these years from your best friend who's about to buy you a grand lunch? Give me an answer, Monsignor Ryan.'

"And I'll say in reply that no two of God's creatures know the heart and soul of each other better than you and I, Lex. And if for one single second you could think that the answer to any of that crap is 'yes,' then I'll say to hell with you, Lex Devlin, and I'll buy my own lunch. Is that clear enough?"

The forced smile on Lex's face was now genuine. "You are one piece of God's work, Matthew Ryan. But it changes nothing. There never was, and there never will be, a fraction of a second that I'd believe 'that crap,' as you call it. So your speech was a grand piece of oratory, but totally superfluous. And you better damn well know it."

"I do, Lex. But it felt good to say it."

After two beef briskets on rye and a couple of Sam Adams arrived, they got down to the heart of it.

"Who is this man with the accusations, Matt?"

"He's just what I said. His name is Finn Casey. I've known him since he was about twelve. His father was a drunk and his mother couldn't handle him. He and another kid with no roots broke into a little candy shop over in Chelsea. They looted the cash register and ran. It turns out they were on the turf of a gang of Italian kids from the North End. Finn got word that the Italian gang wanted the money back plus a pound of flesh.

"Finn's mother came to me to sort things out. I went to our mutual friend Dom Santangelo. He offered to square it for me, but I told him no. I had a better idea. We got both sides to agree to settle the squabble with a fair fight, one-on-one, Finn and one of the Italian kids, at a neutral gym. Finn didn't know a boxing glove from a ham sandwich, so I agreed to give him six months of lessons. He was scared enough of facing the Italian kid to take me up on it."

"And that's how you got into his life."

"That was the idea. Once I had the kid in the gym, I could get him to knuckle down in school and keep his nose clean. For about five years, that's how it worked out. After high school, he drifted away. I lost contact with him until this week. I still haven't had a chance to talk to him. But I will."

"No, you won't, Matt. You'll stay the hell away from him."

Matt looked up. "Why?"

"Because if you approach him, the D.A.'ll make it look like you're trying to intimidate the witness. Leave that to me. I'll talk to him."

"And that's not the same?"

"No. I'm a lawyer doing what I'm supposed to do to prepare a case. Until we get a handle on this thing, I'm the quarterback."

Matt held up his hands in resignation. "So what do I do?"

"Go on with your life."

"Not so simple. The cardinal's put me on leave. I can say Mass, but no other parish functions. My assistant picks up the reins."

"Holy crap. Guilty until proven innocent. I don't like how that'll play to a jury to have your own church convict you."

"I understand what the cardinal's doing. When you think of the slimy way these things have been handled by some Church hierarchy up till now, the pendulum's bound to swing. It may even be a good thing."

"*Not for you,*" Lex thought, but there was no need to say it.


Lex drove the five blocks to the address of the row house on Pearl Street. It took three rings of the bell before he heard footsteps. The face of the woman who opened the door a few inches painted a picture of a life that had aged her beyond her twenty-some years. Lex took off his hat and tried a smile.

"Mrs. Casey, my name's Lex Devlin. I'd like to speak to your husband."

She seemed stuck for an answer. She finally stammered, "I don't know where—"

She got that far, when a male face appeared behind her. Lex saw

the familiar lines that years on the hard stuff can etch with indeli-
bility. There was something else in the eyes that bespoke a hardness,
born of either anger or fear. Lex couldn't tell which.

"Who is he, Annie?"

"He says he's Mr. Devlin."

The face stayed in the background, but the voice addressed Lex.

"I know who y'are. I have nothin' to say to ya. Close the door,
Annie."

"I just want to get your side of the story, Mr. Casey. That's all."

"You'll hear my side in court. That's all I've got to say. Close the
door. Do it, Annie."

Lex saw through the small opening a small, thin girl of about
seven. She started to come into the room, but her father waved her
back.

"I see you have a youngster, Mrs. Casey. I'm curious. Shouldn't
she be in school?"

The man pulled his wife away from the door and looked directly
into Lex's eyes.

"She's sick. And I'll thank you to stay out of things that are none
of your business. Leave us alone!"

The words were as much a slam of the door in his face as the real
thing that followed. What stunned Lex in the instant between the
two was the look of abject terror that contorted Casey's face. It was
so out of sync with Casey's words that it left him at a loss.

Lex stood frozen for a few seconds. For the moment he was
stymied. He sensed that whatever was putting the fear in Casey's eyes
could also be blocking him from asking for help. The immediate urge
was to pound open the door to give whatever help he could. A quick
reconsideration convinced him that that move could turn desperation
into disaster.

He turned and walked to the car in the best performance of unflustered calm he could give to whatever eyes might be on him. He
drove slowly away from the curb while his right thumb hit a speed-
dial number on the cell phone.

"Mr. Devlin. What's up?"

"Tom, I need a good man at Thirty-three Pearl Street in Charlestown. Pronto."

"I don't have any good men, Mr. Devlin."

"Say what?"

"My men start at 'the best' and go up from there."

"Point taken. Can you do it?"

"He's already on his way."

"Good. Here's what I need."

# CHAPTER EIGHT

I was in the office about three p.m. when Julie gave me the word that Mr. D. was back, requesting the pleasure of my company anytime within the next ten seconds. She braced me with the warning that those wrinkles he gets in his forehead were sending up flares.

I was still unprepared for what he told me. I hadn't known Father Ryan long, but it was long enough to take the measure of a good man.

Mr. D. told me about the call he was expecting from Tom Burns while he hit the numbers for the district attorney's office.

"Are you calling Billy Coyne?"

"No point. There's not a chance in hell she'll give up the head-lines this case'll draw."

That was shorthand for the fact that the princess of prosecution, Angela Lamb, who currently held the elected title of district attorney in Suffolk County, would indict, prosecute, and personally lock up Billy Graham if it would generate headlines that might grease her upwardly mobile rump into the governor's seat.

I always suspected that Mary Cornelius, the receptionist in the D.A.'s office, favored Mr. Devlin in his set-tos with her employer.

"Mary, would you do me the kindness of telling the Dragon Lady I'd like a word with her?"

"Good afternoon, Mr. Devlin. I believe she said she's in confer-ence with the mayor." I noticed she never questioned the title.

"The hell she is. She's picking the brains of Billy Coyne so she won't look like an ambitious buffoon in front of the press. If I were to bet you ten dollars that she's in Billy's office right this minute, would you take the bet?"

I could hear a stifled giggle. "Mr. Devlin, may I simply say, no bet."

"That's what I thought. Then let's change the message. Would you tell her I've called to offer settlement of the civil action?"

"And she'll know what I mean?"

"She will when you tell her I'm suing her and the city for six million dollars for violation of Monsignor Ryan's civil rights. Make that eight million. Tell her unless we settle now, she can read about it in the *Globe* tomorrow. And Mary, when you tell her, don't be standing in the doorway."

Mr. Devlin cast a disturbed look down at the floor and just shook his head. "Dear Lord, I wish I were dealing with Billy Coyne on this."

"Devlin! Are you out of your mind? What the h—"

Mr. D. put it on speakerphone, but there was no need. I could have heard her in my office.

"Relax, Angela. Relax. I just wanted your attention, not your obituary. I take it you're ready to go into high gear over this Monsignor Ryan business, assuming you're not there already. I'm sure there's no point in telling you that of all of the priests from here to Rome, you've got your claws into the one who couldn't do these things if his life depended on it."

"No more than in my telling you that I'm personally going to put this predatory animal away for the rest of his life."

I could see the words stung. "Uh-huh. That should play well in the *Globe*. Here's what I want, and I mean while the ink is still wet. I want a copy of the indictment with a full statement of all the particulars. Dates, times, locations, specific acts. If I sense you getting cute with any general allegations without details, I'll smack you with a motion for a bill of particulars even Billy Coyne couldn't fight."

"Are you threatening a public official?"

"No, Angela. I'm giving you a very accurate prediction. You're playing with the life of a man who's worth ten of you on your best day. And make no mistake. I am personally involved. And, Angela, keep this in mind. You're not the only one with access to the boys at the *Globe*."

Mr. D's phone hit the cradle, and I could see the steam go out of him. He'd been looking more tired in the late afternoons than I liked to see, but this time he seemed more depleted than ever.

"How's Monsignor Ryan taking all of this?'

That brought him up a bit. "A hell of a lot better than I am."

He finished telling me about his encounter with Casey and his wife when his phone rang. His secretary of many years, Lois Drury, knew to put the call directly through.

"Tom, what did you find out?"

"Your instincts were, as always, on target. A man went out the back door about five minutes after you left. My man followed him to a bar on Prince Street in the North End. Collini's."

Mr. D. and I exchanged confused looks.

"My man did some discreet checking. His name is Tony Napolitano. He's mid-level muscle for the North End Mafia."

Tom interpreted the silence that followed. "You're wondering what a lush in Irish Charlestown has to do with the boys in the Italian North End. Do you want me to do some more checking, Mr. Devlin?"

"Not yet, Tom. This is very delicate. I'll be in touch."

Mr. D. hung up and did a lap between his desk and the window that gives a long view of Boston Harbor. I knew this was a time to clam up and let his gray cells connect.

It took twenty seconds for him to reach a decision. He was back at the phone dialing numbers with the speakerphone on. Apparently, I was invited to listen in. I wasn't completely surprised to hear him connect with his old friend and former don of the Boston family, Dominic Santangelo.

"Dominic, I said I wouldn't do this. Your old business is laid to rest. And thank God."

"My friend, when you call me 'Dominic' instead of 'Dom,' I get nervous."

"I need one more favor. Some inside information. If you can. It'll go no further. And Dom, this is for Matt. Have you heard?"

"He called me. He didn't want me to hear it on the television and not know what to think. Can you imagine? That I wouldn't know what to think about Matt."

"I know."

"Someone's behind this despicable lie. I could find out who it is and handle this in the old way. You understand, Lex? It's only my promise to you and to Matt that's keeping blood off my hands in this matter."

"I do understand, Dom. And no one would want you to live up to that promise more than Matt. You can help in another way. I'm representing Matt. I need some unorthodox information."

"Like what?"

"I'm going to mention a name. I need background, and—I'm sorry, Dom—an assurance that I won't read his name in tomorrow's obituaries."

"I gave you my vow once, Lex. Don't dishonor me by asking for it again."

"I won't. Forgive me, Dom. I'll never ask again."

"What's the name?"

"Tony Napolitano."

There was a heavy hanging silence for five seconds.

"What do you have to do with this man, Lex?"

"I'm sorry. I can't say. Someday I'll explain. What can you tell me?"

"Stay as far away from him as you can."

"Do you know him?"

"Yes. Tony Nap. He's, we say *pazzo*. He's crazy. I'll be frank. There are those in our organization who will kill for business. This man will kill for no reason. For his pleasure. The slightest insult. You do well to fear this man."

"Who does he work for?"

"This goes no further?"

"Of course."

"I'm out of the organization, but I still hear things. He's a 'mechanic,' a 'cleaner.' You know these words?"

"I can guess. For whom?"

"He was number one boy for Sal Barone. Barone was a *capo*, a big shot in the organization. He was the one found dead in the trunk of his car. I have to assume that Tony Nap works for Barone's successor, Pasqual Salviti. Packy, they call him."

"And where can I find this Packy?"

"You haven't been listening to me, Lex."

"I've been listening. This is for Matt."

I could hear another five seconds of silence.

"I'll tell you two things, Lex. Packy does his business from a bar on Prince Street in the North End. It's called Collini's."

"Thank you, Dom. What's the second thing?"

"Just this. As I promised you and Matt, I'll restrain myself as far as humanly possible. You understand? A man can be pushed beyond his limits. I'll be clear. If anything should happen to you or Matt, the rules of the game will change."

He hung up and we were back in conference.

"Michael, I know we handle every case together, but this one's mine. I know what I have to do. You've got your hands full with the O'Byrne kid anyway. Just one thing I'd like you to do with me."

"Anything."

"I want to set up a meeting with Billy Coyne. I need to work with someone in that D.A.'s office with an ounce of sense and an eye on something other than her career."

"Agreed."

"Let's meet at Marliave's for dinner. Six o'clock. I'd like you there. You sometimes see things these old eyes miss."

He said it as a passing thought, but if I live through the next century, I'll remember every nuance of how he said it. It was Babe Ruth asking a rookie for batting tips.

I left the office about four thirty. I had a few things to do, but I made sure that I was at Marliave's before six o'clock. Roy, the maître d', part owner, and occasional chef, brought me up to the private room on the second floor. I always got special treatment because I stood in the shadow of Lex Devlin.

Billy Coyne, who to my knowledge has never been either late or early for an appointment, appeared shortly, and I could set my watch at six o'clock on the dot.

We both ordered club soda and deliberately kept the conversation to the Bruins, the Celtics, and the Patriots until Mr. Devlin might appear.

That never happened. By six thirty, I had tarantulas in my stomach the size of groundhogs. Billy Coyne's increasingly sour mood showed that he had his share as well.

I excused myself and went into the hallway to make a call. There was no answer at the office. Mr. D. never carried a cell phone, so I dialed up the cell phone of my secretary, Julie.

"Julie, was Mr. Devlin at the office when you left?"

"No. He left right after you. He said he had something to do before meeting you."

"And that was what?"

"He never said. He'd made a couple of calls on his private line. I could see the lights on my phone. Then he left."

"How was he?"

Silence.

"Julie, how was he? Speak."

"I didn't like how he looked. His face was red. He looked like he could have a stroke any minute. I even tried to get him to sit, but— Then he said—"

"What, Julie?"

"Tell Michael this one's all mine."

# CHAPTER NINE

When Michael left the office, Lex decided there was no time for anything but the direct approach. The longer the lie about Matt was allowed to fester, the more indelibly the stain would set.

He called the number for Collini's bar in the North End. The bartender took his name and put him through to Packy Salviti.

"Yeah, what?"

"Mr. Salviti, My name's Lex Devlin. You and I have some business to do. I suggest we meet."

"Oh, yeah? Just like that. What business do I have with you?"

"I represent Monsignor Matt Ryan."

Silence.

"I want you to understand two things. I know you've got your hand in this. Frankly, I don't give a damn about your business. You have nothing to be concerned about from me."

"Oh, there's a relief. I can stop shakin' in my boots."

Lex heard laughter on the other end. That meant he was on speakerphone, and Salviti was playing to his gang of thugs. It also meant that nothing constructive would come of that conversation. He needed Salviti alone.

"I'm a lawyer, Salviti. I'll give you some advice. No charge. If I were you, I'd take that phone off speaker and treat this as a personal call. I told you I represent Father Ryan. Like I said, we have business. It's personal business you may not want broadcast to every baboon in the cage over there."

"Who the hell do you think—?"

"I'm the one who can do you some good if we sit down and talk. We can do it alone or it can happen in a police interrogation room under an arrest warrant for subornation of perjury. I prefer alone, but the other's looking more attractive all the time."

There were three seconds before Lex heard the speakerphone click off.

"What do you want to talk about?"

"Let's meet and see how the conversation develops."

"When?"

"This afternoon."

A few seconds' pause.

"I'll be here."

"I won't. The sooner you get over the idea you're dealing with the class idiot, the more we'll be able to do for each other. Someplace neutral and public. Boston Common. Corner of Charles and Beacon Streets. I'll be on the bench. Five o'clock."

The beginning of rush hour brought a flow of professional suits and tourists by the bench area on one of the busiest sections of Boston Common. Lex knew none of them, but he got a feeling of security in their presence.

The sun was just down. The chill that followed made it all the more difficult to control the urge to catch the first cab out of there. This was not an arena in which he felt on solid ground. He knew he was about to bargain with the devil on a matter in which he was blind-sided from every direction.

It was a quarter past five, and the prospect of a dead end was looming, when he heard the repeated blast of a horn from a black Lincoln stopped at the curb on Charles Street. The driver seemed to be summoning him to the passenger side with the window down.

Lex walked to within five feet and leaned down to check it out.

"Get in, Mr. Devlin."

"Like hell. Where's Salviti?"

"He's waiting. I'll take you to him."

"That wasn't the deal."

The driver held his coat open to show that there was no hardware hidden. "I'm just the driver. Mr. Salviti said you wanted someplace private so's you could talk freely. C'mon. We're holdin' up traffic."

The horns of the Boston drivers behind the Lincoln were in fact getting into the conversation. Lex knew that Salviti had put the decision squarely on his back under pressure. The odds that a decision to get into the car would insure that he'd seen his last Boston sunset were overwhelming. On the other hand, a decision to walk away might quench the last spark of hope for Matt's redemption. Without weighing the matter too rationally, he went against the odds and slipped into the backseat.

The Lincoln jumped into the flow of traffic on Beacon Street toward the Berkeley Street entrance to Storrow Drive. With one hand on the wheel, the driver reached an open hand toward the backseat.

"I'll take your cell phone, Mr. Devlin. Just a precaution."

"Against what?"

"Like I said. Mr. Salviti wants to keep this little meeting private."

"I don't have a cell phone."

The driver gave that a few seconds' thought. "Just so you know. I'll be watching you. I got my orders. Mr. Salviti was very particular. If I see you doin' anything funny, do I need to spell it out?"

There was no need to answer.

The man at the wheel had the Boston driver's knack of cutting across lanes and slipping into openings barely a foot or two larger than the Lincoln. Their speed was well above that of the flow of traffic as they passed Mass. General Hospital and made the circular lane changes that put them in the fast lane heading north on Route 1.

They were over the Danvers line when the driver used an exit to make a U-turn. He went a mile before making a second U-turn back onto Route 1 north. This time he cut a sharp right-hand turn into the darkness that covered a strip of parking spaces in front of a set of wooden cabins that made up the Seaborn Motel. The "No Vacancy" sign was dimly lit, but there was only one car parked on the strip in front of the cabins. The driver of the Lincoln pulled in beside it.

"Let's go, Mr. Devlin."

There was no point in conversation. Lex knew from the moment he shut the door of the Lincoln on Charles Street that he was completely in the hands of the devil. Whatever bargaining power he thought he had vanished with the locking click of the car door.

Lex forced his mind to squelch nerves that approached the panic level with the constant reminder that he was Matt's last frail chance. He followed the driver to the door of the cabin. The driver gave three knocks, then two. The door was opened by a trim man in a dark suit with the eyes of a barracuda.

The barracuda made a two-handed motion that said lift your arms. Lex did. The thorough body search revealed that he was unarmed and telling the truth about the cell phone. The next gesture was more a command than an invitation to enter the room.

A short, dark-skinned, balding man in a gray suit that made him look like an overstuffed sausage sat in an upholstered chair across the room. A straight-back chair was set in front of him.

"Now, Mr. Smart-ass Lawyer, suppose you sit, and we have this conversation you wanted."

A jab in the back set Lex in motion toward the chair. He sat down in silence.

"You go first, lawyer. What's this thing you want to talk about?"

"I think you know. I assume you're Salviti."

Lex felt the point of something sharp at the base of his skull.

"That's 'Mr. Salviti' to you."

"Easy, Tony. Mr. Devlin's a big shot lawyer. He thinks he can threaten me with arrest for something about perjury. We should treat him with respect. Up to a point. What's this business you have with me, Devlin?"

"There's a charge of child molesting against Monsignor Matt Ryan in Charlestown. It's a sham. It's brought by a man named Casey. He's been scared out of his wits by a Tony Napolitano. I hear he's your man."

Salviti looked at the man standing behind Lex. A grin crossed his face.

"Tony, you know anything about this?"

"I'm just listenin', Mr. Salviti."

"So I take it this Monsignor is a client of yours. Maybe an old friend. Yeah?"

Lex nodded.

"And you think that I can make all this trouble for your friend go away. That's why you wanted this little meeting."

"I hope we can do business."

Salviti stood up to his full height of five foot four and walked to the window. "You're a lawyer, Devlin. You should know what business means. It means I maybe do something for you—after you do something for me."

"I'll do whatever I can to get this thing off Matt Ryan's back. You know that or we wouldn't be here."

"Ah, very perceptive. Then you're ready to deal."

"I said I'll do what I can."

Salviti walked back to within a foot of Lex's chair. His pointed finger was inches from Lex's face.

"No, no. You'll do what I tell you. No limits. You do, and maybe I'm grateful. You don't, and I'll let Tony take over my side of our conversation. He explains things more clearly than I do. Is that understood?"

There was no point in debating the unchangeable. Lex just nodded.

"Good. Then here's what you'll do for me."

# CHAPTER TEN

When I left the Marliave, I went back to the office and waited in case Mr. Devlin tried to reach me. Neither Julie nor Mr. D's secretary, Lois, had a clue, and the phone was deadly silent. By ten o'clock, I was jumping out of my skin.

I strained every ounce of memory fiber for what I could recall of Mr. D's telephone conversation with Dominic Santangelo. The only thing I could pull back was the mention of the name, "Packy." That rang a bell. That was the name mentioned by the Irishman, Burke, as the right-hand man of the deceased occupant of the trunk, Barone.

Those two names rattled around a restless, sleepless mind all night. It was not until six o'clock the next morning that an idea broke through. When you keep hitting dead ends, go back to the starting point. This whole disaster began because young Kevin O'Byrne made a misguided trip to Patrini's Restaurant in the North End, allegedly for pizza.

I checked back in the office for any message and did a number of useless, time-killing things through the morning. Still no word.

At quarter past eleven, I walked into Patrini's Restaurant on Endicott Street in the North End. I was just short of planless, but my senses told me that I was in the right area. Even an Irish/ English/ Puerto Rican kid from Jamaica Plain like me could tell you that if you wanted to put a few dollars on a number or an illegal sports bet, or get in on a variety of other illegal enterprises courtesy of the Italian mob, Patrini's was the spot.

When I walked in, the waiters were setting up for the lunch

crowd. Instinctively I went to the nerve center of any place with a bar—the bartender. He gave me a coaster and a smile. The first words out of his mouth rang of a higher intellect than I'd expected.

I ordered a draft Sam Adams and said something snappy about the weather to break the ice. We chatted easily until I leaned over the bar and tried the only name I had in my kit.

"How do I get in touch with Packy?"

The smile remained the same, but the alert code in the eyes went from green to high orange.

"Who's that?"

"Tell you what. I'll give you the first bet of the day. I'll bet a ten spot at ten-to-one odds that you know exactly who I'm talking about."

He went on polishing glasses. "And if I did?"

"Uh-huh. Then we're on first base. Let's try for second. I'll make it easy. You don't have to say anything to me. I just need to get a message to him. Don't say no until I give you the message."

He just kept smiling.

"If you can get word to Packy that Michael Knight, the partner of Lex Devlin, has what he wants and is ready to deal, I'll pretend I lost the bet."

I took out the hundred dollar bill I carry in the back of my cash roll for just such an occasion. I put it on the bar and kept my hand on top of it. His eyes were on it, and then on me.

"And if I should know such a person and he got your message, where could he reach you?"

"I'll make that easy too. You see that booth down there in the back? Right there. The office'll be open."

I picked up the beer and took my hand off the hundred dollar bill. As I walked to the back booth, I checked back. The bill was gone from the bar.

By twelve thirty, I'd nursed two and a half pints of Sam Adams fine lager. At twelve thirty-one, the bartender left a now-thriving business at the bar to walk to the booth. He set another Sam in front of me on a coaster that was upside down. I lifted the frosty glass before the moisture ran the writing on the coaster. The message was terse: "Pi Alley off School Street. Four o'clock. Alone."

Terrific. I had what I wanted. A date with Satan and who knows how many of his fallen angels with just me alone to deal for the life of the man I loved like a father. I had baited the hook with the promise that I "have what he wants," when I could more easily have guessed Rumplestiltskin's name than whatever the hell it was he wanted. Not too promising, longevity-wise, but I could think of not one single alternative.

I'd walked the narrow Pi Alley with my father as a kid more times than I could count. It was the location of most of the printers' shops back in Ben Franklin's day. It was called "Pi Alley" because the printers would throw the used pieces of type said to be "pied" out the window into the alley. It held good memories, but I was dead sure this was not going to be one of them. Today that narrow, darkened path between tall buildings felt like a cattle chute to the slaughterhouse.

At four o'clock, the sun was behind the buildings, and a brooding darkness was settling in. From the first step I took off of School Street, I had to will my legs to take every step. If this Packy didn't show, I was desperate for ideas. If he did, I had absolutely nothing but my life to trade. With those comforting notions, I moved one lead foot after the other into the totally vacant, soundless, dark alley.

I had crossed half of the two-hundred-foot stretch with my heart dropping closer to the pit of my stomach with every step, when I saw two silhouettes at the far end. They looked like Abbot and Costello, one short and fat, the other tall and slim, but not a trace of humor. They were moving in my direction.

We were fifteen feet from each other, when I caught the faint glint of light reflected off the barrel of a gun. The thin one gave the order.

"Right there, Knight. Hands behind your head."

I froze and obeyed. My eyes scoured the scene for an escape hatch. There was absolutely none. The fat one spoke.

"So you got what I want, do you? Let's have it."

"I don't know what—"

I got that far before a hand came from behind. It locked my forehead in a grip like a vise. I could feel the steel edge of a blade at my throat. My body went rigid when the cutting edge started to draw liquid. I couldn't have taken a deep breath without the blade cutting deeper.

"I didn't come here to bargain, Knight. I see it this way. Maybe you don't give a damn about your own life, but I figure you wouldn't be here if you didn't care about the old man. So, here's the deal. You got what I want, cough it up. I don't see it in ten seconds, you'll both be food for the mackerel in Boston Harbor. Can I make it any clearer than that?"

It was nearly impossible to speak. I could almost taste the panic of knowing that, as promised, in ten seconds I'd be on the ground with a bullet or a slashed throat. I had nothing to give him, and even if I did, I knew I'd never leave that alley alive.

I could hardly move my throat muscles to speak. I squeezed out a whisper of the only thing I could think of to buy time. "I don't have it with me."

The fat man moved closer.

"You just bought another ten seconds. Where is it?"

"I can't talk. Give me some slack."

The fat man thought for a second before nodding to the ape behind me. I felt the blade move an inch away from my throat. At least I could speak, but I had nothing to say.

"So talk. I make one call, and you can hear your old partner's last words before it's your turn. Your ten seconds are counting."

I had no words left. I used the ten seconds to speak to God rather than the fat man.

At the count of five, I was pulled out of my prayer space by an incongruous sound. I heard whistling behind me. I was even aware of the tune. It was "The Fields of Athenry." I'd heard it in a pub in Dublin.

The footsteps from the same direction were calm and deliberate. I had no idea who had wandered into that alley, but I thanked God for the brief freeze it put on the fat man's plan.

When the footsteps were nearly abreast of us, they stopped. The fat man spoke first.

"Keep movin' or you'll get a piece of this." The man beside him flashed the gun on the new arrival. I expected a panicky dash in the opposite direction. Instead, I heard the quiet, unflustered Irish accent that I had heard on that porch in Dorchester.

"Now that wouldn't be the smartest thing you could do, Mr. Salviti. Do you see this here? And do you know what it is?"

The Irishman held his two hands in front of him. The light from the side windows was just enough to make out a roundish object the size of a baseball in his right hand and his left hand holding something attached to it.

"What the hell are you—?"

"Come now, Salviti. You're old enough to recognize an old-fashioned hand grenade when you see it. This here's the pin. If I should separate the two, you'd have three seconds to clear the alley before tiny pieces of steel would rip every inch of your body. Do you think you could run that fast?"

Salviti just stared. Now he was planless, but only for a few seconds. It was still a standoff, and the blade was still an inch from my throat.

"You won't pull that pin. You'd be blown up with the rest of us."

"Ah, now that's perceptive. I'll make you a bet, Salviti. I'll bet my life that you're a sleazy skunk of a coward. I'll bet all your useless life you've had others do the killin' for you without ever puttin' that fat, pampered ass of yours in danger."

There was no answer.

"And that's the difference between us. I've lived with death an inch away all my life. I'm not afraid of it. So let's put it to the test. Now I'll give you ten seconds. Let's count them out together before I pull this pin. One—"

Salviti stood fast. His voice never shook when he gave the command to the two thugs with him. "You boys stay where you are. He's bluffing."

"Two—three—four—"

Burke held the grenade straight out and closed his fist around the pin. I could hear the feet of the man behind me shuffle. He held me with one hand, but the knife dropped away from my throat.

"Stand your ground, men!"

"Five—six—seven—"

The count was slow, but relentless. What was relief at Seamus Burke's arrival turned to the certainty of another kind of death, only this time with company.

When the count hit "eight," the man behind me threw down the knife and ran for his life. Salviti shrieked at the man beside him.

"Shoot him down before he pulls that pin!"

Burke's voice never quavered. "No use in that, Salviti. I'll still have time to pull the pin. And that brings us to nine."

The man beside Salviti broke. He bolted for the end of the alley as fast as his shaking legs could carry him. Salviti knew he was alone. All of his weapons had been in the hands of his thugs. It was his turn to face death. He fell to his knees and begged.

The calm voice of the Irishman simply said, "Ten. It's all over."

Salviti watched with tears streaming from his eyes and saliva running from his mouth as the Irishman pulled the pin and threw the grenade down beside him. Salviti fell flat on the ground whimpering. I closed my eyes and counted the three seconds to the explosion.

When I got to five seconds and was still breathing, I opened my eyes to see the Irishman walk over and pick up the grenade from where it landed beside Salviti. He took a cigarette from his shirt pocket, pressed a switch on the grenade and lit the cigarette from the little flame that came out of the top of it.

It took me ten seconds to adjust to the idea that I was not going to die in that alley. Salviti just lay on the ground blubbering.

"I don't know how you knew I'd be here, Burke, but you're my guardian angel."

"I don't know about the angel part, but I've been keeping an eye on you. I've said it before. You've got rocks like boulders, but they'll put you in the grave if you don't pick a better grade of companion."

"Why? Why did you do it? I don't mean anything to you."

"Well now, you could be wrong about that. Either you or your partner might yet do me some good."

He threw me the hand grenade/cigarette lighter. "You can keep this as a souvenir. It's from the joke shop on Bromfield Street. Now take a walk to the end of the alley and wait for me. I've got business with Salviti."

He reached down with both hands and grabbed fistfuls of the back of Salviti's coat. He lifted him off the ground like a sack of potatoes and plastered his well-padded body against the brick wall. He turned back to me.

"Go on, Knight. End of the alley, and don't look back. This won't take long."

"What are you going to—?"

"If you want to see Lex Devlin one more time, go. End of the alley."

It was pointless to argue, and pointless to stay. I walked slowly. By the time I got to the opening of the alley on School Street, I heard Burke's fast footsteps behind me. He passed me and called me to follow him at a run.

We reached a Ford Crown Vic parked on Cambridge Street. He jumped into the driver's side. I took the passenger side. There wasn't a word spoken while he hit speeds through incipient rush hour traffic toward Route 1 that would have blanched a Boston driver.

We were cruising through Saugus at somewhere between seventy and ninety before the silence was broken.

"Could you tell me what the hell we're doing, Burke. At least tell me if you've got me kidnapped or what."

He broke a brief smile. "You really don't know if you're afoot or on horseback, do you, Knight?"

"If you mean I don't have a clue about what this whole nightmare's about, it's the first thing I've heard that's made sense."

He just drove and thought for the next ten seconds. Finally, without slackening the pace, he spoke. "Then maybe it's time you were let into the game."

# CHAPTER ELEVEN

The darkened row of cabins that were the Seaborn Motel could have passed at that moment for the Bates Motel. Burke cruised the Crown Vic onto the grass of an adjoining vacant lot.

I knew enough to whisper. "What's the plan, Burke?"

"The plan is for you to keep your mouth shut and stay two feet behind me. Come on."

We passed silently through the darkness, hugging the fronts of cabins that all joined each other until we reached the one that gave off a thin line of light at the shaded window. I could see Burke put his ear to the door to check for voices and then quickly scan the surroundings.

He put his mouth to my ear. Still, I could barely hear him. "There are two of them. Follow this to the letter, Knight. You're going in that cabin next door. No lights. You're going to count ten seconds. Find the biggest chair you can lift. When you hit ten, throw the chair with everything you've got in that skinny body of yours against the wall it shares with this cabin. Have you got that?"

I just nodded. He moved silently to the next cabin. I was on his heels. I could see him slip something out of his pocket to pry open the door.

"In with you, Knight. Start counting now."

The open door caught just enough scant beams of light from cars on Route 1 to outline the furniture. I was up to the count of "three" when I found a solid wooden chair that I could lift over my head. Between "five" and "seven" the thought flashed through my mind that this is one hell of a sketchy plan to hang our lives on, but nothing better suggested itself.

I hauled back at "nine" with my elbows cocked and the chair held high. On "ten" I said, "God help us," and threw the chair with every ounce of force I could put into it. The glass in a picture frame shattered, and the two of the legs drove holes through the thin wall into the next cabin.

There wasn't a fraction of a second between the crash of the chair and the sound of the front door of the lighted cabin next door being kicked off its hinges. Another fraction of a second and the deafening staccato bursts of automatic weapon fire filled the silence.

I ran to the door of the cabin next door. The bullet-punctured bodies of two men I didn't know lay at odd angles on the floor, but the only point of interest to me was the slumped body of Lex Devlin tied to a chair in the center of the room.

I ran to him, praying for any sign of life. Burke was already there, feeling under the jaw for a pulse. In seconds, he was hitting the emergency number on the cabin phone. My hopes rose when I heard him call for an ambulance and EMTs.

Together we cut the ropes and gently laid Mr. Devlin on the bed. His face was white as a sheet, and I could barely hear sounds of spasmodic breathing. There were no signs of injury on his face. Whatever they did to him must have been to the body.

It was less than five minutes before the sirens wailed and an ambulance ground to a stop by the door. The EMTs were professionals. They worked like a team at double time. Within three minutes of their arrival, Mr. Devlin was in the white wagon with oxygen and intravenous going, and gadgets I couldn't identify taking readings of heaven knows what.

I jumped into the ambulance without asking and just hovered out of the way while the tires threw stones on the driveway to Route 1. The siren and lights went full bore to clear the way for what I thanked God was clearly a Boston driver at the wheel.

We reached a hospital where the waiting crew took charge without a wasted motion. Mr. Devlin was out of sight and into their good hands within what seemed like seconds. For the first time since I took that first step into Pi Alley, I took a normal inhale and exhale.

From that moment until the first rays of sunlight lit a horizon in the direction of Boston, I sat alone in the hospital waiting room with a notion I had never before considered—walking into those offices at 77 Franklin Street and not dropping in for morning coffee with my quasi-father/partner. Since that notion was more than I could face, I replaced it with the words that have often straightened my spine: "Be not afraid. I go before you always. Come follow me, and I will give you rest."

Sometime toward dawn, I must have given in to exhaustion, because I woke to the gentle nudge of a man in pale-green hospital clothes.

"He's going to make it. Can you hear me?"

I could hear him, but I couldn't speak. He sat down beside me. "I have to ask you something. He had some strange welts on his body, but they'll heal. It's his heart. Has he had an attack before?"

I said to hell with the moisture coming out of my eyes and just focused on the question.

"Yes. About three years ago. He seemed to come out of it. He's a criminal trial lawyer. They make 'em tough."

He nodded. "I think he'll come out of this one too, but he needs rest. I want to keep him here for a few days. Are you a relative?"

"As close as you can come to one. There are no others I know of. When can I see him?"

"Let's give him until tonight. He seems to have been through a lot. I want to keep him sedated for a while. We'll do everything we can."

He was up and gone and hopefully back to "doing everything we can." I felt totally washed over by relief, gratitude, and pure exhaustion. Everything ached, but there were things to do. First in line was a call to our faithful Tom Burns, with whom I figured we were running up a tab that would make the national debt seem like chump change. Clearly, the chance of a follow-up run-in with the boys from the North End was a major concern. I arranged with Tom for private security for Mr. Devlin with no fear of a leak as to his location.

The next step was one of human necessity. I checked into a local motel with three Big Macs, super-sized fries, and a mammoth Coke, since I couldn't remember the last time sustenance had passed my lips. I left a call for five that evening and drifted into blessed unconsciousness.

I woke up to the call at five p.m. A quick shot of motel coffee with two Motrin for chasers got me back on the road. On the drive to the hospital, I checked in with my secretary, Julie, by cell phone.

"Michael, thank God. Are you all right?"

"Never better, Julie. Never better."

If not the truth, at least it would stem the flow of oral chicken soup my mothering girl Friday would have unleashed through the phone.

"Is Mr. Devlin with you?"

"Sort of. Listen, Julie. Take this calmly. Mr. D. had a heart attack."

"What—?"

"He's all right. He's being well taken care of. He just needs a few days' rest."

"Where is he now?"

"Julie, I'm short of time. Check with his secretary, Lois, for any messages. Right now. I'll wait. Go."

That last diversion was partly to avoid letting one more person in on Mr. D.'s whereabouts. I was also curious about any follow-ups by the company we were keeping the previous night. Julie was back in a minute.

"He had a lot of the usual calls. Lawyers, clients. The usual suspects."

"Skip those. They can wait. Anything unusual?"

"Father Ryan called. Just to check in. Then this."

"What's 'this'?"

"Lois said someone with a rough Italian accent called three times. When she says he's not there, he just hangs up. Michael, is that anything?"

"No. Just a crank. They go with the territory. Listen, Julie, I want you to tell Lois that Mr. D. had a mild heart problem. Emphasize mild. He's recovering nicely. He'll be in touch with everyone in about a week. That's all. Not one word more. Lois can use that to stall off calls. Got that?"

"Of course, but—"

"Next, on Mr. Devlin's private line. Call Father Ryan. Tell him personally about Mr. D. Emphasize he'll be fine. In the meantime, we're on top of his situation. Got that?"

"All right, but—"

"Last one. Tell Lois that if the Italian calls back, before he hangs up, tell him Mr. Devlin wants to meet. Ask him where and when. Don't mention the heart attack. Have you got all that?"

I could sense the temperature rising. "Michael, this is not nothing. This is something. What have you two gotten into?"

"Absolutely nothing that can't be handled by your following instructions to the letter. Gotta go, Julie. I'll be in touch."


I soft walked into Mr. D.'s room in the ICU. He heard my approach and turned a weary, drawn, pasty-looking face toward me. Those eyes that could blaze and give palpitations to junior associates and assistant prosecutors looked soft and sedated, but the Irish smile was still quick on the trigger—a bit dreamy and faint, but I knew he knew me.

"How's the old warrior?"

"Fit, and as tough as the day I beat the school bully in the Charlestown schoolyard."

"That was a sweet pair of bullies you took on last night."

"I had them right where I wanted them. Another few minutes and they'd be pleading for mercy."

"Right. You do draw a strange lot of companions."

He just nodded. I thought he was drifting back to sleep, but he caught my eyes with his and I saw a trace of the old fire. "Truth told, I guess the Lone Ranger rode to my rescue again. Thank you, Michael."

"Actually, more like Tonto. Last night's Lone Ranger is someone I hope you'll meet someday. One of our Irish countrymen."

"What's he got to do with all this?"

"I haven't figured him out yet. We both owe him our lives. At least maybe a good dinner at the Top of the Hub."

"Soon as I get out of here."

I scanned the wires and tubes he had running in and out of everywhere.

"About that. I want a promise."

The old eyebrows could still rise up at this reversal of roles.

"I want you out of sight and out of action till we can take them on together. I need that promise. Or else I may have to rough you up all over again."

I didn't know how he'd take that, but he just started to laugh until his worked-over ribs cut it short.

"I'll be gone for a while, Mr. Devlin."

That canceled out the humor. The old scowl was back. He could always smell danger on my part, and he always forbade me to get into it—which is why I seldom told him in advance. This was different.

"Where? How long?"

"Ireland. And I don't know. Maybe a few days. We'll see."

"Why in the damned hell—?"

"Because it's necessary. Listen, they'll be throwing me out of here in a minute. I'll speak fast. It's like this. You know about the mess our client Kevin O'Byrne got into. You also know about the trouble that suddenly dropped on Father Ryan. I think there's a connection, and I think you agree. We've run out of leads here, but I got a name that might open up something. It's someone in Ireland."

"Where did you get it?"

"The Irishman who pulled your chestnuts out of the fire last night. He let me in on a piece of what this thing is all about. I better go. Remember, I'm holding you to that promise. Out of sight till I get back. Those boys don't play nice."

I beat a quick retreat before he could grill me for particulars that would only give him worrying fits. His voice caught me at the door.

"Michael, for the love of the saints, what is it about?"

I said it in the lowest voice that would carry to his bed.

"Diamonds, Mr. D. The kind they call 'blood diamonds' from Africa."

# PART TWO

# CHAPTER TWELVE

Sierra Leone, West Africa, 1999

This was the start of a good day. No, better than that. This was to be the best day of all nine years of Bantu's life. The first rays of sun were just cracking the pall of constant rain clouds of the rainy season. His red dirt village of Koinu in eastern central Sierra Leone on the Atlantic coast of Africa had been soaked by unremitting rainfall for five months. Soon the red clay floor of his family hut would have the respite necessary to absorb the unending drenching of everything in and out of the hut. Even the suffocating hundred-degree heat would subside slightly.

That meant that his father would leave him, his mother, and younger brother and sister to walk deep into the all-but-solid mass of jungle palm and banana bushes to neighboring villages to trade for food and clothing. But what made this year and this day special was that his father's last words to him were a commission, a deputation of trust in his budding maturity.

"You are the man while I'm gone, Bantu. Keep them safe."

In the years before Bantu was born, those words would have been merely a symbolic gesture of a father's confidence in his son. Since the events of early 1991, they took on a darker significance and laid a ponderous weight on Bantu's immature shoulders.

In leaving, his father counted on the fact that the menace had so far kept its distance from Bantu's village. Word had spread through the mud villages of the Kono region of horrors so inhuman as to be beyond belief. Some villagers avoided the unthinkable by considering the reports mere offshoots of the superstitions of the neighboring Kamajor tribes. Disbelief kept pace with tales too hellish to be fact.

Then the sounds began echoing off the distant hills and penetrating the protective wall of vegetation. The static bursts of AK-47s punctuating human cries were chilling, but still distant enough to be of another world.

One reassuring thought freed Bantu's father to make his annual trek to the neighboring villages. The sounds were still sufficiently distant that if the monster should approach his village, there would certainly be time for his family to flee into jungle undergrowth so thick that anyone passing within three feet of them would be oblivious to their presence.

His father had been gone a week. Bantu was settling into the self-esteem of his recently elevated position in the family. There were still sporadic reminding echoes from a distance, but nothing to change the village routine.

On the eighth dawn of his father's absence, Bantu was sleeping a short distance from the family hut, close to the slight coolness at the jungle's edge. There was no transition. There was not a split second between his life of sanity and kindness, and the rupture of everything human.

They exploded out of every pore of the jungle wall. Staccato, deafening bursts of automatic gunfire strafed every hut within view. He saw friends he had known since birth, polka dotted with crimson holes, blown off their feet, turning the once red dirt crimson.

The invaders came in hordes, screaming curses and spraying death until Bantu could not count the loss of people who had been his life. And worst yet, if there could be such a thing, their invaders who followed with razor-sharp machetes worked horrors so stunning that he was frozen to the spot.

His father's words, "Keep them safe," stung him to the core. He started to run through the numbing evidence of death toward his own hut. But he could only cover half the ground before his mother's and sister's cries from inside the hut went suddenly silent.

He saw two of the invaders half drag, half carry his six-year-old brother off toward the jungle. He ran at an angle to cut them off. He had no idea of what he could do against machetes, but he had to try.

His scrawny legs carried him at their best speed around an outlying hut to charge the two pulling his wailing brother into the brush. He never saw it coming from behind. In the flash of a blade, he was in the mud with a gaping wound in his side. One seized him by the back of his neck and lifted him to his feet. A second came at him with a machete raised.

An instant before the blade came down, an order barked from one in command stopped it in midflight. Another order was barked. His two captors pulled him with feet dragging to the center of the village and threw him in the center of a circle with four other terrified boys of his age.

For the first time since the furies of hell exploded into what was now unrecognizable as his village, he saw their faces, and the horror of what was happening was magnified twofold. They were the faces of boys not three years older than his nine years. But they were faces such as he could never imagine. They were human faces without the least trace of humanity. The eyes were glass, lit with the unnatural fire of what he would come to know too well as drugs.

The terror around him continued as if feeding on itself until Bantu's mind could no longer bear the assault and shut down. The merciful balm of unconsciousness let him keep a slim grasp on his sanity. But the Bantu who had laid down by the jungle's edge the night before was gone forever.

He woke with no sense of time, tied to a tree in the center of the camp of the child soldiers who had taken all but his life. Boys and girls within two or three years of his own age, dressed in faded camouflage T-shirts and brown slacks, wandered among the refuse of their camp as if in a drug-induced abandonment of reality. Most carried the omnipresent AK-47 assault rifles slung over their shoulders. Others wielded machetes in sporadic outbreaks of fights among themselves.

Bantu noticed an older boy, probably as old as fourteen, giving the orders. Each order was accompanied by a gesture with the automatic rifle toward one of his village friends tied to a tree. Each was, in turn, untied and raised to his feet. He was pushed toward the center of the circle while the leader watched him walk. If he was unable to walk steadily, the execution order was given and carried out immediately.

When Bantu's turn came, in spite of the pain from his wounded side, he knew he had to walk upright for his life. He apparently passed the scrutiny of the leader because an order was barked. Two of the child soldiers tied his hands in line with the other prisoners who had passed the test, and the trek began.

He walked on the heels of the boy ahead of him from that morning's sunrise until the scant light that penetrated the growth of jungle ceiling was below the horizon. The pain in his side was all that kept him conscious to move one foot ahead of the other after exhaustion had set in.

Not all of the boys survived the trek, but Bantu allowed one thought to keep him on his feet when his strength could no longer sustain him. Somewhere in the horror the world had become were his father and younger brother, and if God could still find Bantu in all of this hell to deliver him, he'd find them. In the years that followed, he never let that thought diminish.

On the evening of the third day of endless slogging through jungle mud, the small band of survivors came to a sight so foreign to Bantu that he had no idea what he was seeing. The jungle opened onto a clearing with a massive sixty-foot circular pit of mud at the center. Ten or twelve bone-thin male figures clad only in torn shorts stood knee-deep in the reddish-brown fetid liquid, covered in mud and slime.

Their bodies moved in the macabre rhythm of exhaustion. They appeared to dredge pails full of solids from the bottom of the pit and dump them onto mounds of the sludge by the bank. Another five or six of the cadaverous figures filled circular wooden pans with sieved bottoms from the piles of sludge. They shook and sluiced the material in the pit's liquid until small stones collected in the center. They scanned the stones in the pans, emptied them, and refilled the pans from the sludge pile on the bank. Occasionally, one of the stones caused an alert. It was taken from the pan and immediately handed over to the armed guard hovering over the ritual.

While Bantu soon realized that his life had been spared to become one of the skeletal workers in the pit, driven by the child guards with AK-47s overseeing the operation, he had no notion of what was worth the suffering that was spent on the task. Clearly, nothing edible could survive in the noxious sludge of the pit.

His confusion was lifted his first day in the pit. The few forbidden words that could be stealthily exchanged between laborers when the attention of the guards was drawn to something in one of the pans opened a world to Bantu that no one of his age, or any age, should experience. He came to realize that all of the killing, the torture, the satanic inhumanity was driven by the insatiable lure of the small chunks of milky-white rock that occasionally appeared in the sluicing pans. Now he knew what, but he still had no idea why. Even the name meant nothing to him, but he knew it would rule whatever was left of his life—diamonds.

# CHAPTER THIRTEEN

Bantu's days ground on in the monotony and painful exhaustion of work in the pit. The days, then the weeks, then the months, then the years. Thoughts of escape died early in the first week. Instead of chains, his captors used the weapon of sheer exhaustion. The back-breaking labor began at first light and ended with darkness. There were no breaks, and the only sustenance was a cup of rice at day's end if his labors were judged worthy of keeping him alive.

The other prison wall was the jungle itself. One man or boy running alone would be unlikely to survive the swarms of malarial mosquitoes, poisonous snakes, and what was worse than both of those—venomous black ants.

In the enforced isolation from communication with other prisoners, it was years before Bantu was able to piece together an understanding of what it was that had so completely despoiled every spark of humanity that had originally been born in the child soldiers who dominated every painful moment of his day. What he didn't know was that the seeds of the country's devastation began in the 1930s, when a British geologist discovered rough diamonds strewn on or just under the ground in certain regions of eastern Sierra Leone. No other substance on earth could have so thoroughly cursed the life of the entire country.

What Bantu did come to know was that in 1991, the year he was born, a rebel group called the RUF, the Revolutionary United Front, trained in the inhumane arts in Libya, poured across the border of Sierra Leone out of neighboring Liberia. It was not liberation or political revolution that ultimately drove them. It was the soul-sucking lust to capture and control the regions of Sierra Leone that held the earth's bounty in rough diamonds.

The RUF swelled its ranks of killers by capturing young teens and subteens from the jungle villages in eastern Sierra Leone. They trained them to kill at the point of an AK-47, the cheap, light, plentiful weapon of choice of most African rebel groups. Whatever residue of human conscience remained in their child captives after their first compelled killings, sometimes of their own families, was drowned in a sea of drugs to produce an army as destructive and devoid of conscience as any on the face of the earth.

The evil fed on itself. Once the RUF had control of a diamond rich area, captured child slave labor in the pit gave them a continuing source of the rough gems. Mules in the form of other young slave laborers under close guard trekked the gems across the easy border of Liberia, where the RUF found willing buyers who would pay for the stones with the Russian-developed Kalashnikov AK-47s, ammunition, and even rocket launchers. And, of course, the other weapon of choice, drugs.

Once the sale was completed, the cases of weapons and ammunition were loaded on the backs of the human mules for the twenty-five-mile return trek. Any mule that could not keep pace under the crushing load was disposed of on the spot. His load was then distributed among the remaining mules.

What Bantu came to learn later was that the rough gems, harvested illegally by the rebels in captured territory through the agonies of child slave labor, once across the Liberian border, made their way into the hands of diamond merchants, and then into the mainstream of legal diamonds. From there, it was a direct route to the diamond cutters of Antwerp or London or Mumbai, and then onto the necks or wrists of fine ladies throughout the world with no notion of the price in human suffering that had been paid for their privilege.

Bantu's years in the pits followed seamlessly one on another, interrupted only by an occasional forced march from one pit to another when the government army would mount an assault to take back a particular diamond-rich area from the rebels. The only extraordinary part of Bantu's subjugation was that it went on years longer than any of the other child laborers who eventually succumbed to the ravages of starvation and exhaustion and were no longer capable of justifying the cup of rice at day's end.

What kept Bantu's aching arms moving and his back bent over the fetid sludge day upon day to earn the cup of life-sustaining rice was one single thought. *My father and my brother are somewhere waiting for me. I am the man of the family. I am the man of the family. I am the man of the family.*

It had been nine years since the world he would never see again had imploded. It was a day like any other. The rainy season had relented. The jungle trails used by the human mules to trek harvested rough diamonds were carpeted in a greasy mud base solid enough to permit movement.

A band of mules had just launched its twenty-five-mile trek to the Liberian border. The turnaround between trips had been shorter in time than usual because of the rebels' need for a resupply of weapons and ammunition to fend off attacks by government troops. The effects of lack of rest on the mules became obvious to the rebel guards before they had been gone half a day. The band of mules were weaving, some dropping from exhaustion within five miles of the start of the trek. The others had little chance of standing under the added weight of cases of bullets and assault rifles on the return trip.

The child leader sent a runner back to the pit for fresher legs. The pit boss barked a command at Bantu to come up out of the pit. Caked in the slime and grit of the pit, he stood, confused by the order. A burst of fire just over his head from the pit boss's rifle jarred him into climbing out of the pit to be marched to where the column of mules had stopped.

Bantu was given a small leather sack to hold ahead of him in plain view of the rifle-bearing guard by his side, and the march began. Bantu knew the sack contained the rough, milky stones that would be traded for weapons and drugs. He also knew that if he should drop his hand out of sight, the AK-47 would instantly end his dream of finding his father and brother.

While the march under the tightly packed banana and mango vegetation brought relief from the blistering sun and the exhaustion of the pit, it substituted the constant whine of infectious mosquitoes, and wariness for deadly mounds of poisonous ants on the path and snakes that could drop out of the trees.

Each day's march was suspended when darkness made finding the path impossible. By the end of the second day, they were a day's trek short of the Liberian border where one load would be exchanged for another.

They were a half mile from the usual camping spot as the sun's last rays barely lit the path. The three guards in the lead went on ahead to clear the camping ground of anything deadly. That left four of the rebels to guard the halted column of six mules.

Bantu noticed that there was a sudden stillness in the air, a slight absence of the surrounding amalgam of sounds that made the jungle seem a living, breathing creature. The rebel guards who remained with the mules had helped themselves to the white powder contained in one of the sacks. They were arguing in the agitated state the powder always produced. They never noticed the slight change in the atmosphere.

The odd stillness was almost complete, when it was broken by the hoarse rush of air from the lungs of the rearmost rebel guard who plunged headlong into the mule at the back of the line. The mule screamed in shock, as the limp body of the guard rolled off of his back to expose the hilt of a machete jutting from his back.

That scream touched off a cacophony of yells and high-pitched chants out of black bodies that leaped out of the vegetation wielding killing blows of machetes to each of the rebel guards before any of them could swing a rifle into firing position.

Amid the panic of screaming rebels, attackers, and prisoners, Bantu dropped to the ground and rolled his body into the dense mass of vegetation that hid him completely within two seconds. He froze every muscle, hidden just off the trail, clutching for his life the small sack of gemstones he had been forced to carry.

He barely breathed. He was sure the attackers were Kamajor tribesmen, the only force other than the army that challenged the strongholds of the rebels. Their physical weapons were basic knives and machetes, easily outpowered by the rifles and rocket launchers of the rebels. But they combined these with the clever use of surprise and an emboldening superstitious belief in the power of chants and fetishes to make them impervious to bullets and even invisible to their enemies.

Bantu froze where he was in the bush. He knew that what he held in the bag would ensure his death under the blade of a diamond-hungry Kamajor as quickly as from a rebel bullet. The only light now came from flashes of fire and tracer bullets from the rifles of the re-turning patrol of the rebels. Within seconds, the firepower of the rebels laid waste the Kamajor warriors and spread the bullet-ridden bodies of the mules caught in the fire across the path.

When the firing ceased, the night blackness was absolute. Bantu listened to the confused squabbling of the rebels over their next move. The dark was a major ally of any other Kamajors in the area and neutralized the rebels' superiority of weapons. In spite of the dangers of night travel in the jungle, they had to move out. The shouting was over which direction. The decision to advance toward the Liberian border was driven by the fear of returning to the rebel leadership without fresh rifles and ammunition.

Bantu's decision was easy. He couldn't go back to life in the pit. He couldn't stay where he was or go deeper into the jungle for a dozen different natural deadly reasons. He chose to follow in the wake of the rebels to the border. If he stayed just out of sight, he could follow the dim light of their flashlights in the hopes that the sound of their movement might clear the way of anything lethal—human or other-wise.

Before leaving, Bantu stripped the camouflage shirt and brown pants off the rebel closest to his fit. The clothes were streaked with blood, but that would not appear totally out of character for a rebel.

By dawn, the foot-weary train of rebels and mules had crossed the border into Liberia. Since Bantu had never in his life left the immediate area of his village until he was taken captive, the rest of the world was an unexplored labyrinth.

He watched from a distance as the exchange of gems for weapons with men waiting in trucks was completed close to the border. The rebels themselves had to replace the human beasts of burden. Once they cleared Bantu's line of sight on their return across the border, there was no choice but to go forward on the path to whatever town or village lay ahead.

It was mid-morning when the path led Bantu to the largest village he had ever seen. What had been mud huts in the only village he had ever known were mostly decrepit thatched-roof cinder block shacks, crowded together along a wide, garbage-strewn mud road that carried the main coagulation of humanity's dregs. Refugees in every state of dysfunction from lost limbs to untreated malaria and polio wandered in what seemed aimless begging paths among those with business to do. And the only business was obvious. The main street was rife with crude signs over doorless entrances that announced "Diamond Merchant."

Even given his previous nine years in the pit, Bantu thought this town, with its stench of stagnant water and festering wounds, was a way station to hell.

The bloodied camouflage shirt and brown pants he was wearing clearly identified him as RUF, but his boney face and skeletal body said otherwise. His first concern was that any of the dozens of RUF child soldiers who wandered the same street could put the two together and spot him as an escapee. His worst nightmare of the moment was recapture.

As he moved farther through the amalgam, he began to realize that the RUF there were too heavily drugged to take notice, and no one else could see beyond their own plight. His fears of recognition and return to the pit fell away as he blended into the disconnection of each of the wandering souls from all of the other lost souls.

Bantu's body was screaming for two immediate needs: rest and almost anything to eat, in that order. He found an alleyway between two cinder block shacks wide enough to accommodate his body and fell in a state of exhaustion. His last move before giving in to unconsciousness was to find a chink in one of the cinder blocks large enough to stash the leather bag of rough gems he had clutched for his life.

# CHAPTER FOURTEEN

The sun was well down when Bantu felt light blows to his feet. They pulled him out of one darkness into another. He became aware that a massive figure, lit from behind by the faint glow of a bulb from the main street, was casting a large shadow over him.

"Hey dere. How's wichu? You alive?"

The voice was accompanied by gentle nudges to the bottom of his feet. Bantu went rigid. For nine years he had not met a single human being who did not want to do him harm.

The voice laughed. The laugh had the kind of hearty, good-natured sound that Bantu had not heard since the day his world fractured. He sat up, but braced himself against the cinder block wall.

"Don't chu have no fear 'bout Jimbo. I don't mean you no harm a'tall. Come on outta dere."

The wall of distrust built over nine years did not fall in an instant.

"Hey you, fella. Come on now. Jimbo take care of you. You hungry?"

The words brought him back to the type of English Bantu had learned in his village school. The last word in particular stung his awareness. He had passed hunger two days ago. Whatever this giant had in store for him, if it included anything edible, the temptation overcame all fears.

The voice continued to tempt him. "You don't worry a bit. I'm Mandingo. No RUF here. I got no trouble for you. Maybe even good for you. Come on."

Bantu seized on the word, "Mandingo." He had heard his RUF captors talking about this breed of wandering dealers in rough diamonds. They had no scruples about the legal or illegal source of the stones, but he had never heard of them doing anyone harm. They were apparently go-betweens, arranging sales from the RUF to whoever was willing to pay a price in cash or guns.

Bantu got to his feet and moved out into the dim light.

"Come on, lad. You need food, yes? How you called?"

Bantu followed this largest man he had ever seen, but remained silent. They moved through the waves of begging humanity to a building larger than the rest with a hand-scrawled sign, "Cantina." Bantu wondered why this giant ignored every desperately needy beggar at his knees, and yet offered to feed him. No matter. He'd worry about that after food had passed his lips.

While the fetid smell of the street seemed magnified in the captured heat inside the cantina, all Bantu could think of was the possibility of food. The unlikely twosome weaved through some tables, at which the local alcoholic product was already taking its evening toll, and others where whispered deals for the buying and selling of every illicit substance known to man were the business of the day. While drugs, arms, and other substances were on the trading block, it ceased to surprise Bantu from the snatches of whispered conversation that the overwhelming subject of trade was raw diamonds.

The giant, Jimbo, led him to an empty back corner table. A heavy fist on the table caught the attention of one of the cantina workers. Jimbo bellowed two words: "Food. Drink."

Within a minute, the worker brought a bowl of thick stew, a dish of rice that would have fed him for a week in the pit, and some kind of liquid smelling of alcohol. It was the first food he had eaten in more than starvation portions in nine years. Bantu could not identify anything but the rice, but it made no difference. The giant let him eat in silence. The plates were cleaned in less than two minutes.

The giant pounded the table. "Again!"

The worker brought more of the same. This time Bantu slowed to a pace that was merely ravenous. In the midst of it, he paused just long enough to look up with one word. "Bantu."

"What?"

"Bantu. You asked my name."

The giant laughed that hearty laugh again, and Bantu went back to eating.

"Ah, so you speak. You call me 'Jimbo.' It's not my name, but everyone else does."

Bantu kept eating for fear that any interruption might see the plates disappear. When he finished, he looked up again with curiosity in his eyes.

"Why?"

"Why what, lad?"

Bantu just nodded to the plates.

"Ah! Why I treat you to this wonderful meal?"

What Bantu was really asking was why this man was treating him with the kind of human decency that would have been common in his village, but that he thought no longer existed in the world.

"Well now. Here's my thinkin'. When I see you in the alley, I say here's this boy dressed like any one of them RUF slime. But he don't look like 'em. He look like what they do to them young boys in the pits."

The panic of recapture and return seized Bantu. He braced to bolt at the fist sign of restraints by the giant. But they never came.

"No fear, Bantu. Looka me. You know I'm no RUF. But I say to myself, he most likely escape from the pits. This boy must be something. Damn few make it out. Like, I think no one I ever hear of. Then I say something else. You wanna hear?"

Bantu looked into his eyes and let the question hang.

"Okay, so I say, maybe this boy bring something with him. You know what I sayin'?"

Bantu shook his head slowly.

"Sure you do, Bantu. You know. Like maybe you bring some them funny stones with you."

Bantu just shook his head. The giant just smiled.

"Because you and me, we maybe help each other. See here, Bantu. I don't steal. Not my way. But if you have them stones, what you do with 'em? Can't eat 'em, right?"

Bantu just sat in silence. Trust had been too completely stamped out of him to return in an instant.

"Okay, Bantu. We say this. You get hungry tomorrow. You come back here. I be right here this table. You think 'bout this. I know people. I get you good price. Maybe even somethin' else. I don't know. We'll see. You hear me?"

Bantu rose from the table on legs more steadied by the meal than he could remember in years.

"So, tomorrow maybe, Bantu."

Bantu nodded and made his way through the tables toward the door. His head was down to avoid eye contact, but a sense of something watching drew his eyes to a table toward the front corner. It was just a glance, but it put near panic in his step. He saw the faces of two of the RUF who had kept guard over him in the pit.

Did they see him? Did they recognize him? He couldn't be sure one way or the other. Once outside, he weaved his way into the motley crowd buying, selling, begging, or just aimlessly moving up and down the main street. He walked for at least an hour until he felt that as nearly as he could tell, no one in the crowd was paying him any particular attention.

He found his way back to the alley where he had stashed the bag of rough diamonds. He crawled in on hands and knees with the intent of retrieving the bag to find a more secure stash. He was about to put his hand in the hole in the cement block when a sense of impending danger washed over him. Something about the rapid cadence of two sets of footsteps approaching set off alarms.

Bantu just lay himself flat on the ground as if he had just found a quiet place to sleep. His eyes were shut, but he could tell that someone had blocked the dim light in the alley. This time the kick to the bottom of his feet brought a shock of pain through his spine.

"Get up, you!"

He was on his feet before another blow could cripple his feet. He was staring into the cold, lifeless eyes of the two RUF from the cantina. He could feel the rising surge of hope drain out of him.

"Outta there, you!"

The AK-47s in their hands emphasized the order with a gesture. He thought at that moment of letting them just end his agony with one burst of rifle fire. But again the words came back. *You are the man in the family.*

He moved in the direction indicated by the rifles. The only effect of the weapons on the disparate mass of humanity they passed through was to clear a wider path and discourage most of the begging.

A block beyond the cantina, the weapons gestured a command to enter one of the cinder block buildings. It was deeper than the others with a second room in the back behind a long cloth hanging for a door. The way was blocked by another child guard with a rifle. He stood aside as one of Bantu's escorts planted the butt of the rifle between Bantu's shoulders and shoved him into the second room.

The only light in the room came from a dust-covered kerosene lamp on a low table that barely lit the eyes and forehead of another RUF rising from a frayed army cot. He looked up at the two escorts for an explanation.

"This one's from the Koido pit, Captain. I know him. He was on the delivery that was ambushed. There were stones missing."

The one sitting on the cot looked over at Bantu. He couldn't see features in the dark, but no matter. They were all alike to him, except this one had information. He spoke in a tone that was devoid of warmth, hatred, anger, anything human.

"I'll ask this just once. You can answer and we end this. Otherwise, I give an order you won't like. Where are the diamonds you stole?"

Bantu had no fondness for the diamonds that had caused all of his misery. But these in particular could mean his chance for a life, a chance to find his father and brother. He simply stood silent.

The one on the cot shrugged. "All the same to me."

He looked at the two who had brought him and again spoke without emotion. "Take him. Don't come back without the diamonds."

One of the two grabbed Bantu by the arm while the other held open the cloth door. Light from lanterns in the first room fell full on the face of the one on the cot.

Bantu looked straight at the face. He screamed, "My God, my God!"

The one on the cot was beyond being moved by the anguished pleas of his victims, but something caused him to look up at this one.

Bantu's eyes filled with tears. He could only whisper, "My God. Sinda."

For a brief second something alive came into the eyes of the one on the cot. He caught himself and stood slowly. He said to the two soldiers, "Never mind. I'll do this myself. Go to the cantina. Get me whiskey. Take him with you." He gestured to the guard who had been standing at the door.

The three hesitated until he gave them a look that said his orders would not be questioned. When they had cleared the outside door, he came slowly around the table and stood looking at the one standing alone in front of him. Bantu spoke first. His face was covered with moisture.

"My God, my God, how could it be? Are you Sinda? Are you my brother?"

It had been so many years since the boy soldier in front of him had been permitted to feel anything remotely human that he was stunned that there was any spark to reignite. He just said in a whisper, "Bantu."

Bantu moved close to him. This figure in a hated RUF uniform was a part of his flesh from a time he could hardly remember.

His tears would not stop. He held his arms out to the stone figure in front of him and slowly closed his hands around his brother's arms. The frozen shell that had encased Sinda's heart began to crack. He fought it, because he knew that that shell was his only protection against an unbearable self-hatred for the things he'd had to do since that day in his village.

Bantu held his brother close to his heart. Sinda's face was washed with Bantu's tears, and the shell dissolved. Soon it was impossible to tell whether the tears were coming from Bantu's or Sinda's eyes.

When he could speak, Sinda whispered, "There's so much to say, and so much I can't say. But they'll be back. You have to leave."

"One thing has to be asked. Is our father alive?"

Sinda looked down. "Yes. He was taken by the RUF when he came back to our village."

"Tell me quickly. Is he all right? Where is he?"

"He's alive. That's all I know. They keep him somewhere around Kenema."

"How do you know?"

"I know because they let me see him once a year. That's how they keep me. After they took me from the village, they brought us together. They threatened to do things to him in front of me unless I followed their orders. As long as I do, they keep him alive."

Bantu's heart ached at the thought of their father in RUF hands, but at least he was alive.

"Could we buy his freedom? I could give myself back to them in his place."

Sinda shook his head. "They can get a dozen of you in a raid on one village. And younger. They only listen to money and the weapons it can buy them."

"How much?"

"Does it matter? We don't have it."

"Perhaps. Those men were right. I have a small bag of rough diamonds."

"Probably not enough. The buyers in this hellhole won't pay much for the dirty ones."

"But somewhere else. Keep your faith, Sinda. Nothing's impossible. Look at us standing here together."

Sinda nodded without conviction.

"How much will it take?"

Sinda shook his head. "A lot. More than you could get for a bag of rough diamonds in this town. I've been of great service to them. They want to hang onto me."

"Then I'll go somewhere else."

Sinda pulled back the cloth curtain. He looked through the outer door for the returning soldiers.

"You have to go now, Bantu. They'll be back."

"What will they do to you if I'm gone?"

"They won't question me. They'll assume I took a bribe. They probably expect it. Besides, I have the power of life and death over them. Go, Bantu. God go with you. I never thought I'd say that word again."

# CHAPTER FIFTEEN

Bantu left and blended seamlessly into the mass of weaving derelicts and RUFs in the street. He knew now that it was only a matter of time before other guards from the pits would spot him. He went directly to the alley. He knelt down and pulled the bag of stones from the cinder block. His only plan was to run somewhere beyond the edge of the town. He felt he had better odds against the lethal creatures of the jungle than the human ones with AK-47s.

Before he could turn and straighten up, he heard a sharp, commanding voice behind him. He knew that if he looked back, he'd be looking into the muzzles of two AK-47s in the hands of the two RUF who had found him in that alley before. His fear both for himself and for his brother was that they had overheard the conversation.

At the sound of the voice, the breath went out of him. He was certain they'd take the diamonds, his only hope for his father. Then they'd take him back to the pit or kill him, which amounted to the same thing. For the first time in all of his captivity, he lost the will to cling to his life. He just lay down flat. They could do what they wanted to him.

He closed his eyes. Just as he was surrendering himself, he heard a resounding crack that echoed off the walls of the alley. He spun around to see the giant figure of Jimbo with one of the RUFs under each arm. They just hung there lifelessly. Bantu knew then that the crack was the collision of the RUFs' heads in the arms of Jimbo.

"Come on you, Bantu. My goodness, what you do widout Jimbo? Gotta get you outta here. Move fast. Bring them stones you got wicha."

Bantu sprang to his feet. Jimbo dropped his two armloads into the alley. He led the way at quick march through the main street and down a side passageway to a dark spot behind a pile of garbage. He pulled a large sheet off an old battered Jeep.

"Get in, Bantu. No questions."

Bantu followed the order. In an instant they were coursing along the rough ground behind the buildings. When they cleared the last building, Jimbo cut back onto the main road and turned away from the town. The lights of the Jeep found the dirt-and-gravel path that penetrated the solid jungle mass of vegetation. The ride through the jungle was rough, but Jimbo seemed to know it well.

Bantu grabbed the roll bar over the seats for stability. He let his tightly strung nerves unwind. Their destination was a complete mystery beyond the short reach of the headlights, but he knew that he was out of immediate danger, and Jimbo had so far shown no inclination to do him harm. In spite of the roughness of the dry dirt road, Bantu's hands locked on the roll bar, and he managed to slip into a sleep of exhaustion.

His first awareness that they had driven all night came with his waking glimpse of sunlight on an expanse of windswept water that stretched beyond his sight.

"I bet you never see the Atlantic Ocean, Bantu."

Bantu just shook his head. His second awareness was that they were driving along a paved road that skirted the largest village he had ever seen.

"This here Freetown. This the capital of Sierra Leone. But you don't care 'bout that. You just wanna sell what you got in dat bag. Right?"

Bantu was still leery of giving too much information. He just continued to look at sights that were beyond anything he had ever imagined. Jimbo pulled the Jeep over to the curb and put it in neutral. He turned to face Bantu.

"Looka here, Bantu. We gotta make some understanding. You hear me?"

Bantu looked over at him with his full attention and some newly aroused flares of caution.

"Here's where we are, Bantu. You got them rough stones and no way to get a good price for 'em. They what these people call 'conflict diamonds.' Sometimes they say 'blood diamonds.' I guess you know why. Ain't no one in this country gonna give more'n a tenth their value. You hear?"

Bantu took it in. He had no argument.

"Okay. So here's me. I got no diamonds, but I got good contacts. I got people, got a way to turn them stones into enough money to make us both happy. You hear me?"

Bantu slowly nodded with clear hesitation about where Jimbo was going.

"See now, that's no good, Bantu. The only way this works is we gotta trust each other. I never done you nothin' but good, right?"

Bantu nodded again.

"Den say it. You gotta talk to me. Can't just hide behind them nods. Gotta talk."

Jimbo sat back and waited.

Finally Bantu spoke. "Why do you do this for me?"

"All right. Now we talkin'. I be honest. I know you got the rough diamonds in that bag. I can help you get more money for 'em than you think in the world. I won't steal from you, and I won't betray you. I just want a fair share for my part. There be more'n enough for both. But you gotta believe in me. Else I leave you right here and I say to hell wichu. So what's gonna be?"

Bantu knew he was at the crossroads of his life. He had only his intuition to guide him. With nothing else to go on, he looked into Jimbo's eyes, and the decision was made. He nodded.

"You gotta say it."

"I believe you."

"Okay, den, Bantu. You gimme the bag. You hand it to me."

It was like handing over his soul. It was one thing to say it and another to actually part with his hope for his father's life. Again he was moved by intuition. He reached inside of his shirt and took out the bag. He held it out to Jimbo.

Jimbo looked deep into Bantu's eyes and took the bag of rough diamonds out of his hand. He just held it for ten seconds. Then he handed it back to him.

"Good. Now I know you trust me, Bantu. No matter what happen, we never go back on that trust. You hear me?"

Bantu spoke the word. "Yes."

"Then we got things to do."

Jimbo put the Jeep in gear and drove farther along the beach road. He stopped at a beach house where, for a few coins, Bantu could shower the crusted grime of the pit off of his body. Back in the Jeep, they drove to a shop such as Bantu had never seen. It held men's clothing finer than anything he had ever encountered.

"First, we get you outta them RUF rags. They not so popular here."

Bantu stripped off the RUF shirt that still had the faded blood stains from the Kamajor ambush in the jungle. Jimbo grabbed it out of his hand and threw it into the gutter before they went into the shop.

Jimbo told the man who greeted him with a broad grin what he wanted. In fifteen minutes, they walked back to the Jeep. Bantu was wearing new chino pants, new sandals, and a collared shirt that bore no political associations. Jimbo looked him over before they got into the Jeep.

"You look good. Now we go do business."

As Jimbo drove into the center of the city, every block of Freetown was a revelation to Bantu. Most of the buildings still bespoke the waste and desolation of decades of civil wars and the uselessness of a government more devoted to corruption than rebuilding.

They drove through streets of the city teeming with refugees from the conflicts between government soldiers, the RUF, and the Kamajors—all for armed control of the pits that held the diamonds in the eastern half of Sierra Leone.

Jimbo mused to Bantu along the route that even the name of the city—Freetown—was a contradiction. It had been founded in the eighteenth century by the British as a free refuge for African slaves in America who had agreed to fight against the colonists in the American Revolution. That high moral purpose never stopped its later denizens from profiting from the ongoing traffic in newly captured African slaves.

In no less a contradiction, the swarms of refugees showing scars and lost body parts Bantu saw on their route through so-called Freetown gave clear evidence of the ongoing slavery of the Sierra Leone population to the rough gems that cursed the land.

Jimbo pulled up in front of a building on Charlotte Street. There were many signs throughout the city declaring simply "Diamond Merchant" in neat stenciling, as opposed to the crudely scrawled lettering in the town they had just left. The sign over the front door here bore the added legend, "Morty Bunce. Diamonds Bought and Sold."

Bantu looked at the sign. "You know him?"

"I know him for more years than you've been alive."

"Can you trust him?"

"I trust him as far as I could throw this fine building. Maybe less."

"Then why—?"

"Because he got contacts. He's English and Irish. Ninety percent them other diamond dealers Lebanese. They do us no good. He might."

He turned to face Bantu. "You gonna have to talk here. So be on your toes. Now listen. Here's how we do."

Jimbo was sucking air by the time he reached the second-floor landing. He knocked and opened the office door to the voice inside. The short, round man with a perspiration-covered bald pate jumped to his feet when he saw Jimbo. His short legs carried him around his desk to grab Jimbo's hand and pump it.

"Long time, my friend. What brings you out of that rotten jungle?"

"Business, Morty. Only kind of business that keeps either of us in this crazy country. Right? This my friend, Bantu."

Both Jimbo and Bantu noticed the hesitation before Bunce offered his hand. Jimbo knew Morty could see through the new clothing to a boy who still showed unmistakable signs of RUF treatment. Morty had no scruples about dealing for stones from RUF, Kamajor, or the devil himself, but not at close quarters in his own office.

"You say business, Jimbo. I'm intrigued." He held up his hands to ask what business.

"My friend has some merchandise. I told him you give him fair price."

Bunce took his seat behind his desk. He locked a grin in place and leaned over the desk toward Bantu. "Perhaps I could see the merchandise?"

Jimbo nodded to Bantu. With some uneasiness, Bantu took the bag out of his shirt and laid it on the desk. Bunce's small hands wrestled with the strings and opened the bag. He poured the small nuggets out on a piece of black felt. His expression remained as flat as a poker player's. Jimbo watched for the dilation of his eyes as he picked up one stone after another and raised them to the eyepiece held to his right eye. What he saw raised Jimbo's expectations.

When Bunce had examined the last stone, he put down the eyepiece and went into deep thought. Jimbo knew it was a game. He had reached a figure the instant he poured the gems onto the felt. He had even calculated the profit he'd make on them.

Bunce leaned back with a doleful look and spoke directly to Bantu. "I know where these came from. They're from the conflict zone around Kono. They don't bring much around here. Not like the legitimate stones from Namibia, South Africa, Botswana. You know what I'm saying? Isn't that right, Jimbo?"

Jimbo gave a noncommittal shrug to emphasize that he was keeping out of the bargaining.

Bunce looked back at Bantu.

"But, since you're a friend of Jimbo, I'll do better than anyone. I'll be generous. I'll give you three thousand English pounds."

Bantu looked down at the diamonds, which he had not seen out of the bag until that moment. Bunce took that instant to wink in Jimbo's direction. That meant another three thousand pounds to Jimbo for not interfering with the deal.

Bantu slowly gathered up the gems and put them back in the bag. He looked at Jimbo who simply shrugged to say, "It's up to you. It's your game."

Bantu looked back at Bunce. He remembered Jimbo's instructions. "You give me the money now?"

"Right this minute. Wait here."

Bunce got up and hurried his little body into an adjoining room and shut the door. In a minute, he called to Jimbo to join him. In a few minutes, Bunce reappeared with a stack of British pound notes. Jimbo came back behind him smiling.

Bantu laid the bag on the desk with his hand still holding the string. He pointed to a place beside it. Bunce was slightly surprised by the formal procedure, but he caught on and laid the stack of bills where Bantu pointed. At the same time, they each picked up what they had bargained for.

Jimbo and Bunce grinned at each other, shook hands, and Jimbo led Bantu out of the office and down the stairs. When they reached the sidewalk, Jimbo and Bantu leaned against the Jeep.

They waited ten seconds before the mélange of city sounds was split by the high-pitched shriek from the second-floor window. Bunce was leaning halfway out the window until he spotted Bantu and Jimbo casually resting against the Jeep.

His yells were punctuated by air-stabbing thrusts of his little fists.

"You get the hell up here, you little blighter. And you too, you Mandingo trash. Who the hell you think you're dealing with?"

Jimbo eased his body off the Jeep. "Don't get yourself in a stew, Morty. You'll have a stroke, and then you be no good to us. We have more business with you."

Together they climbed the stairs slowly to give Bunce time to get control of his blood pressure. They came into the office to find Bunce pacing like a small tiger.

"What the hell you think you're doing here?" He was stabbing his finger at the bag Bantu had given him on his desk, and the pile of small pieces of common gravel he had poured out of it. "You think you can cheat me. I could have you—"

"Sit down, Morty. Sit down."

"The hell I will."

"Morty. Sit yourself down. No one's cheating. You notice we still here."

Jimbo took the packet of pound notes out of his pocket and threw them on the desk. He nodded to Bantu, and Bantu did the same.

Bunce scooped up the notes and dropped back into the chair behind his desk. "You are one crazy Mandingo. You trying to kill me?"

"No, Morty. Educate you. Now let's do real business. I know you got some of them blood diamonds from those RUF pits around Kono. So does my friend, Bantu. Like you said, ain't neither of you gonna get a tenth what they worth anywhere on the African coast. You remember you told me you could do a deal with some buyer in Ireland. You remember?"

"So."

"So, this. You said you gotta get 'em there. You gotta smuggle 'em in. Meet the people. Do the deal. Get back out. You remember?"

Bunce looked over at Bantu. He was not comfortable with Jimbo's laying out details in front of a stranger.

"You listen, Morty. Who gonna do all that for you? You told me you can't leave this place. So never mind. I got a man can do that for you."

"Who?"

"My friend here, Bantu."

Bunce started to laugh and then just shook his head in disbelief. "I think those ants in the jungle have been eating your brain. You playing another trick on old Morty here, Jimbo?"

"No. No. No. Sit there. You listen, Morty. This man twenty years older'n he looks. Nine years now, he took everything the devil in hell could throw at him. You know them RUF. He survived it. It made him strong. Gotta cool head too. He don't panic at nothin'. I seen it."

Bunce raised his hands with a half smile.

"Jimbo, you idiot Mandingo, this is business. This is a business deal. What the hell does he know about business?"

Jimbo picked up one of the wads of pound notes and threw it into Bunce's lap. "He just did a scam on you. Cool as can be. Took you for six thousand pounds, countin' my kickback. Who else ever did that?"

Bunce still had the half smile, but he looked over at Bantu.

"How the hell did he do that?"

"When he had you go into the other room to the safe, get the money, he switch'd 'em. He picked up the pebbles from the street before we came in. He had 'em in his shirt."

"Except that was your idea, Jimbo. Not his."

"Don't matter whose idea. He pulled it off. And, another thing, he's honest. Won't cheat you. He made his point and, look here, he give you back your money. He could be heading for Conakry right now. You never find him."

The smile was gone from Bunce's lips. He just sat there in thought.

"So, what's the deal? What are you suggesting here?"

Jimbo leaned forward. "Give him some your rough stones to take to Ireland. Make it a test. He'll take his own. You arrange the contacts in Ireland. He can do the deal since they speak English in his village. Maybe better'n me. He bring you back the cash for your stones. He keep the cash for his."

Bunce continued to look at Bantu. "And what's your take in all this, Jimbo?"

"I take my share from Bantu. We're good on that. I trust him all the way."

Morty was looking at Bantu with his noncommittal poker face.

" 'Nother thing, Morty. Before he go, I teach him everything I know 'bout this business. He already met the devil a hundred times over. He know to watch his step. So what you think?"

Bunce leaned back in his chair with a searching eye on Bantu for a full ten seconds. Slowly his business grin began creeping across his lips.

"Well, I'll be damned."

# CHAPTER SIXTEEN

It was just after dawn three days later when a thirty-foot motor vessel, painted black and flying a Liberian flag, tied up at one end of Government Wharf on the shore of Freetown. Within minutes, a figure approached from one of the open warehouses carrying a single suitcase.

The captain of the vessel raised his hand and said quietly, "Mr. Walker?"

The man nodded and stepped aboard. Lines were cast off, and the vessel moved slowly into open water.

It took three weeks of hugging the coast northward along the west coasts of Africa, Spain, France, and England to reach the rocky west coast of Ireland. It was a pitch-black, drizzling night when the vessel reached the waters a mile off the shore of Achill Island. It anchored at rest while the crew scanned the shore.

Within an hour, a faint light cut through the fog to mark the approach to a quarter-mile expanse of sandy beach. The timing was right to catch a high tide so that the vessel could cruise toward the light to within fifty feet of the shore.

A boat rowed by a man dressed completely in black pulled alongside the vessel to take the passenger ashore. A small van was waiting to drive him through the heather-filled peat bog lands south to the city of Galway.

It was ten in the morning when the van deposited the passenger at the entrance to the Hotel Meyrick in the center of Galway City. The neatly dressed, carefully groomed, gentleman of color was greeted cordially by the host in reception.

"Most welcome, sir. First time in Ireland, is it?"

"Yes, it is."

"And your name, sir?"

"Johnny Walker."

"Ah, grand. A coincidence. We serve a fine blended Scotch whiskey by that same name. I have your reservation right here."

Every time Bantu used the name, Johnny Walker, it brought him back to his first meeting with Morty Bunce in Freetown. Among Morty's many misgivings about Bantu, the name stood out.

"Jimbo, none of that Irish crowd are going to pull out their checkbooks for a man with one name—especially if it's 'Bantu.'"

Jimbo gave a quick scan through Bunce's fine liquor shelf. In an instant, the name, Bantu, disappeared, and Johnny Walker was born.

"We have a fine room with an excellent front view of Eyre Square, Mr. Walker."

"Thank you. But do you have a room facing the back?"

The receptionist hid his puzzlement at the choice and complied. "Anything else, sir?"

"Yes. I'd like a second room. Next to the first room. If anyone asks for my room number, you'll please give them the number of the first room. The second will be just between us."

Without either man looking down, a twenty euro note found its way from Mr. Walker's palm to that of the reception clerk.

"I see no problem, Mr. Walker. If there's anything else?"

"There is. This may seem unusual. May I count on you for a small favor?"

"Most certainly, sir. Discretion is our hallmark."

Mr. Walker had a few more whispered words with the reception clerk to outline his request. Before he had left Freetown, certain precautions had been worked out by Jimbo and Bunce.

"In ten minutes, I'll be in the dining room. You'll know where to find me."

"Excellent, Sir. *Bain taitneamh as do bhéil,* as we say. In other words, *bon appetit.*"

◆  ◆  ◆

Mr. Walker took the lift to the third floor. He found his first room and unpacked his clothes. He left his one suitcase closed but unlocked on the bed. He went to the second room and locked the door between them. He deposited a small leather case in the second room's safe and went back down to the Oyster Bar and Grille.

He took a table at the far end of the dining room and, since it was the crossover hour, he ordered a full Irish breakfast.

Fifteen minutes later, a bellboy brought a note to his table from the reception clerk. Within a few minutes, a tall, well-muscled man in gray slacks and an Irish wool sweater stood in the doorway scanning the people at table in the dining room. He slowly walked among the tables, paying no attention to tables with couples or small children.

When he passed by, Mr. Walker said quietly. "I believe you're looking for me. Sit down, please."

The Irishman hesitated. He gave the room one more scan for a more likely candidate. Finding none, he sat.

Mr. Walker just nodded to the man across the table. "My name is Johnny Walker. You're expected. Now you have my name. I don't have yours."

The Irishman grinned. "I doubt it."

"You doubt what?"

"That I have your real name."

"Ah, but does it matter? I'm not here to propose marriage. How shall I call you?"

The Irishman leaned closer with a sneer. "Jack. Jack Daniels."

This time Mr. Walker grinned. He remembered another black bottle with that name on Morty Bunce's liquor shelf.

"That'll do for our purpose, Mr. Daniels. Excuse me."

He looked up at the bellboy who handed him another note from the reception clerk. He read it and nodded to the bellboy. He looked toward the door and saw a second man dressed in Irish clothing who had taken a table alone by the dining room entrance.

"Ah, now, Mr. Daniels. This is not polite. We should ask your friend to join us."

"What friend?"

"The one you came here with. The one who seems to be watching us by the door."

Mr. Walker stood. He easily got the attention of the second Irishman who had been keeping them under surveillance. Mr. Walker smiled and waved to him to join them. The man seemed flustered at the turn of plans. He looked to the first man for orders. Mr. Daniels gave a grudging nod to the second man who silently walked to the table and took a seat.

"Now, gentlemen. As you say, all the cards on the table." He looked at the second Irishman. "And I suppose your name is Jim Beam."

The second Irishman was flustered. "It isn't. My name's Paddy—"

"Shut up, Paddy. I'll do the talkin' here."

Mr. Walker leaned across the table. "Good. Then you do the talking, Mr. Daniels. But before you say a word to me, be kind enough to tell your man Paddy to put it here on the table."

"What the hell are you talkin' about?"

"You're wasting my time. Just have him take the pouch he stole from the suitcase in my room and put it here on the table."

Paddy broke in, "I didn't do—"

"Shut up, Paddy. The hell you get off accusing us—"

Mr. Walker lowered his voice to bring down the tone before attention was attracted.

"Mr. Daniels, again, all the cards on the table. You were watched by the hotel staff at my request, Paddy. You asked for my room at the reception desk. One of you came to find me here while the other—that was you, Paddy—went up to my room. You asked the maid to open the door. You told her you forgot your key. At my request, she was told to open the door if she was asked. You were watched while you went through my suitcase and came up with a small leather pouch."

Neither of the Irishmen spoke.

"We're wasting time. There'll be no trouble. Place it here on the table, Paddy. I have no wish to call hotel security."

The two Irishmen looked at each other in confusion. Finally, Mr.

Daniels gave the other a scowling nod. The one called Paddy slowly took a small leather case from inside his shirt and put it down in front of Mr. Walker.

Mr. Walker opened the leather case and poured out onto the white linen tablecloth a handful of milky stones the size of rough diamonds.

Mr. Daniels turned his frustration to anger to get some control of a situation that had gone completely against his expectations. "What the hell is this, Walker? This is not a tenth of the number of diamonds we bargained for."

"No. it isn't, Mr. Daniels. Would you be kind enough to hand me your shoe?"

The frustration was back. "What the hell is this?"

"Right or left. It's no matter. Here, let me have it."

Daniels slowly removed his left shoe and put it in the outstretched hand of Mr. Walker. Mr. Walker took one of the pieces of diamond and placed it in his white linen napkin. He held the shoe by the toe and hit the napkin a sharp blow with the heel of the shoe. He opened the napkin and poured out fine dust-like particles of crystal.

"It's glass, gentlemen."

Mr. Walker held up the leather case.

"I suppose if it held as many pieces as you were expecting, you'd have been out the door, and we'd never have had this little chat."

The two Irishmen looked at each other for some way of responding. They found none.

"It's all right. Just so you know, I'm here to do business. I was warned that I'd be dealing with common thugs and thieves. This little test was set up to send a message to whoever sent you, hopefully someone brighter than either one of you."

Mr. Walker leaned forward over the table. He reduced his voice to a whisper. "You'll please pass this message to your man in charge. I have what he's looking for. I'm ready to sell for the price that's been arranged. If there is one more trick, I'll be gone and the diamonds with me. Is that clear enough?"

Mr. Daniels stood. He finally got enough of a grip to speak. "You'll be hearin' from us, Walker."

"If I do, Mr. Daniels, in fact, if I ever see you or Paddy here again, you'll never see one of those stones. You tell your man to contact me directly. He has one more day. No more. He can leave a message with the clerk at the desk. Is that clear?"

They both simply looked with no response.

"One day. No more."


Mr. Walker spent the afternoon in his second room as a precaution. It was three p.m. when the phone rang. The reception clerk said that a gentleman was asking to speak with him.

"I'll take the call."

The reception clerk connected the call.

"Mr. Walker, my first word is one of apology. The men you met this morning were not following my orders."

"And your name is?"

"I'm sorry. I'd rather save that for our first meeting face-to-face. Our business is a bit delicate. I'm sure you understand that."

"Actually, I understand very little. I came to do business in your country. First you sent two thieves to steal the objects, and now you say they were not under your orders. No offense, but I think that's a lie. Neither of the thugs you sent had the wits to plan a theft. And now you won't share a name. I'm wondering if we can do business."

There was a pause.

"Mr. Walker, I'll be honest."

"That would be refreshing. I'm listening."

"This is our first dealing with each other. I'll be frank. I underestimated you quite badly. It won't happen again. You'll be treated with respect. That said, the people we represent will both make a substantial profit if we can work together. I'm extending my hand, so to speak, for a new beginning."

"And you'll understand if I take your hand with eyes in every direction."

"That's fair. On that basis, a car will be at your hotel in ten minutes."

"To go where?"

"Again, I don't trust telephones. Bring your suitcase, and please bring the items in question. I believe we can do business."

It was a short ride to the tarmac of the Galway Airport. A small, two-engine Cessna aircraft was already in the warm-up phase when Mr. Walker was escorted aboard. An hour later, the plane touched down at the Dublin Airport. A car was waiting to drive him to the Gresham Hotel on O'Connell Street.

Mr. Walker was just entering his room when the phone rang.

"Mr. Walker, I trust you've been made comfortable. Are you ready to meet?"

"As soon as possible."

"I'll be at your room in ten minutes."

"You'll find it empty. The flight was pleasant. The room is comfortable. But I still have no basis for trust. I noticed a quiet, public room off the lobby. People are enjoying a small meal."

"They're having afternoon tea, Mr. Walker. And, if that suits you better, that's where we'll meet."

The single man of about fifty years in a conservative dark suit and tie at a table in a far corner before the window on O'Connell Street rose and waved when Mr. Walker appeared. They shook hands, sat, and placed an order for tea and scones. The hum of voices at a sufficient distance assured privacy.

"And now may I have a name?"

The man smiled an ingratiating smile, but Mr. Walker had seen smiles on the faces of RUF guards at the pit.

"Of course, Mr. Walker. In fact, while I suspect your name is adopted for the occasion, my true name is Declan O'Connor. I have no reason to hide it."

"I'll take you at your word."

"That's good. This may be the beginning of a long and prosperous business relationship."

Mr. Walker hid his revulsion at the thought. He knew he was dealing in a product he detested to the bottom of his soul—smuggled diamonds harvested on the blood and pain of his countrymen. He would do it this once because it could lead to a windfall of money to ransom his father. But not once more.

"Now we have names, Mr. O'Connor. Where do we go from here?"

"A simple exchange. I assume your people have a private account. I'm prepared to transfer the amount we agreed on with Mr. Bunce to that account. I have a man waiting in a room upstairs to examine the items. As soon as he verifies the quality and quantity, I give the word to transfer funds. It's that simple."

"Perhaps not quite that simple."

"Why not? I assume you have the items with you. Perhaps in your room."

The waitress appeared with cups, a pot of tea, and a plate of scones and clotted cream. When she left, Mr. Walker leaned back to look Mr. O'Connor eye-to-eye.

"If you assume that, then you're still assuming that you're dealing with an idiot. That won't get us anywhere."

Mr. O'Connor's expression remained unchanged except for the slightest narrowing of the eyes. He held up his hands. "Then, what do you suggest?"

Mr. Walker laid out the process explained in detail to him by Jimbo and Bunce in Freetown. He handed a slip of paper to Mr. O'Connor.

"First, you transfer the complete price to this account. It's a bank in Belgium."

"Ah, Mr. Walker, now who's making assumptions?"

"Hear me out. The account is opened jointly in the names of both you and Mr. Bunce. Neither will be able to get the funds without the permission of the other. Your money is safe."

"Go on."

"When the transfer is made, I'll give you the key to a particular room in the Meyrick Hotel in Galway. I also give you the combination to the room safe. Your man can see the items and report back to you. When he does, you release the funds in the joint account to Mr. Bunce."

Mr. O'Connor sat back with a piece of scone and took a sip of tea while he considered the option. When he set the cup back down, his smile was more relaxed.

"Mr. Walker, I'll say it again. I underestimated you badly. This will take time. I'll do the transfer of funds this afternoon. Mr. Bunce can check with the bank this evening. When he notifies you that it's all there, you can leave the key to the room at the Meyrick and the combination of the safe in a sealed envelope with the concierge here. My man will fly to Galway this evening. We should be able to wrap this up tomorrow at breakfast in the dining room here if that suits you."

"Very good."

Mr. Walker followed O'Connor's lead in standing up. He accepted the offer of a handshake on the deal.

Mr. O'Connor leaned close to Mr. Walker's ear to say in a quiet but unmistakably firm tone, "I'm doing it your way, Mr. Walker, because you're entitled to exercise caution. Also, because it seems fair. Don't for a fraction of a second take it as weakness. My organization has a long reach. If matters should become—unsatisfactory from my point of view, there will be no hiding place on earth for you or your Mr. Bunce. You'll convey that to Mr. Bunce, won't you?"

# CHAPTER SEVENTEEN

Mr. Walker was well into his full Irish breakfast when Mr. O'Connor joined him at the table. The smile on Mr. O'Connor's face told him that the exchange had gone smoothly.

"Johnny, before you leave Dublin, can I buy you a pint of Guinness? A bit early, but we'll drink to happy conclusions. I guarantee you'll taste nothing like it in Sierra Leone."

Mr. Walker smiled and accepted the outstretched hand. "I'll accept, if you let me buy you a late breakfast."

"A fair exchange. And a fitting end to a profitable business. I suppose you'll be off to Africa."

Mr. Walker had no reply for the moment. He had accomplished half of what he had come for. The less important half to him.

"I have something to show you, Mr. O'Connor."

"I think it's time you called me Declan. We have a bit of history with each other now."

"So be it, Declan. That makes it easier."

He took out of his shirt the bag of rough diamonds he had carried out of the jungle of Sierra Leone after the Kamajor attack. He set it on the table in front of Mr. O'Connor.

Mr. O'Connor looked down at the pouch and back up at him. "You seem to trust me now. Why?"

Mr. Walker leaned forward, "I've had an interesting life. Sometimes my intuition is all I've had to guide me through difficult times. I won't bore you with details. My intuition tells me you're a man who doesn't hesitate to do business on either side of the law. But something says to me there's a strong sense of loyalty inside of you. I sense you won't easily go back on your word if you give it. I'm trusting in that."

Mr. O'Connor sat back. "I've said it twice now. Here's a third time. I underestimated you badly before we met. There's a good deal more to you than meets the eye, Johnny, or whatever your real name is. I've had no occasion to say this to another man. Your trust won't be broken by anything in my power. What are we talking about here?"

Mr. Walker opened the bag. He poured out onto the linen tablecloth twenty-two milky rough stones similar to the ones that had just been successfully transferred.

"I need to sell these. I need money. A lot of money."

"How much?"

"As much as I can get. Much more than you paid for the other stones."

Mr. O'Connor looked at the rough gems. He looked around for curious eyes and covered the stones with his linen napkin.

"I don't suppose you'd tell me why you need that much money. You don't strike me as a man who hungers after wealth."

"You're from a different world, Declan. I could tell you, but you might not understand. Or you might not believe me."

"You've never lied to me yet. Try me."

The room was empty but for the two at that table. Mr. Walker thought long and hard before he spoke. Where to begin to bring this Irishman into the world of Sierra Leone; the world of the pit, the loss of his family, the incomprehensible cruelty of the child soldiers of the RUF, the desperation of every waking moment in slavery to those whose only emotion was lust for the diamonds.

Somehow he began talking, and for some reason, he laid open his soul to this stranger. At the points where he could not hold back the tears, he simply let them flow.

Mr. O'Connor listened without speaking, and the words dug deeply into his own soul. Mr. Walker finally told him about his chance meeting with his brother, and the news that their father was alive and held captive by the RUF. He spoke of the chance that his father could be bought out of captivity if the price could be raised. The only chance of that happening lay in the stones on the table in front of them.

When he finished, Mr. O'Connor made a call on his cell phone. Within ten minutes, another suited man of about his age joined them at the table.

Mr. O'Connor put his hand on the napkin and looked up at Mr. Walker. "You can trust Lannie McLaughlin as far as you trust me. He knows the value of diamonds better than any man I know. May I?"

Mr. Walker nodded his assent. Mr. O'Connor lifted the napkin. Lannie McLaughlin took every diamond individually in hand and held them to the jeweler's eyepiece. When he laid down the last one, he just sat quietly. Four eyes were on him.

"What do you think, Lannie?"

He turned to Mr. O'Connor and spoke quietly. "I've never seen a collection of rough diamonds so pure. These are rare. They're worth ten times the amount you paid for that whole batch in Galway."

"How much, Lannie? Fair price."

"Rough estimate. One million euros."

Mr. O'Connor gave a low, expressive whistle.

"And that's a fraction of the profit to anyone who can get them into the legal mainstream of the cutters in Antwerp."

Mr. O'Connor and Lannie McLaughlin locked eyes for a few seconds as if they were exchanging the same thoughts.

"You're thinking what I'm thinking, aren't you, Lannie?"

"I am. With all deference to Mr. Walker, stay the hell away from these, Declan. You've stayed under the radar of the international enforcers so far. That's because you deal in pedestrian diamonds. When word of these gets out somewhere along the line, you could have the full attention of black market law enforcement that could shut you down. Or worse."

"Worse meaning jail time."

He nodded. "Could happen. I've seen it."

Mr. O'Connor breathed a long sigh. He turned to Mr. Walker. "I hoped I could help you, but it's out of my league by a long shot. Lannie, can you think of a buyer?"

"Around here? No. Anyone who knows diamonds will spot these. No offense, but good as they are, they're blood diamonds. Probably from the Kono region of Sierra Leone. To begin with, they're smuggled. Then, on top of it, the buyers are beginning to get a conscience about paying for diamonds that buy guns and drugs for that gang in Sierra Leone. You'd be lucky to get ten percent of what they're worth from the people we know around here, if they'll take them at all."

Mr. Walker asked, "Are you saying the market for diamonds is that bad?"

"Oh, hell, no. The market for mainstream legal diamonds is as puffed up as it has been. It'll never drop. It's something of a fiction to begin with. Diamonds are not the rare gems people think they are. Years ago the De Beers crowd bought up every diamond source they could get their hands on. They held such a monopoly that they could release them in small amounts so the public would think they were rare. That still keeps the price up."

"Then there is a solid market for diamonds."

"Ah, that's just the beginning. Then they put together the greatest marketing device in advertising history. They came up with the slogan, 'Diamonds are Forever.' Worldwide, people would hardly think of getting engaged without the biggest diamond ring they can afford. Sometimes bigger than they can afford. It was ingenious."

Mr. O'Connor added, "But not these diamonds?"

He shook his head. "Not blood diamonds. Not now. Not unless they get blended into the mainstream flow of clean diamonds to the cutters and polishers in Antwerp. Once they do that, nobody can tell the difference. They'd get their real value."

"And how's that done?"

"Connections. Connections to the world diamond merchants you don't have, Declan. Not for these diamonds. Connections to people up around the top of the chain who're willing to take the dirty ones with the clean ones and don't care whom they deal with."

Mr. Walker's expression said that he had come to a dead end. Mr.

O'Connor leaned toward him and spoke just above a whisper. "Maybe there's a possibility. Someone approached me a while ago. He was talking about getting into the diamond business with us for rough diamonds. He knew we had a source. He says he has the connections to go from there. This was someone in America. How soon do you have to go back to Sierra Leone?"

"I have nowhere to go. I have no home in Sierra Leone. I can stay as long as necessary."

"Then, do. I'll make a call. I'll get back to you here at the hotel tonight. Nothing promised. But like they say, 'Nothing ventured, nothing gained.'"

It was nine p.m. when the phone rang in Mr. Walker's room.

"Johnny. It took a while. I was calling a man in Boston in the United States. Six-hour time difference. "

"Thank you, Declan. Any luck at all?"

"I don't know. It may be something. Or not. Can you stay a couple of days?"

"I think so." Mr. Walker knew that his expenses were being paid by Bunce and Jimbo, but if he could make a major sale, he could repay them.

"Good. This won't be easy sailing. The one I talked with is a big shot with an organized crime gang in Boston. They call them the Mafia over there. Basically a gang of thugs, but they can do big business when they're interested."

"How do you know him?"

"Interesting. He actually approached me a week ago. He wants to get his beak wet in the diamond trade, as he puts it. The black market side. He knew some of the former IRA were into it. He heard we have a source. I think he's looking to make a big killing on the kind of diamonds you're selling. That could serve your purpose."

"Maybe. Depends on how much he can pay."

"I get the impression he can handle the kind of price you're talking about. What do you think?"

"I think he's my only hope. How do I meet him?"

"I thought you'd say that. He's flying in tomorrow."

"Great. I'll be ready."

"Johnny, move easy here. I don't know if I made the point. This guy's no choirboy. I've heard of him. Do you know what a 'stone killer' is?"

"No."

"Well, you can guess. You took a chance trusting me. Don't do it with him. And watch your back. People who deal with this guy frequently wind up dead. That would not suit your purpose."

"Could he be worse than the ones I've dealt with for nine years?"

"Point taken. Just don't underestimate him. He sounds like a brainless thug when he speaks. Don't let him fool you. He didn't get to be the number two man in the Boston Mafia on the brains of an idiot."

"I'm forewarned. How will we meet?"

"Not in your hotel. I don't want him to be too sure of how to find either one of us outside of the meeting. There's a pub on Fownes Street, just off the Temple Bar area. I know the owner. He'll have a private room for us in the back."

"Sounds good. What time?"

"This guy'll fly into Dublin tomorrow morning. I'll send a car to pick you up here at the Gresham at three tomorrow afternoon. I'll warn you. He'll have his diamond expert with him. You'll have to show him the diamonds. I'm not sure that's the best place to do it."

"Will you be there, Declan?"

"Hah. You think I'd miss it?"

"What's this man's name?"

"Salvatore Barone."

# CHAPTER EIGHTEEN

Irish weather had been soaking the streets of Dublin all day. At three on the nose, Mr. Walker came out of the Gresham Hotel under the umbrella held by the doorman to the waiting black limousine. After enduring five months of constant soaking through nineteen Sierra Leone rainy seasons, he marveled at the extent of the hotel staff's concern that a few drops of rain not fall on their guest.

He met Mr. O'Connor at the door of O'Doole's Pub.

"He's inside. Brace yourself. He comes equipped with his personal goon."

When they reached the door to a small private room with a long table and chairs at the back of the pub, Mr. Walker went in first. He was less than a foot into the room, when an arm shot across his chest and barred his way. He looked back at Mr. O'Connor who just shrugged. "It's apparently how they do business in the colonies. Just pretend you're at an airport."

The heavily beefed individual with the arm turned him toward the wall and ran his massive hands over any part of Mr. Walker's body that could conceal a weapon. When he was satisfied, he stepped back, leaving Mr. Walker facing a pudgy, bald man of about fifty with an obvious air of control. He was seated beside a taller man with glasses.

"You Walker? You the guy I'm supposed to meet with?"

"I am."

"So, sit yourself down. I ain't got all day."

"Thank you. Most gracious."

"And don't gimme no smart-ass answers. You ready to do business? I gotta get the hell outta this joint. It don't do nothin' but rain over here."

Mr. Walker reminded himself of his ultimate goal, and swallowed the indignities. He sat facing the speaker.

"Are you interested in buying diamonds?"

The man leaned back with an affected air of indifference. "I don't know. Depends what you got. Lemme see 'em."

Mr. Walker glanced back at Mr. O'Connor who took a seat at the far end of the table. He gave a nod of the head that conveyed, "It's your game, Johnny." At the same time, his calm attitude suggested that there would be backup if matters got out of hand. It gave Mr. Walker the confidence he needed.

He straightened in his chair and paused long enough to indicate he was not on Mr. Barone's short leash. He looked at the man in glasses beside Mr. Barone.

"I didn't get your name. I assume you're the diamond expert."

Mr. Barone came straight forward. "Listen you, you talk to me. I do the business here."

"Really. I assume you're Mr. Barone."

"You assume right, kid. Now get out the diamonds. I don't wait too good."

Mr. Walker looked straight into the eyes of Mr. Barone and lowered his voice. "Mr. Barone, I'm not a kid, yours or anyone else's. I'm here to do business, man-to-man. If I decide to sell, and if you pay the price, you'll make more money than you ever dreamed of."

Mr. Barone's color went from pasty sallow to steaming red. He grabbed the arms of the chair to bolt upright.

"Mr. Barone, if you get out of that chair, the deal's off. You'll never set your eyes on those diamonds. I think you should understand this. You're out of your kingdom now. You're on Irish soil. I make no threats, but if you or that goon at the door make one threatening move, I think my friend and I can assure you that you'll never leave this country in the fine health you seem to enjoy now. And just so you have no doubts about that—"

Mr. Walker stood up slowly and walked to the door. He opened it to give Mr. Barone a full view of the eight tall, well-muscled men in loose-fitting sweaters that could conceal anything Mr. Barone might imagine, sitting at the long bar. Mr. Walker had noticed them on the way in. He knew they probably had nothing to do with Mr. O'Connor, but Mr. Barone had no way of knowing that.

Mr. Walker called out to the bar, "Gentlemen."

They all looked in his direction. Mr. Walker called out again, "Everything's fine so far. This won't take long." He waved to them. They had no idea what he was talking about, but they all waved back.

Mr. Walker closed the door and walked back to his chair. Mr. Barone sat back in silence. Mr. Walker glanced over at Mr. O'Connor who simply raised his eyebrows and smiled.

"Now, Mr. Barone, if we're through with the power plays, let's talk about things that can make both of us very rich."

Mr. Barone remained silent, while Mr. Walker addressed the man in glasses. "I was asking, are you the diamond expert?"

"I am. My name's Vincent Mangione."

"Good. I'm going to show you a collection of diamonds. And I'm going to make you a bet, Mr. Mangione. I'll bet you one Irish euro that you've never seen anything like them in your life. I'll bet you'll conclude they're worth far more than I'm asking for them, which leaves room for an enormous profit for anyone who buys them from me. Will you come with me?"

Barone came out of his pout and shot forward. "Wait a minute. What the hell? You got the diamonds here or not? What the hell is this?"

"This is the way we do business or not at all. I take Mr. Mangione to see the diamonds. He'll come back in twenty minutes and tell you that if you can buy them for one million euros, you'll be able to make at least three times that amount in profit when you sell them to your connections in America. And that's how it works. You can say yes or no. There are other buyers. Your decision."

Mr. Mangione looked at Mr. Barone for orders. Mr. Barone fidgeted like a man with an uncomfortable decision. When his hunger for money finally trumped his need for a show of dominance, he nodded to Mr. Mangione.

When Mr. Walker and Mr. Mangione passed through the door,

Mr. Barone yelled out an attempt to recoup face in front of his goon. "And make it snappy. I ain't got all day."

Mr. Walker took Mr. Mangione on a short walk to the campus of Trinity College in the heart of the city. He bought the tourist tickets and led him across the campus green to the mammoth Old Library. They climbed to a secluded alcove with a table and two chairs on the second floor.

Mr. Mangione had a seat while Mr. Walker took a bag from behind the two books on a lower shelf where he had secreted it earlier in the day. Mr. Mangione spread a velvet cloth on the table. Mr. Walker poured the twenty-two stones onto the cloth. He stood back by the rail while Mr. Mangione completed his prolonged examination of each of the stones.

When the inspection was complete, Mr. Mangione exited the library to wait for Mr. Walker to choose another hiding place for the diamonds. When Mr. Walker joined him, they began the walk back to O'Doole's Pub.

They walked in silence until they reached the statue of Oliver Goldsmith by the campus gate. Mr. Walker addressed him quietly. "I don't ask you to betray any confidences, Mr. Mangione. I'm only wondering if you have anything to say about what you've seen."

Mr. Mangione continued walking another fifty feet before speaking. "I know Mr. Barone well enough to know he'll ask me if I said anything to you. My answer will be 'No. I've said nothing.' You can perhaps surmise that my life could depend on that."

"I can. I'll ask no more questions."

"Good." As he said it, he took out a one euro note and quietly handed it to Mr. Walker.

When they returned to the room in O'Doole's Pub, Mr. Barone was pacing like a hungry tiger.

"Where the hell you been? I coulda had supper by the time you two get through messin' around. Mangione, get over here."

They walked to a corner and whispered with their backs to the room for a minute or two. When they turned around, Mr. Barone spit out in the direction of Mr. Mangione, "Awright. Awright. Shut up."

When they were seated, Mr. Barone said to Mr. Walker, "So, he says they're okay. They ain't nothing special. But hell, I come all this way. I'll give you ten thousand. Go get the rocks."

Mr. Walker smiled. "I have one price. It's not negotiable. You can say either yes or no. The price is one million euros."

Mr. Barone slapped the table and grinned. "You're jokin', right? How the hell much is that in real money?"

"I take it you mean American dollars."

"Yeah. What else?"

Mr. O'Connor broke his silence. "At today's rate of exchange that would be one and a quarter million dollars."

That set off another outburst accompanied by pacing by Mr. Barone. Mr. Walker sat in silence for ten seconds. Suddenly he stood and slapped the table with both hands and shrieked, "Stop!"

It caught Mr. Barone in mid-tantrum. He looked at Mr. Walker in silence. Mr. Walker stood while he spoke, this time in a room-filling tone. "This is not business. This is idiocy. There's only one question to be answered here. Do you want to make a profit of at least three million of your *real* dollars or not? If you do, you'll pay me one million euros for the twenty-two diamonds. I'll be at the Gresham Hotel until tomorrow. You can leave a one-word answer. Yes or no. Nothing more."

On that last word, Mr. Walker turned and strode through the door without looking back. Mr. O'Connor followed him out the door. They caught a cab at the pub entrance. Mr. O'Connor gave the address of a restaurant on the other side of the River Liffey. They settled back in the seat and Mr. O'Connor spoke first. "I'm going to buy you the finest dinner in Dublin and many pints of Guinness to go with it. Forgive me for saying it like this, Johnny. You've got rocks harder than those twenty-two diamonds."

He started to laugh, and before they turned the first corner, the both of them were rocking back and forth in the first actual laugh that had passed Bantu's lips since he was nine years old.

◆  ◆  ◆

It was ten o'clock that night when Mr. Walker and Mr. O'Connor returned to the Gresham Hotel. There was a message in three words rather than one. "Yes. What now?"

At Mr. O'Connor's suggestion, they planned to meet with Mr. Barone at ten the next morning at the office of the Ulster Bank on O'Connell Street. The deal was struck. Mr. Barone would have one hundred thousand euros deposited in an account in the name of Mr. Walker immediately. He signed an agreement to deposit the remaining nine hundred thousand euros when he got to his bank in Boston the following day.

Mr. Walker had serious doubts about handing over the diamonds to Mr. Barone on the basis of words on a piece of paper. Nothing he had seen in Mr. Barone inspired trust. The deal was at a stalemate until Mr. O'Connor took Mr. Walker aside for a private word.

"Johnny, I know you need this deal. You're not going to find many other Barones out there. I'll give you something you can put your trust in. I'll send my best man back to Boston with Barone to see that he does his part. You don't know my man, but you know me. There's not a man from the old war days in the IRA I'd sooner trust with my life. He's smart as a whip and tough as a tank. It's your choice."

Mr. Walker thought hard for a minute. He knew he was gambling with his father's life, but other options did not seem to exist. Again, he followed his intuition.

"I'm going to put my trust in you, Declan. Someday I'll repay the favor. What's your man's name?"

"Seamus Burke."

That afternoon, Mr. O'Connor drove Mr. Walker to the airport in time for his flight to Sierra Leone.

"Johnny, I'll miss you. You've made my life exciting. Why don't you stay?"

"I can't. I have business in Sierra Leone. I have to know that my father's still alive. Maybe I can get a message to him. I know what it means to need hope."

"I understand. Will you be back?"

"When you notify me the money's in my account. I'll come back to collect it. You can reach me at the Mammy Yoko Hotel."

They shook hands. Mr. Walker went to the entrance of the terminal. Before he went in, he turned back with one last thought. "Maybe someday I'll even bring my father and my brother to this wonderful country. Wouldn't that be something, Declan?"

Less than a week later, Mr. Walker was back in Freetown, Sierra Leone, when word reached him from Mr. O'Connor. He had read in a Dublin newspaper that shortly after returning to the United States, Mr. Salvatore Barone had been found murdered in the trunk of his Cadillac.

# PART THREE

# CHAPTER NINETEEN

Boston, Massachusetts. The present.

The most pressing question was where to begin. Loose ends dangled in every direction. I did an inventory of the ones giving me the most spiking headaches. For one, we had a boy-client, Kevin, who stacked up in my mind as a major player in a game that I hadn't really identified. The question of how to defend him on a murder charge was a challenge since his whereabouts, in fact his alive/dead status, was anybody's guess.

On another front, the man who means more to me than all the rest of the characters involved in this mess unquestionably remained the target of an Italian organization not known to belay a grudge. That situation needed immediate defusing.

A further complication, if one were necessary, was how to pick up the reins of Father Ryan's defense on a trumped-up charge that stood to do increasingly more uncalled for harm to a good man the longer it remained open.

I felt strongly that based on something Seamus Burke had said on that flying drive to our little incident at the Seaborn Motel, a trip to Ireland would probably lie in my near future. On the other hand, one of those enumerated leaks in our boat needed immediate plugging before I went anywhere. Even considering an eventful upbringing in the rough-and-tumble bowels of Charlestown, Mr. Devlin had just taken the beating of his life. If there were one more, I'd most certainly lose the best friend I have on this planet.

That settled the order of priority. What had gotten Mr. D. into this mess in the first place seemed to be his visit to the rather shaky witness against Father Ryan, one Finn Casey, also of Charlestown. I recalled that at Mr. D's request, Tom Burns had followed a thug later identified as Tony Napolitano from Casey's home to Collini's Bar in the Italian North End of Boston.

In the choice of which lead to follow first between Casey and Napolitano, Casey won hands down. Napolitano had been identified in Mr. D's telephone conversation with his friend, Don Santangelo, as the right-hand thug of Packy Salviti. Run-ins with Salviti had so far not only been unpleasant, but also unproductive.

Judging from the stone wall Mr. D. ran into when he approached Finn Casey in his own home, I knew I had to corral him on a more neutral turf. I knew in my heart he was lying about Father Ryan. His propelling impetus was easy. He was scared out of his wits by Packy Salviti's goon, Napolitano. The more obscure question was exactly why Salviti was putting the attack on Father Ryan in the first place. Casey may or may not have known, but it was worth a shot. A devilish notion began taking shape.

I checked out the neighborhood around Casey's address on Pearl Street. I knew he had a taste for the sauce. With a wife and child at home, the odds were that he was a regular at whatever neighborhood bar was closest to his house. In a working-class Irish neighborhood, it was no trick to find a bar within half a block's walk of his address.

It was shortly after two in the afternoon when I walked into Bob G's Shamrock Bar and approached the bartender. The lunch crowd had thinned, and I had his undiverted attention for some conversation. I ordered a pint of Sam Adams, and we got on a first name basis. I needed a message delivered with no red flags, and Bones, as they call him, the bartender, seemed to be my most promising route.

Since Finn Casey and I were close to the same age, and since the chances were outstanding that both he and Bones had gone to the local Charlestown High School, a rough plan began to fall into place.

When Bones and I had chatted ourselves to somewhere between acquaintances and reminiscing buddies, I asked if "my old classmate," Finn Casey, ever came in. It did not knock me off the stool to learn that he was a regular.

I mentioned that I'd been working in Chicago since graduation from Charlestown High. This was my first chance to get back to The Town, as locals like to refer to Charlestown. I only had a day at home, and son of a gun, wouldn't it be great to get together with Finn for a couple of drinks to rehash those great high school memories. My figuring was that Casey's high school days were probably the happiest times of his life. And if that didn't do it, the prospect of a couple of drinks certainly would.

My new pal, Bones, thought Finn would go big for the idea. He happened to have his phone number by the bar telephone.

Within ten minutes, from my seat at a table in the dark back end of the bar I could see a man of the right age and the typical facial lines a career of hard drinking can etch, approaching Bones.

Bones pointed, and Finn Casey came my way. On Bones's advice, I had a full bottle of Tullamore Dew, one of Ireland's finest whiskeys, uncorked beside two glasses on the table.

I stood with my hand out to my "classmate," and dredged up the best imitation of a Charlestown accent I could muster.

"Hey Finn. The Finnster. Been a wicked long time."

His first glance was at the bottle, and then at me. I could see him searching what he could see of my features, which was not much in that darkness, and trying to pull back a name from our high school days.

I gave him a clue. "Yeah, it's me. You remember, Patrick, Pat, from homeroom senior year."

I figured if there was not a "Patrick" or three in the senior class of Charlestown High School, I was in the wrong town altogether. To jog his memory, or imagination, further, I poured two very substantial shots of the Dew.

"Sit yourself down, Finn. Let's drink to—um, who the hell was that guy we used to laugh about—taught, um, English, was it?"

I noticed by the speed and accuracy with which my new classmate found his mouth with the Dew, he'd have happily toasted the Commander of the Ulster Constabulary.

I continued to babble in generalities about those wicked great high school times, while Finn continued to accept and consume each refill.

By the fourth round, he was in a maudlin state of sharing the misfortunes of the post-high school years and recounting all that life had done to impede his personal rise to fame and fortune. I noticed that two particular barriers to success in his life were significantly left unmentioned. One was whiskey. That was no surprise. The second was his alleged abuse by Father Ryan.

I ignored the first and probed the second in subdued tones.

"Hey, Finn, I was at Mass this morning at our old church, Sacred Heart. I heard the damndest thing. I heard you said you were molested by Father Ryan. No kiddin'?"

I slipped it in as delicately as you can slip an eight-hundred-pound gorilla into a conversation, but it straightened him up. I only prayed it didn't snap him out of the sweet buzz that had him conversational. I poured him another substantial shot to get him past the shock of the jarring shift of subject.

His silence told me that I was losing him. I tried to keep the flow going. "That was a real shocker, Finn. Who'd a thought? He seemed like such a great guy. Wasn't he giving you boxing lessons?"

More silence. His eyes seemed to sink deeper into his head, and I thought he was losing focus. I tried a diversion. "Hey, you were a pretty good boxer in those days. Didn't you fight that Italian kid?"

Nothing. He was sinking deeper into himself. More Dew would have been counterproductive. I realized I was stymied. Time to cap the bottle and cut my losses.

"Well, Finn, old pal. It was good to see you again."

"That's the damn hell of it."

"What?"

He checked back over his shoulder. We were alone in the bar except for Bones at the far end. The faint light picked up pools of moisture collecting in both eyes.

"Damn it! I had to do it."

"Had to do what, Finn?"

"You got a wife and a kid? What the hell would you have done?"

"Done about what, Finn?"

"I hadda do it. That scumbag, Napolitano. That hood. He woulda killed 'em. He told me that."

The tears were flowing freely now. He dropped his head onto his arms on the table. I leaned in close and whispered.

"Tell me about it, Finn. Maybe I can help you."

He just shook his head and sobbed. I gave him a minute and then took his shoulders and gently held him back to face me. "Finn, I can help you. But you've got to tell me about it. What did you do?"

He focused on my eyes with the most desperately pained look I'd ever seen. The words were fighting to get out, but they were bottled up in fear. I pulled his shoulders close to me so I could speak directly into his ear. Without eye contact, I thought it might have brought back the safe feeling of confidentiality of the confessional. I fired my last, best shot.

"Finn, I can help you. I can relieve your pain. I can get protection for you and your wife and your daughter. I can do it. Can you hear me?"

For seconds I had no idea whether or not I was getting through. I could feel the struggle going on inside of him through the layers of clothing.

Then the dam cracked slightly open with that one whispered word. "Yes."

"It's true, Finn. I can. I can do it right now. But you've got to say it. You've got to tell me what you did. I'll understand."

His shoulders were shaking almost to the point of convulsion. I could feel the struggle for freedom from the grip of his personal devil that was going on inside of him. I just held him until he suddenly froze. The words burst out of him.

"I lied. God forgive me. I lied. He never done anything to me. I lied. And I can never take it back."

"You can, Finn. You can make it right. I'll help you. But you've got to say it. Why did you lie?"

"That scumbag, Napolitano. He told me what he'd do to my wife. My little daughter. He said he'd kill 'em. I didn't want to hurt Father Ryan. I had no choice."

The sobs came in full force now. I held him back so he could look in my eyes. "Listen to me, Finn. I said I'd help you. I will. Right now. But I need one more thing. Did they tell you why they made you do it?"

His breathing was coming in short gasps, but the sobbing had stopped. I could see him thinking. I believed him when he said they never told him why.

"Okay, Finn. Just sit there."

I walked to the empty bar and sat on the last stool. I made two fast calls. The first was a speed dial to Tom Burns. "Tommy. Guess who. I've got yet another one for you. This could be more dangerous. Same address on Pearl Street in Charlestown. The man, his wife, and daughter. I'm working to get them into federal protection. That thug you followed, Napolitano. He and his crowd have a vested interest in seeing he doesn't get there. What do you recommend?"

"Are any of that mob at the house now, Mikey?"

I checked with Finn. "Casey says not right now. They come and go."

"Tell him to go home. I'll put a perimeter of protection around the house."

"Good. How soon?"

"Ten minutes."

"What would I do without you, Tom?"

"Not well lately, Mikey."

The second call was to the District Attorney's Office. When Mary Cornelius answered, I asked if she recognized my voice. She said yes. I stopped her before she could mention my name.

"Mary, I need you to connect me to Billy Coyne's private line. No one else hears this conversation. And no names. Understood?"

She was enough onto the game to know that I meant no word to the Wicked Witch of the East. Billy Coyne was on the line in ten seconds.

"I'm assuming this is not just boyish dramatics, kid."

"Judge for yourself, Mr. Coyne. Are you alone?"

"Just me and the King of Sweden."

"Then tell the king to get the hell out of there. I need you to take this seriously, Mr. Coyne. Do you think you can do that?"

He must have caught my tone. "Go ahead, kid. What is it?"

"Listen to this. This is a recording of a conversation I had about two minutes ago with your star and only witness against Father Ryan. It's legitimate. Take it seriously. Then we'll talk."

I played the recording I'd made of my conversation with Finn on my never-leave-home-without-it pocket recorder. The tear-filled words of Finn poured through the cell phone. You could not fabricate the sincerity of the voice. When it finished, I was back on the line.

"That's your case against Father Ryan, Mr. Coyne. Now, do I have your attention?"

There was a slight pause before a taut voice came through the phone.

"Damn it! I knew it. I thought that accusation stunk to high heaven. I wished we could have let it rest till I could check it out."

"I know, Mr. Coyne. She smelled blood and went for a quick kill. The question is, what now?"

"I'll check it out. If it's what it seems, I'll move to kill the indictment before it goes public. Then I'll go after Napolitano. Get that recording to my office, pronto."

"In due time, Mr. Coyne. There's something more pressing. Can we agree you owe me a big one?"

"Don't press your luck, kid. I said I'll check it out."

"This is not pressing my luck. This is saving three lives. If word gets to Napolitano or Salviti that their fish is off the hook, Casey and his wife and daughter have been promised a death sentence. Casey's with me now. I'll be taking him to his home. Tom Burns's boys can protect them for a while, but I've got to get them into federal witness protection. He'll testify against Napolitano. That could lead to Salviti on federal racketeering charges. That should have the U.S. Attorney salivating. Can you move fast?"

"I'm ahead of you, kid. I've got the U.S. Attorney on the other line. Just sit there."

I held the line for thirty seconds before Mr. Coyne was back on the line.

"Tell Casey to go home and stay there with his family. There'll be a United Parcel Service truck at his front door in fifteen minutes. A man in a UPS uniform'll come to the door. Tell them to come out with him and get into the truck. You got that?"

"I got it. Go easy on him, Mr. Coyne. He's brittle."

# CHAPTER TWENTY

Two messages needed delivery at warp speed. The first was to Cardinal Ferrigan with no intermediate relays. One word of my connection with Mr. Devlin got me an instant pass into the inner sanctum.

The relief in the cardinal's eyes when I played the tape of Finn's heartfelt words made it easy to ask him to take immediate and unpublicized action to reinstate Father Ryan. There was actually no need to ask.

"You have no idea what this means to me, Michael. I get the idea Matt Ryan's one of the best on our team."

"If not *the* best."

"I'll get in touch with him right away."

I thought he might be in a mood to grant a personal favor. It had been a week of mostly losses. My psyche felt a selfish desire for a shot of jubilation. "If it's all the same, could you let me give him the word?"

The cardinal saw it in my eyes. "You've earned it, Michael. Tell him I'll be in touch. I might even have a promotion in mind for him."

We said our good-byes, but when I reached the door, I had to get rid of one small nagging thought before leaving. "If I could, Cardinal Ferrigan. You might give it a lot of thought before promoting Father Ryan. Especially if it took him out of Sacred Heart parish. You should see him down there. You'd think it was the Lord Himself holding those people's lives together."

"That's high praise, Michael."

"It was intended to be."

I left him smiling. "I won't do anything hasty."

The spiritual bounce I was anticipating from passing the word confidentially directly to Father Ryan was underestimated. I left the parish house on a temporary, but invigorating, cloud of faith in the joy of life. It carried me right through a drop-in to see how my senior partner was recuperating.

He had the staff of the hospital hopping to provide him with whatever he needed to function in what had become his out-of-the-office office. The head nurse explained that it was the only way they could keep him from pulling out tubes and getting back into the legal fray.

His secretary, the faithful Lois Drury, made two visits a day to take dictation and relay phone messages. She told me it was the only way she could screen the usual daily messages from cantankerous opposing counsel that would have sent his blood pressure through the top of the machine. In other words, he was rapidly getting back to normal.

Nothing in the entire realm of medical science could have done for his heart and soul what my news about the reinstatement of Father Ryan did for him. He glowed. He even seemed content at last to let the rest of the legal world's skirmishes struggle along without him while he got his physical act together.

When the good news had been conveyed and savored, we closed the door of his room for privacy. We rambled through possible reasons as to why the Italian mob took such an invasive interest in the life of his friend, Father Ryan. There was no question in either of our minds that it was tied to whatever shenanigans our vanishing client, Kevin O'Byrne, was up to. That connection would call for some delicate probing into areas I could have lived a contented lifetime without facing.

Just before I left, Mr. D. got a call from his old friend, Dominic Santangelo, the former don of the Boston Mafia family. I had filled Father Ryan in on Mr. D's heart condition without giving the details of what had triggered it. He had apparently passed the word to the third musketeer.

Father Ryan called at about the same time. We were able to make it a three-way conference call with the speakerphone on.

"Lex, what happened?"

"Dom, I'm good. Getting better every minute. In fact, pretty *damn* good for the number of courtroom wars this old ticker's been through."

"Tell me the truth. Did anyone I might have reason to know cause this?"

The tone was spiked with elements of a Sicilian hair-trigger sense of retribution. Mr. D. deflected it with a nonanswer. "This has been building for years, Dom. Heart attacks are endemic to trial lawyers. It's not the first. Did you hear about Matt?"

"Thank God, Lex. Matt says your Michael pulled off some of the old Devlin magic."

Mr. D. looked over at me with a grin that ran deep. "Michael's capable of pulling off his own magic. We can all thank God."

"And we do," the voice of Father Ryan added.

Mr. D. signaled me to be sure the door was closed tight.

"Dom, we still can't figure out the connection of this business of Matt with the boys in the North End. Any word?"

The voice became quiet. "My friend, who's there with you?"

"Only Michael. I have a secure line. What is it, Dom?"

"I've been in touch with Mr. P. Are we clear?"

We knew he was referring to Antonio Pesta, the "reputed," as the newspapers say to cover their legally vulnerable posteriors, successor godfather of the Boston Mafia family.

"We're clear."

"This is delicate, Lex. I had to burn more bridges than you could know when I kept my promise to you and Matt to start a new life. No regrets, but I was fortunate to be permitted to live. Most of them did not want to make that concession."

"What held them back?"

"Two things. I was the don of a family. Rule One. They needed permission of the dons of the other families to take my life. I've done favors over the years. The short of it is, the other dons wouldn't give the permission."

"You said two things. What was the other?"

"The man of whom we speak, Mr. P., is my godchild. I was his godfather in two senses, you might say. When he succeeded me as don, he kept tight reins on his capos and his consigliere in regard to me. There was a time some years ago, just before I took over, when his life was forfeited by a previous don to settle a dispute with another family. When I took over, I put myself between him and an execution. He never forgot. Is your Michael there?"

"He's right here, Dom."

"You see, Michael. Even among those of us you consider savages without consciences, there is loyalty. Honor of a sort."

"Nothing is black and white is it, Mr. Santangelo?"

"I think your young partner is beginning to open his mind, Lex."

I added, "You're truly an education to me, Mr. Santangelo."

He laughed, and then the tone turned serious.

"This stays between us. In spite of what I just said, I tell you this literally at risk of my life. Is that understood?"

We all chimed in in agreement.

"The man of whom we spoke shared a confidence with me. This can never be spoken of again in any way whatsoever. It's a matter of the utmost trust. I reemphasize that."

We all sensed the thin line of conscience Mr. Santangelo was walking. We again voiced our commitment to silence.

"This man we're talking about, he recently discovered disloyalty in one of his capos. Apparently this capo had ambitions he kept to himself. Ambitions of the sort that could put him in a position to take control of the family."

"Can you say what it was, Dom?"

"I'm getting there, Lex. This is difficult."

"I understand.

"This man, Mr. P., had the loyalty of one of the soldiers in the ranks of this capo. The soldier came to Mr. P. with the information that his capo had conspired to do business with his enemy."

"What business?"

"Diamonds. Smuggled diamonds taken from a mine in Africa, in Sierra Leone, held by some rebels."

"How could he make contact with these people?"

"By dealing with the Irish. The Irish have been our enemy in this city since before I was born. The group he dealt with in Ireland is a splinter group of the IRA. This capo apparently made it known he was in the market for these things they call 'blood diamonds.' Someone in the IRA arranged for him to buy a quantity of these diamonds a week or so ago in Dublin. He brought them back here to resell them at a large profit."

"To whom?"

"He'd been buying them from someone in Ireland. Then this deal came along with the capo for diamonds of a higher quality than he'd ever seen before. O'Byrne apparently has connections with diamond merchants somewhere in Europe to get these blood diamonds into the flow of the legal ones."

"I'm beginning to see the connection. Go ahead, Dom."

"This capo, the traitor, was Salvatore Barone. When the disloyalty was discovered, steps were taken by Mr. P. to deal with it. Barone died, you might remember, in the manner of a traitor. His body was found in the trunk of his own car by your client, the boy, Kevin O'Byrne."

Mr. D. and I looked at each other as some of the pieces of the puzzle began to fall into place.

"And the diamonds, Dom?"

"I'm told they were never found. And there's your connection. After Barone's death, he was succeeded as capo by Packy Salviti. My source tells me Salviti's still looking for the diamonds. That boy who stole Barone's car is your client, Kevin O'Byrne. My guess is Packy Salviti thinks the O'Byrnes have the diamonds. He wanted to put pressure on you to get the boy or his father to give them back. What better way than to trade the life of your close friend, Matt, for the diamonds? If he couldn't get the O'Byrnes to give them up any other way, sooner or later he'd have come to you with a deal to take the pressure off Matt. That was his ace in the hole. He may still play that card. None of them know yet that Matt's accuser is off the street."

It felt like the deck had been reshuffled and a whole new set of questions had been dealt. Our Mr. Frank O'Byrne had been up to his pink Irish ears in a sleazy business with the man in the trunk.

If, in fact, the death of Barone by many symbolic weapons had been at the hands of the Italians, as seemed likely, O'Byrne must have jumped out of his skin when he saw the face of the dead man in the trunk. Not because it was a mutilated body. He'd "allegedly" seen his share of those. And possibly not because of a deal gone sour. He'd undoubtedly experienced those. But this one had sucked his straight, clean son, Kevin, into the mired vortex. And that was enough to cause him to suck me right in there after him.

Mr. Santangelo had plugged a number of vital pieces into the puzzle, but a number of pieces still sat on the table. Just how did young Kevin get his hands in the mud, and how dirty were they? And how much of Kevin's involvement was known to Papa O'Byrne? And the winner and still champion of all of the unknowns—who actually had the diamonds? And how many more people would die to find out?

# CHAPTER TWENTY-ONE

It was time to get a few renegade ducks in a row. What started a week ago as a one-time request for a simple mediation by O'Byrne was beginning to show shadows behind the shadows. I left the hospital trying to get my mind around the true dimensions of what O'Byrne had originally presented as young Kevin's boyish prank. The more I digested the full implication of what Mr. Santangelo had tipped us to, the more my quietly smoldering resentment at O'Byrne's concealment of the risks was turning into a fully bugged-out rage.

And that was fortunate. In a collected, dispassionate state of mind, I would never have had the grit to beard that particular lion in his den. I had worked up a fully stoked head of steam by the time I walked into O'Byrne's bar, marched straight up the stairs, and knocked on his office door. I passed the two thugs on watch at the bar below before they could lift their bulk off the bar stools.

My knock had enough insistence in it to bring O'Byrne to the door about the time the two on watch caught up with me.

"Mr. O'Byrne, a word with you."

The force of the words seemed to stun O'Byrne, his two guardians, and me as well. He waved off the guardians with a look that said he'd have a word with them later about the level of security.

"What? What the hell is this all about?"

I took the seat in front of his desk and waved him to his desk chair. He sat, in spite of the inconsistency of being invited to sit in his own office.

Now that I was there, I came back down to cool rationality in time to put on the brakes. I realized that whatever I was about to say to O'Byrne could not divulge anything I'd learned in confidence from Mr. Santangelo. That was limiting.

"A couple of things turned up, Mr. O'Byrne. Most immediately, I need to talk to Kevin."

"Why? What?"

"Because, you may remember, about a week ago you hired me to represent him. He's indicted for murder. That means things have to be done in court that require at least speaking with my client."

That produced a wrinkled forehead and silence.

"The question is: where is he? Have you heard from him?"

He paused and leaned back, I think to get a grip on what I had dropped in his lap before he said anything compromising. The question was relatively simple. I figured the pause meant more hiding of the eight-hundred-pound gorilla that was now inhabiting both of our lives.

"No. I haven't heard from him. You?"

I held up my hands with a look that said, basically, "Would I be here asking?"

He caught the logic. He seemed to pass over the impertinence of the way it was asked to focus on an appropriate answer. "I'm worried as hell. The place in New Hampshire was a mess. I'm sure someone's got him. Funny I haven't heard from anyone with any demands."

I heard the words, but this time I was tuned in to the lack of deep-seated paternal panic behind them. I had about a dozen questions on the tip of my tongue. The problem was that every one of them was premised on the confidential disclosures of Mr. Santangelo. I asked the only untainted question that stood a chance of getting a truthful answer.

"The place in New Hampshire. Where is it? Maybe if I took a look I'd see something that might give us a lead."

I could almost hear the wheels grinding behind his solemn look. *If I let him see it, could he find anything I'd rather he didn't?*

"Yeah, sure. Why not? Maybe you'll come up with something. You'll let me know if you find anything."

"You'll be the first to hear." I figured a lie to a liar is not exactly a lie.

It was mid-afternoon, so I put off the trip north till the following morning. That left me an afternoon to follow a lead that I had let lie dormant in the back of my mind. That first night, Kevin gave me the names and addresses of the two boys who went with him to Patrini's restaurant in the North End, purportedly for pizza. Being South Boston Irish kids and friends of the son of the Irish mob boss, they more than likely had some notion that a pizza—even a North End pizza—was not worth the risk of riding into hostile territory. That, plus the fact the Kevin apparently wanted them along on whatever monkey business hc was into, indicated that there was gold to mine. I also figured I'd probably need blasting powder to get anything out of either one of them.

I drove to the campus of Northeastern University on Huntington Avenue. Kevin had said the two boys were also in their junior year.

My first stop was in the office of the dean of student affairs. I figured most of the employees in the dean's office would be bound and gagged by privacy issues. Fortunately, one of the secretaries in that office had a son for whom Mr. Devlin had performed near miracles in short circuiting an early drug conviction before it could derail his life.

Luisa Espinosa had recently lifted herself and her son out of the barrio in Roxbury with a move to Cambridge. The move was financed by income from her recently acquired job at Northeastern—another fix up by Mr. Devlin.

I found her in an office occupied by four other people. She recognized me from her visits to our Franklin Street office, saving the need for introductions. Thanks to an early upbringing by my mother, who was more fluent in the Spanish tongue than English, I was able to smile and speak to Luisa in the Puerto Rican dialect we shared. Her pure-white office mates seemed to take no offense, in the spirit of inclusiveness the university fostered.

I wanted the class schedules of each of Kevin's two friends. Innocuous as that information seemed, I knew I needed some leverage to crack the gagging rules of privacy. Luisa's gratitude to Mr. Devlin provided the leverage. While we chatted amiably in words no one else in the office understood, she fingered the keys of her computer and handed me a printout of two class schedules, facedown.

At three thirty, I was standing to the side of the stream of twenty students flowing out of Churchill Hall. I asked the first girl in the flow to point out Chuck Dixon. She complied with a smile. I fell in alongside target number one.

I flashed my business card and invited him to a bench for a quick word. He seemed immediately on edge, but when I mentioned that I was Kevin's attorney, he appeared willing to suspend the defensiveness—at least to the extent of a sit-down.

I was on a tight schedule, since I had to catch target number two coming out of class in fifteen minutes. That meant a more direct approach than I'd have liked.

"Chuck, you were with Kevin that night in the North End, right?"

I could see the defenses go back up behind the withdrawn posture. "I'm sorry. Who are you again?"

I slid over closer. "I'm quite possibly the best friend you've got in this city. Maybe you've heard. Kevin's been indicted for murdering that guy in the trunk of the car Kevin stole. You were with him at the time. The D.A.'s out for all the blood she can get. Nothing would tickle her small heart more than widening the net to include you in the indictment."

That produced the look of shock I was going for. Time for a full-court press.

"Hear this, Chuck. It's just possible I can keep you out of it. It depends on one thing."

I paused in the hope of drawing him into the conversation. It worked.

"What's that?"

"Information. I need to know exactly what happened that night. I'm listening."

I could see him weighing how much or how little information to give in answering a question that had caught him without time for preparation.

"Like, what do you mean?"

That was a staller. I checked my watch. "Start at the beginning of the evening. I need all the details. Just pretend you're writing a thesis for a history course, except that the next thirty years of your life depend on your answer. It's that simple."

He was looking off in the distance at nothing in particular. I could tell he was searching for a safe path. "We'd been at the library. It was about midnight. Kevin said he felt like a pizza. He said the best in the city are in the North End."

He looked over to see how it was going down. "No argument so far."

"So we drove over."

"Who else?"

"Another classmate. Bob Murphy."

"Who drove?"

"I did. My car was closest."

"Go ahead."

"We were going into Patrini's. We saw a guy pull up in a Cadillac. He just left the motor running. He ran into the restaurant. Bob dared Kevin to take the car for a spin around the block."

"It was Bob's idea?"

"Yeah. I thought he was joking. Anyway, before we knew it, Kevin jumped into the car and drove it down the street."

"And?"

"The guy came running back out of Patrini's. He was yelling and screaming. Kevin must have heard him. He stepped on the gas and took off."

"Would you know the guy if you saw him again?"

"I guess so. It was dark, but I got a good look. It scared the—I was kind of panicked. Bob and I ran back to my car and got out of there. That's all I know."

"Have you talked to Kevin since that night?"

He looked away and took the moment to wave at a couple of students in the distance. It could have been a significant body-language sign of a stall or I could have been just desperate enough to see clues where they didn't exist.

"Um, no. Not since then."

"Did you call him?"

"No. I don't think so. I've got to get to another class."

I leaned in closer. "I've got a better idea, Chuck. As I said, we could be talking about an accessory-to-murder charge. Suppose you finesse the class and meet me in twenty minutes in the Curry Student Center. I'll find you in the cafeteria."

I left him with a blank look on his face, tinged with just enough panic to insure he'd be there. I hustled over to Hayden Hall in time to catch Bob Murphy coming out of class in the same way I caught Chuck.

The scene played the same, with me sitting on a bench beside a kid who was digesting the thought of a possible thirty-year sentence as an accessory to murder. The dialogue was remarkably similar. In fact, his telling of the tale of that night came out in practically identical words. That much could be coincidence, but there was one jarring, at least to me, dissimilarity in the telling. According to young Bob, it was Chuck who dared Kevin to take the car.

I took Bob in tow, and we joined Chuck at a table in an unoccupied end of the student center cafeteria. I left them alone at the table and picked up three Cokes from the counter. My arrival back at the table cut off a whispering session in midstream.

I sat down with a smile and distributed the Cokes. "Now, boys, here's where we're at. You've both told the same story with remarkable consistency, except for one point. Let's see if we can work out the truth. Which one of you dared Kevin to steal the car?"

The silence hung like a cloud. They stared at each other for a few seconds. Chuck pulled out of it first. "What difference does that make?"

"Ah, Chuck, good question. Who cares, right?" I leaned in and dropped it to a whisper. "I care. You might wonder why, right?"

They were drawn in closer to catch every word.

"I care because I think you young gentlemen and your buddy, Kevin, are three of the lyingest scumbags I've had the displeasure of meeting this month. This little tale of a boys' night out is a crock. Damn! You boys are in college. Couldn't you do better than that fairy tale? Don't they teach you creative writing these days?"

No answer. None was expected. The blank stares were fixed, but the level of tension was clearly rising.

"Now, gentlemen—forgive the inappropriate title—here's the score. Both of you are looking at a possible stretch of prison life as accessories to murder. I mentioned that before. It's true. But it doesn't have to be that way. One of you can bail out. The price is the truth. All of it. And the prize goes to the swiftest. Whichever one calls me first at this phone number gets the best get-out-of-jail-free card I can offer. Are we clear so far?"

Neither one wanted to be the first to put it in words. I took the pained, blanched expression on their faces as an affirmative answer.

"Good. Then here's what I need to know. When did you really talk to Kevin last? Where was he? And what did he say? So far, so good?"

Same nonresponse response.

"Also good. And here's the last question. What in the hell were you three really doing at Patrini's that night? And if the word 'pizza' pops up in the answer, there'll be no prize."

I stood slowly and dropped the price of the Cokes on the table. "It's been a pleasure getting together with you boys. One way or another, we'll talk soon."

## CHAPTER TWENTY-TWO

It was a two-horse race, and my money was on Chuck Dixon to crack first. There was, however, no point in babysitting the phone. Given the tight lips I'd run into on the Irish side of this weeklong debacle, the odds were against either of them cracking the wall of silence.

That's why I was surprised when I got back to the office to hear from Julie that the phone had been ringing like a telethon. It was the same voice each time, but no name and no callback number. The second surprise was that when I answered the next ring myself, I recognized the voice of Bob Murphy—not Chuck Dixon. Live and learn.

"Mr. Knight, don't use any names. You know who this is?"

"I do. Go, Paws."

I figured the mention of the Northeastern University mascot, Paws the Husky, would establish contact without compromising anyone.

"I need to see you. Has the other guy called?"

"Nope. You won the race. If you give me something worth it, you've got me in your corner."

There was a pause while he seemed to be weighing what he had to give against what I could do for him. That latter was a mystery to both of us, and I let it hang that way.

"Okay, let's talk."

"Shoot. You have my full attention."

"Not here. I can't over the phone. Will you meet me tonight?"

"Done. Where and when?"

"Midnight. You know that strip of land off Storrow Drive just below the Hatch Shell?"

"I do. Beside the Charles River."

"Right. There's a bench under some trees. I'll be there at midnight."

That was promising. It also gave me a chance to make a down payment on a debt. Seamus Burke, the Irish quasi-angel who had pulled my chestnuts out of the fire in Pi Alley and then staged a Navy SEAL rescue of Mr. Devlin at the Seaborn Motel, deserved something for the effort. I called him at his home in Dorchester. No answer. I left a message vague enough to seem innocuous to anyone else, but specific enough to tip him off to the midnight rendezvous with a person of interest.

That done, I could fully appreciate the fact that for the first time since I was favored with the invitation to O'Byrne's office at the point of a switchblade, I had an entire six hours apparently goon-free. There was no question about how I'd spend them. That was my second call.

For well over a year, Terry O'Brien had been the only girl I'd dated, considered dating, or wanted to date. I reached her at her home in Winthrop and asked if I could pick her up in twenty minutes for a quiet dinner at a seashore restaurant that I'd been saving for a special date.

Her answer was yes. The next question that popped to my mind, but that I didn't ask, was why? Why on earth would she still say yes? It had been a year of catch-as-catch-can dates sandwiched between the embroilments of a practice that would make Jack Reacher's life look like that of an accountant. In fact, on several occasions, our dates ended with Terry being slipped into the backseat of the car of one of Tom Burns's operatives just to keep her alive. She was truly the front-runner for the *Guinness World Records* for courageous endurance.

I picked Terry up at her home by the ocean on the north shore of Winthrop. We drove north along the rocky coastal drive to the Molly Waldo Restaurant in Marblehead. She absolutely glowed. It happened to me the first time we went out on an actual date, and it happened to me every time since. The breath seemed to squeeze out of me at the thought that all of this mind-bending vibrancy and beauty was to be with me alone for the entire evening. Just having her beside me in the Corvette on that glorious stretch of seacoast put every unpleasant detail of the previous week on another planet.

When Paul at the desk of the Molly Waldo showed us to our table, I could feel the eyes of other diners turn in our direction. I knew I wasn't the one drawing the attention.

Chef Anthony came out to our table shortly after drink orders. He took the menus out of our hands, and said, "Please, Michael, allow me."

I'd known him for years, but this was the first time he'd done that. The answer, of course, was, "Yes, by all means." I could tell by her smile that Terry was just radiating pleasure in a perfect evening.

About eight thirty, just after the main course, the sweet gentle sounds of the Hammond organ began with "It Had to Be You." I asked Terry to dance, and she had her hand in mine on the way to the small floor before I finished asking.

In the middle of the next song, I couldn't resist asking Terry my favorite sports question. "What player actually played for the Boston Celtics, the Boston Bruins, and the Boston Red Sox?" It was a setup. Not just because Terry knew about as much about sports as I did about molecular physics, but because I was enjoying another small surprise. She did this cute thing with her nose and eyes that said, "Surely, you jest."

By this time I had danced us to a spot directly beside the organist. I whispered in Terry's ear, "This is the guy. He's the one who played for the Red Sox, Celtics, and Bruins."

She whispered back, "He doesn't look athletic."

"He's not. He's John Kiley, the organist."

She gave her face a wrinkled smile that could have greeted a bad pun. John Kiley leaned over without missing a beat and said in that baritone voice, "Michael, are you pulling that old gag on this beautiful lady?"

"You caught me, John. Meet Terry O'Brien."

John played with his left hand while he reached down for Terry's hand with his right. "My dear, but for your choice of dining companions, you are absolutely impeccable."

Terry burst into a smile that illuminated the room. "Thank you, Mr. Kiley. But I thought my choice was the best part of the evening."

John just leaned back and looked at the ceiling, "Oh, my God, Michael. If you don't ask this lady to marry you tonight, I'll personally have you committed."

Before Terry could turn a deeper shade of red, I danced her out of range. We danced in silence through the song John was playing while I did a fast but deep life calculation.

We were alone on the floor. I could see John signal the waiter to turn down the lights. As only John could, he played the most romantic rendition I have ever heard of "There Will Never Be Another You." I held Terry close through the first verse. When he began the second verse, I caught his look over Terry's shoulder. His scrunched-up forehead and wrinkled eyebrows beamed directly in my direction could not more clearly have said "Now!"

I had to say it quickly before my legs buckled beneath me. I whispered, but made it loud enough so I couldn't be misunderstood. "Terry, I think I've loved you since the first moment I saw you. I know I do now. And I will for the rest of my life. I know I'm not good at this. But will you please marry me?"

The whisper was so soft, I didn't really take it in. "Of course I will, Michael. Don't you know I love you too?"

"Terry, you don't have to answer right away. You can— What did you say?"

"I said, of course, I will."

We were dancing, and kissing, and grinning, and almost leaping in the air. John Kiley went into a jazzed up version of the "Wedding March," and all of the other diners, the maître d', and even the waiters gave us a standing ovation. When we finally walked back to our table, I could see John give me the fighter's victory sign with his hands over his head. At our table was a bottle of champagne, open with two glasses.

We toasted the night, and the music, and mostly a love so strong you could almost taste it, and we danced to John's music until ten thirty.

And then the carriage turned back to a pumpkin, and the white horses became mice again. I remembered my meeting with Bob Murphy at midnight by the Hatch Shell.

We said our good-byes to John, who could not stop grinning, and to our other hosts. We were back in the Corvette starting to head south along the coast. Terry was holding my right hand and just seemed to be floating in a silent dream. My own state of euphoria was slightly jarred when I noticed headlights pull in behind us as soon as we left the parking lot.

Something was triggering a definite alert. It might have been the uncomfortable closeness of the car behind us or the fact that it appeared as soon as we were on the road. Without alarming Terry, I turned right at the next street. The car followed. I made two more rights and a left to head back toward the Molly Waldo. The car followed.

If I were alone, I'd have floored the Corvette and used familiar streets to lose him, but not with Terry aboard. I kept the speed moderate and turned into the Molly Waldo parking lot. By now Terry knew this was not an average ride home from a date. She kept her amazing cool. It was not the first time a date with me ended in more excitement than necessary.

I spoke as calmly as possible. "Here's the plan. When I stop the car, you run back into the restaurant. And don't worry. I can handle this."

"What are you going to do, Michael?"

"I have an idea."

I tapped out a number on my cell phone. John Kiley answered. "John, I need a favor. Terry's coming back in at top speed. Will you call the Marblehead police? Get them to the parking lot as soon as possible."

"Oh, Michael, not again. Do you ever live like a normal person?"

"Sometimes. Not today."

"I'm on it. Send her in. I'll stay with her."

I pulled back into the parking lot at an unhurried speed as if I'd forgotten something. I saw other diners just leaving the restaurant. The car behind pulled in right after me. When I reached the door, I stopped and told Terry, "Go. Now. I'll be in to pick you up."

I saw Terry run the ten feet to the door and get safely inside. I hit the gas and swung around a half circle to the right to come in behind the car following me. I was deliberately blocking the only exit from the parking lot. I just sat there. The car that had been following me was boxed in between my Corvette and the other cars leaving the restaurant. I figured that in full view of that crowd, whoever it might be was unlikely to get violent. In less than thirty seconds, two distinct sirens announced the arrival of police cars.

The two men in the blocked-in car made a panicky choice to get out and run. They were both a couple of beefy-looking hoods who were not about to set Olympic speed records. The four officers were quick to respond to my shouted allegations of assault and harassment. They had the two of them in custody before they could make it across the parking lot.

I complimented the officers with a vague suggestion that I was a local resident. In a high-income, low-crime area like Marblehead, pleasing the residents is second only to pleasing the tourists. They agreed to hold the two thugs overnight until I came in to proffer charges in the morning.

I got a good look at the two in the backseat of the police car glaring back at me. They were both of the thuggish cut, but I didn't recognize either of them. I said through the window, "You boys out for the sea air?"

I said it because I wanted to hear the voices to see if they carried a South Boston Irish or a North End Italian accent. The response was salty, and the accent was definitely South Boston Irish.

That was a jolt. Clearly the two thugs were not ambassadors of goodwill. Equally clearly, if I pegged the Irish accents right, they'd be doing nothing without the orders of Frank O'Byrne. I had thought we were playing for that team—at least in a limited way. It made me wonder if O'Byrne was following Shakespeare's proposal in *Henry VI*—"The first thing we do, let's kill all the lawyers." Starting with his own.

I went back inside the restaurant. I took Terry back from the sheltering protection of John and the rest of the staff. She was shaken, but glad to hear that the crisis had passed—for the moment.

I held her close on the walk to the door. When she caught her breath, she gave me a serious look. "Michael—"

"I know what you're going to say, Terry. And you're right. When I get this thing cleaned up, I'm going to practice nothing but real estate law. The most dangerous thing I'll ever do again is cross Tremont Street to the Registry of Deeds."

She smiled the kind of smile that said she appreciated the prediction, but wasn't too sure how seriously I meant it. The fact was, I meant it from the bottom of my soul.

When we reached the door, I could hear John yell, "Michael, you're about to be a family man. Will you for the love of Pete—?"

I yelled back, "I will, John. I will. You take care of yourself too. We need you for the wedding!"

# CHAPTER TWENTY-THREE

By the time I dropped Terry off in Winthrop, I had twenty minutes to get to the Hatch Shell on Storrow Drive for the midnight rendezvous with Bob Murphy. With Friday night traffic, I made it in twenty-five. Parking was not so easy with all the apartments around the Esplanade. I was about ten minutes late by the time I used the overpass and walked along the tree-covered strip of land leading up to the Shell.

Bob Murphy had picked the right spot if he wanted seclusion. It was dark, cold, and totally unpopulated along the pathway. What sparse light there was came only from the passing spillover of lights from Storrow Drive.

There were several benches along the way, but only one held the silhouette of a lone figure. I came up from behind. I didn't want to scare him into a premature heart attack. I called in a soft voice, "Bob Murphy."

No answer. I thought he might be piqued by my late arrival. I figured he'd get over it. The voice that finally came out of the figure on the bench promised something more jarring. I wasn't ready for the Irish brogue of Seamus Burke.

"You're late, lawyer."

"I know. Thank you for noticing. Apparently, Murphy is too. I'd invite you to wait on the bench with me, but he was pretty adamant about us doing this alone. Maybe you could watch from the bushes."

"I don't think either of us needs to wait."

I didn't like the sound of that, especially in that irritatingly calm voice of the Irishman.

"I'm sure you're going to tell me why."

"You can see for yourself."

He nodded his head toward a row of bushes on the other side of the path. The words, "Oh crap, oh crap, oh crap," grew in volume as I slowly made out the outline of the body that was splayed under the canopy of bushes. Another life, this time the young life of Bob Murphy, had apparently been sacrificed to the quest for those damned diamonds.

"How?"

"Knifed. His throat was slit. Someone caught him from behind. He was there when I got here."

I started to go through his pockets with minimal disturbance of the body for the sake of questions I might have to answer later.

"Don't trouble yourself, lawyer. There's nothin' there."

I straightened up and began taking a mental count of the people who could have known I was meeting him at that place at that time. I doubted that he'd have tipped off anyone, and the only one I told was Seamus Burke. Given the way the sides were being realigned without notice, and Burke's sole presence with the body, I asked him the obvious question.

"Lawyer, for all of your book learning, you're not too quick upstairs. If I killed him, why would I be sitting here waiting for you? Do I strike you as simpleminded?"

"I had to ask. All right, that leaves three prime choices. He was about to tell me what happened that night in the North End. That means he was also double-crossing the other two who were there—Chuck Dixon and the elusive Kevin O'Byrne. I doubt he let either of them in on it. The final choice is Frank O'Byrne. Clearly, Murphy didn't tell him."

I hardly finished saying it when Burke was on his feet and moving fast. I caught up and moved with him. I think the same idea hit both of us at the same time.

"You drive, lawyer. You know the shortcuts."

I took every back street I knew through the Back Bay to Huntington Avenue. Luisa Espinosa had given me the address of Chuck

Dixon's dorm room. We were there, parked, and running up two flights of stairs within twenty minutes.

We reached the floor and breezed past a couple of sleepy-eyed students who took an immediate interest in our race to Dixon's room. Their interest peaked when, after two quick raps, Burke slipped something into the lock and sprung the door open.

"Hey, what the hell're you guys doing?"

I faced the two boys in the hall, while Burke flipped on a light and made a quick scan of the room.

"We're from the fire marshall's office. Report of electrical fire in the walls. You better keep out of there."

They just stared at me while I called into the room. "Anything?"

"No. Get in here."

I went in and closed the door. The most immediate thing I noticed with some relief was no dead body. I hadn't allowed myself to dwell on the fact that my afternoon chat with the two boys could have triggered one boy's death. On the drive over, I prayed hard that the count was not up to two.

Seamus had gone through the chest of drawers and was rifling through whatever was in the bedside table. "Take the closet, lawyer."

I did. And then the bathroom medicine cabinet. I came out to find Burke sitting on the bed.

"Well, lawyer, what's your conclusion?"

I sat down beside him. "Two possibilities. One thing's for sure. He made a deliberate choice to leave. No panic. He didn't just cut and run. There's no suitcase in the room. No heavy jacket or coats in his closet. Even the bathroom cabinet. No shaving equipment, no toothpaste. He packed for a trip. What did you find?"

"You're starting to grow a brain, lawyer. Same thing in the drawers. No underwear, socks. He's going to be gone for a while."

"It may have been his choice, but he made it in a hurry. This afternoon he was fully into his classes. Something made him pack up and go sometime after that last class. It's pretty obvious what it was."

"You mean that little discussion you had with him this afternoon?"

"What else?"

"I'm not sure. You're quick to jump to conclusions."

"That still leaves two possibilities."

"And they are?"

"Either he cut and ran on his own when I threatened a jail sentence. We could follow that trail and get nowhere."

"Or?"

"Or, he decided to stay in with the O'Byrnes. He could have tipped off Frank or Kevin that I was onto both him and Bob Murphy. He could have added that Murphy might rat out the bunch of them. No great trick to follow Murphy to the Shell and—" I made a gesture with a finger across my throat that he understood.

"You're not as dim-witted as I thought you were, lawyer."

"You're too kind. Are you still in for the next round?"

"I wouldn't miss it."

It was just past rush hour the next morning when Burke and I were cruising north in my Corvette. I was following the directions I'd gotten from Frank O'Byrne to the place in New Hampshire where he said he had stashed his son, Kevin. I did it with some misgivings. The events of the previous evening left serious doubts as to which side O'Byrne was on. On the other hand, given the paucity of other leads, the choice was fairly mandatory.

We followed Route 93 north across the state line, and then deep into the wooded lake country of New Hampshire. The last turn off two and a half hours later was onto a one-lane dirt road that penetrated a densely pine-forested area. The road skirted the shore of one of the smaller lakes that fed into the massive and more populated Lake Winnipesaukee.

It was two miles of subjecting the suspension of my Corvette to the rivulets, gullies, and washouts that nature had carved into what could only be called a "road" with a healthy sense of humor. It finally brought us to a small cottage in a clearing beside the lake. No question that it was the one O'Byrne had in mind. It was the only evidence of human habitation in the entire two miles.

We had the benefit of the noon sun when we stepped out onto the silent pine spill area near the single cottage door. For all of his cool, I sensed that Burke was feeling the same tension that had my nerves on red alert.

We looked at each other when we reached the door. The question was which of us would reach for the doorknob. Since the mission was primarily mine, I made the move. A count of three, a twist of the knob, and a heart-stopping thrust of the door inward resulted in— nothing. No bomb, no ambush. Just an opening into what was obviously a summer cottage, chilled to the below-freezing temperature of the outside air.

The layout of rooms was easy to see at a glance. We came in at the kitchen, with a living area behind it. Behind that was a closed door that seemed likely to lead to a bedroom. What gave the sensation of going from the serene, harmonious, wooded exterior into the playpen of a demented orangutan was that the two visible rooms looked as if a giant eggbeater had whipped everything into one enormous omelet.

Every piece of furniture was upended. Every drawer was pulled from its socket and not only emptied, but smashed. The few pieces of overstuffed furniture were slashed. The stuffing was pulled out in fistfuls, and even the frames were broken. When O'Byrne had described it as "a mess," he was a master of understatement.

Burke was the first in. He stepped silently between shards of glass and debris to a point between the kitchen and living area. He gave a quick scan to everything visible. Without a word, he turned and pointed to me and then pointed to the kitchen area. He turned to walk into the living area, apparently to give it a closer inspection himself. Given the wide-openness of the cottage, I couldn't resist saying it out loud.

"Hey, Burke, who the hell made you boss?"

He spun around with his finger to his lips.

"What? We're inside. Look around. There isn't a living thing for two miles but bears. Maybe a moose. This damn place is creepy enough without the dramatics."

He gave me one cold look and walked softly to stand beside me. He spoke in a whisper, but the words stung. "This is why I work alone, lawyer. I've lived forty years because I know what I'm doing. You don't. I'll be damned if some Ivy League lawyer is going to blunder my life away. Do you understand that much?"

He had me. I nodded.

"Then shut the hell up. Walk softly and search the kitchen."

It was no time for a smart answer. I started searching the kitchen. The technique was easy. Just look. Everything down to the dust molecules had been pulled out of every cabinet shelf and counter drawer. Even the doors had been pulled off the cabinets, and the counter drawers had been thrown on the floor and smashed.

O'Byrne's description had been that the cottage had been "tossed." That implies "searched." What I was looking at smacked more of anger and malicious destruction. It could have been the result of frustration or perhaps something completely different. There was something about the condition of the room that did not fit any theory I could come up with. That was disturbing.

Since every nook and corner of the room was totally exposed to view, a complete search took little more than standing in the center and turning in a couple of circles.

I checked on Burke's progress. The living room was in the same condition. He was simply standing in the center of the room and doing the same slow three-hundred-sixty-degree scan. The somewhat aggravating lack of any telltale emotion in his face left me totally unable to read his thoughts. I moved as silently as the clutter on the floor permitted to stand beside him.

To keep silence, I tapped his shoulder and gave him a questioning look. He just waved me off. He gave it one more slow, three-sixty scan with a focus that did not admit interruption.

With that, he pointed to the closed door on the far side of the living area. He gestured me to the left side of the door, while he moved silently to the right side. Not only did I feel like a golden retriever on hand signals, he was beginning to creep me out. We were clearly the only humans in that part of New Hampshire. I seriously doubted the need for the silent movie treatment. Nevertheless.

He fixed me in position beside the door with a "stay" signal. He reached slowly across the door to take a grip on the knob that was on my side. In mime, he indicated that he would pull it open toward us on the count of three.

By now he had my nerves in an uproar. I was fully focused. He counted off the "three" with slow nods of his head. When he reached the magic number, he jerked the door open a crack. I caught one glimpse of a string attached to the inside knob. It triggered an instantaneous flash reaction. Without a fraction of a thought, I dove across the door and caught Burke with a tackle in the midsection that would have done Lawrence Taylor proud.

I knocked the wind out of him. The two of us went sprawling through the debris on the floor. At the same moment, our ears went stone deaf with the concussive impact of a blast that ripped two feet off of both sides of the door.

We rolled over clutter to the side wall and just froze. I lay there flat on the floor in shock. I could see Burke sitting back against the wall, propped upright with both fists around a .45 pistol aimed at what was formerly a door frame.

Burke was on his feet first. He moved with the handgun extended into what had probably been a bedroom before the demolition crew had torn it to pieces. I followed him in. It looked just like the other two rooms, littered with splintered remnants of furnishings. The one exception was the pair of shotguns solidly mounted to a heavy chair that was blown backward. The strings that had run to the door were still trailing.

I thought I saw two tiny wisps of smoke from the guns fading into the chilled atmosphere. The chill moved into my bones when I realized that those wisps could easily have represented our lives.

# CHAPTER TWENTY-FOUR

By the time we moved outside the cottage into what by comparison looked like the real world, my hearing was slowly coming back. The concussive mental cloud was beginning to lift. Thoughts, mostly questions, started pouring in. Leading off in both of our minds I'm sure was the big one. Was this reception planned in our honor, or did they have someone else in mind? That was closely followed by the question of who the hell had taped those shotguns to the chair.

The two of us sat quietly beside the gentle lapping of the lake on the small sandy beach. For the first time since I'd met him, I saw the slightest emotional reaction in Burke's eyes to what was happening around him. It took a near-death experience, but it finally proved he was human after all.

"That was close, Burke."

He gave me a look that seemed to congratulate me on my fine grip on the obvious. At least he didn't disagree.

"Who do you suppose—?"

I got that far before his hand went up. By now I was obeying his hand signals instinctively.

"I've got to say this to you, lawyer. You were quick and right on the money. If you hadn't been, we'd not be having this conversation. I owe you."

I was touched, but I had to seize the moment.

"Mr. Burke. Seamus, if you will. I'm not one to take advantage of a situation. But I'd like to claim one bit of compensation."

I had his attention.

"Will you, for the love of all the saints in heaven, stop calling me 'lawyer'? You make it sound like 'child-molester.' My name's Michael."

"Done. Now, what're you thinking? What's your take on all this?"

I was doubly shocked that he'd ask, but since he did, "If you mean who set the trap, no one knew you'd be coming up here. It wasn't for you. The only one who knew I'd be here was Frank O'Byrne. Any one of his thugs could have done the rigging."

"Damn, lawyer—Michael, I thought he hired you. You have to pick your clients more carefully. You must have pissed him off royally."

"I seem to have a talent for that."

"Did you notice anything else in there?"

Apparently, he was tuned to the same signal I had picked up.

"I think so. I can understand them searching the place. Obviously, for the diamonds. Apparently, someone's pretty sure Kevin had them. From the looks of the total wreck, they never found them. But I agree. There's something else."

"Like what else?"

I had a feeling he was testing me.

"It looked like more than a search."

"True. A demolition. What else?"

"It was like they were sending a message to whoever came into that cottage. I'm still trying to figure out the message."

"When we get the answer to that one, we'll be one up in the game."

"Then there's the question of where the hell Kevin is—alive or dead? My money's on alive. How about you?"

"We think alike."

"And if I read you right, Seamus, the question that trumps them all is where are those damn diamonds."

He gave no response. He just jumped to his feet and headed for the car. I'd have followed him, but an idea struck me at that moment. I headed back into the cottage. It took me about two minutes, but then I was back in the car. I tortured the shock absorbers of the

Corvette over the two miles of washboard road to get back onto Route 93.

The first words were mine once we were headed south on a paved road. "Kevin's alive. He's in touch with his father and, wherever he is, they're working together."

He looked over at me. "You developing psychic powers?"

"Not quite. I noticed the phone was still hanging on the wall in the kitchen. When I went back in, I hit the redial button. If Kevin used the phone, it'd redial his last call."

"You're a bloody genius. What'd you get?"

"The phone dialed a number. One guess who answered."

"Frank O'Byrne."

"Right on. There's more. Frank must have checked his caller ID to see who was calling. He could tell it was from the cottage. He answered it, 'Hello, Kevin.' That's all. No panic. No 'Where the hell have you been?' Just a calm, 'Hello, Kevin.'"

"He must have figured Kevin went back to the cottage for something. What'd you say?"

"Nothing. I hung up. I didn't want to tip him off that his little mousetrap missed. Probably not too bright on my part. If it was Kevin calling, he'd have spoken to him. The only other one who'd be up there is me. That would tell him I'm still alive and some kind of a threat."

"Maybe not. Maybe he thinks you used the phone trick before you went into the bedroom. At least he could be in doubt."

"Possible."

We rode another ten miles in silence. I was absorbed in my own thoughts. The primary question on my agenda was simple and wide open. What do I do next?

I hadn't noticed it brewing, but when I looked over, I could see fire in Seamus eyes.

"What, Seamus? You look like a bomb about to go off."

He was looking straight ahead. "This is damn bloody embarrassing. I'm losing my edge. Twenty years of the wars in Ireland people minimize with the paltry words, 'the troubles.' Another twelve years of things that are none of your damn business. And here I come within a rat's whisker of getting my arse blown off by some pissant of an American gangster. It takes a bloody lawyer, no offense, to pull my arse out of harm's way. I'm definitely losing it."

I was stuck for a comment. Except for the "bloody lawyer" part, I had no clue to the personal history that went into his tirade. I went with what was still on the table for discussion by me. "Does that mean you're pulling out of this mess?"

He looked at me as if I had just materialized in time to say something offensive. "Are you out of your mind? I'm committed. If I did drop out, not that I would, there'd be three on my trail to silence me for what I know."

I just shook my head. "I'll be damned if I understand you people, Seamus Burke. You're like creatures from some God-forsaken war planet. Then what exactly does it mean? If I'm in this thing by myself, I can handle it. But I'd like to know it right now."

"It means I'm fed up with playing this game on the sidelines. It's time I got into the thick of it. Did you ever hear what they say—the best defense is a good offense?"

"It was one of my father's favorite sayings. How does it relate?"

"It's time to go on the bloody offense. We're going to carry this game to that pissant, O'Byrne, and his slippery kid. Have you got the stones for it? Are you in or out?"

I pulled into a traveler's rest station. This conversation was getting into waters too deep for highway distraction.

"I've been in this thing up to my ears since long before you showed up, Seamus. I have no choice."

"I'll take that as a full commitment. Then it's time we exchanged some serious information. I want everything you know about O'Byrne, his kid, the Italians, everything. Right now."

On the implied promise of a reciprocal spilling of information, I laid out everything I knew from the moment Paddy O'Toole stuck a knife in my ribs to induce me to pay a friendly call on Frank O'Byrne to my run-in with the two Irish thugs at the Molly Waldo. Seamus absorbed every syllable. If I touched on matters O'Byrne confided as a client, I figured the two goons at the Molly Waldo, not to mention the double shotgun blast, dissolved any bonds of confidentiality.

When I finished, I waited in silence. I wanted him to break it as a sign of mutual trust. It took a minute, but he finally opened up.

"Given what we're about to get into, you're entitled to this."

He looked over to lock eyes before he continued. "Do I need to tell you that if this ever passes your lips, it'll be the last thing you'll say on this earth?"

I nodded. "I've been hearing that a lot lately."

"Then take it to heart."

He opened his window and fired up a cigarette. If it helped him put it all together, I could stand gagging on the smoke.

"I work for a man in Ireland. I'll give you his name because the day may come when you'll need to meet with him. Declan O'Connor. If you think I know my way around the arts of combat, it's because you never met Declan. That's neither here nor there."

He took a pause to draw a cloud of cigarette smoke to the bottom of his lungs. Perhaps it cleared his thinking.

"Declan teamed up with a man who came from Africa. Sierra Leone, to be exact. For some reason, Declan took an interest in this man who calls himself Johnny Walker. This Walker had a bag of diamonds he'd smuggled out of Sierra Leone. He needed to sell them for all he could get. Some kind of personal problem. But they were what they call 'blood diamonds,' and smuggled to boot. That meant he could only deal with the black market. You listening?"

"With both ears."

"All right. Declan put this Walker in touch with one of your scumbag Italian gangsters from America. That was Barone. I say 'was' because he's the one you saw dead in his own trunk. Barone struck a deal with Walker to buy the diamonds for a lot of money.

Around a million euros. Barone was going to bring the diamonds back here to sell to someone he had a deal with—someone who could get them into the legal flow of diamonds to the cutters. Once Barone sold them, he'd get the money to this Walker. Are you following this?"

"Not completely. Why would Walker give the diamonds to Barone without being paid?"

"Because Barone wouldn't have the money to pay him until he sold them."

"And once he did, what guaranteed payment?"

"You're looking at the guarantee. Declan sent me to see that Barone paid the money."

"I see your problem. With Barone dead, who has the diamonds, and how do you collect the money?"

"You sum it up like a lawyer."

"I am a lawyer."

"Don't be a smart-ass. That brings us to the next phase of the campaign. I've got an idea. It could get us some answers. It could also get us killed. Are you still in?"

I thought about the fact that Mr. Devlin was still under the protection of Tom Burns from whatever thugs Packy Salviti might care to send after him next. On top of that, I'd just been the target of what, thank God, was an *attempted* murder, most likely by the team of Frank and Kevin O'Byrne.

The anomaly was that I was still defense counsel of record in the murder indictment of Kevin O'Byrne. I thought I could make the anomaly go away in short order by snipping the lawyer-client relationship. Unfortunately, that would not lessen the desire of the O'Byrnes to terminate my existence. I felt a strong intuitive sense, for reasons I would have had difficulty putting into words, that both of those life-threatening issues could be resolved if I could get my hands on the damn diamonds.

I held my hand out to the man who had finally chucked the cigarette. He took it, and the immortal words of Oliver Hardy to Stan

Laurel rang through my mind: "Here's another fine mess you've gotten me into."

There was one complication that needed elimination before the
sun went down. I called Julie at the office before I pulled out onto
Route 93.

"Michael. Are you actually back from phantomland? Because if
you are, there are about two thousand messages—"

"Not now, Julie. I'm still in phantomland. This has to be quick.
Would you call the court? Suffolk County. I think Judge DiSilva drew
the Kevin O'Byrne indictment. If so, speak to his docket clerk, John
Murphy. Tell John I need a hearing with the judge. This afternoon,
if at all possible. Preferably in chambers. John'll know it's important.
Can you get right back to me?"

"Should I notify the district attorney's office?"

"No. This is strictly ex parte. I'll fill Billy Coyne in later. Thank
you, Julie. *Chop, chop.* Before they close the shop for the day."

Julie got back to me in ten minutes with a message that changed my
course to a direct line to the courthouse. I dropped Seamus off at an
MTA station and made it to Judge DiSilva's chambers in another
twenty minutes.

It was well after court hours. It was just the judge and I—no law
clerk, no secretary. Exactly what I needed for some delicate maneuvering.

The judge was just hanging up his robe. He waved me to a seat.
"What's up, Michael?"

"Just what you don't want to hear, Judge. I want permission to
withdraw from representation of Kevin O'Byrne."

His eyebrows went up. "And the reason?"

"This is delicate. I'm tap-dancing around attorney-client privilege."

"I take it it's something you don't feel comfortable disclosing."

"No problem there. I'd be delighted to disclose it to the world.
I've just got to get around the privilege."

"Are you inviting me to ask you something?"

"Yes. If you ask the right question, and I think you're about to, you can order me to answer it. Nothing would give me greater pleasure."

"I've played this game before, Michael. I believe the question is this: does the information you have concern the health or safety of someone?"

"It most certainly does."

"And would that someone be you?"

"It most certainly would, Judge."

"Then I'm ordering you to give me that information."

"Thank you. I'm formally requesting permission to withdraw as counsel for Kevin O'Byrne on the grounds that I have credible reason to believe that he, and probably his father, just attempted to blow my body into several New England states. If they know I survived it, I believe they'll go for a second attempt until they get it right."

The judge, even given what he encountered daily in his court-room, seemed stunned.

"Are you sure, Michael?"

"Sure enough to be sitting here. You know I wouldn't make the request lightly."

"I know you wouldn't. Does Lex know?"

"Not yet. I'd rather he didn't."

"I heard he had a heart episode. How is he?"

"Getting stronger. This could give him a setback. I'd like to keep this between us."

"Of course. I've known you long enough to take you at your word, Michael. Your request to withdraw is granted. We'll notify the district attorney's office of the change of counsel."

"Thank you, Judge."

I was up and heading for the door. The judge caught me with some of the tone of concern I get from Mr. Devlin. "Michael, that's a hell of a situation. Do you want to file a complaint? I'll issue a bench warrant right now."

"Won't help, Judge. He's on the loose. Even I don't know where he is."

"Damn it. What are you going to do?"

"I'll be all right, Judge. I have some ideas."

"It sounds feeble, but for the love of God, take care of yourself."

.

# CHAPTER TWENTY-FIVE

I was back in the Franklin Street office in time to catch Julie before she left for the day.

"Michael, is that really you? A personal appearance right here in the office?"

"In the flesh, Julie. Did I miss anything?"

"Oh, let's see. There was that little tantrum I threw this afternoon when one of those miscreants you call clients threatened to sue me personally if *you* don't return his phone call by six o'clock tonight. That was worth watching."

"I can imagine it. My dear Julie, you are my shield, my fortress against the maddening and suffocating onslaught of the communicating world. What would I do without you?"

"Not well at all. Is that a prelude to an announcement of a substantial raise or just the usual let Julie blow off steam?"

"I'm deciding. I take it you left memos of the important calls and e-mails."

"In a mound on your desk. You're in the nick of time. You can still see over it."

"Excellent. Here's the deal. I'm slightly over my head right now in a bit of a mess."

"Michael, is this the kind of mess that could cause you personal harm?"

"Not a bit of it. I could be researching land titles for the amount of danger involved. Your concern does warm my heart. But, no."

"Michael?"

"No. Not even worth the telling. Now, here's what I need. Would you go through those memos? Give a courtesy e-mail to anything below code orange. A thirty-second personal call for the code oranges. Save the code reds for me. Clear?"

"Yes, but—"

"One more thing. Take all the code reds and reclassify them code oranges. Got it?"

"Michael, if you could sit for one hour and listen to your obnoxious clients ream me out. Me! Who am actually here speaking nicely with them!"

"I've decided, Julie."

"What?"

"You need a substantial raise. Put it in a memo, and put it on my desk."

"Really. Is that code red or code orange?"

"I'll decide. Now listen. I need both of those ears tuned to this frequency. You mentioned someone who was calling with a rough Italian accent a while ago. Has he called again?"

"Every two hours. In fact, he's about due. I was hoping to be out of here before the next one."

"I'll take this one. Who does the Caller ID say it is?"

"It doesn't. Just says 'caller unknown.'"

"Okay, thanks, Julie. You're a peach. That's old-fashioned, but it's a compliment. Before you go, can I give you something for an immediate printout?"

I used the next few minutes to dictate a document that I hoped I'd be needing by that evening. Julie typed it as I spoke and gave me a printout before leaving.

I used my office phone to call the hospital. Mr. Devlin was, according to all accounts, alternating between driving them totally nuts with his demands for release one minute and charming the living crap out of them the next. He was supremely capable of both, but only when he was full of the old "piss and hot sauce," as my friend, Big Daddy Hightower, was wont to put it. That was a very good sign.

I spoke with Mr. D. and filled him in on the events of the last two days, including the murder of Bob Murphy and the flight of Chuck

Dixon. I gave him the details of my excursion with Burke, mentioning, but passing over lightly, the shotgun blast. He takes precedence even over Julie in the department of personal concern for my well-being.

The icing on the cake was the news of my engagement to Terry O'Brien. I saved it for last. It left him with a smile that I could hear in his voice.

I cut short the good-byes when a light lit on the other phone line. I clicked it on and dropped my voice an octave.

"Yes."

There was a stunned moment of silence.

"Who the hell is this?"

Julie was right. It sounded like a gorilla in heat. There was no mistaking the gravelly North End accent of Packy Salviti.

"This is an old acquaintance of yours, Mr. Salviti. We last had the pleasure of a chat in Pi Alley. I'll bet a bundle you remember it."

I was sure we were both recalling his sniveling whining for his life on his knees when Burke produced the hand grenade. The flashback had the desired effect on his blood pressure.

"Listen, you little bastard. I get hold of you—"

"I thought you'd never ask. I'm going to give you the chance. How do you like that?"

"What're you talkin' about?"

"Your dreams come true. You and I are going to get together and iron out a few things. Only this time on my terms. What do you say? You got the guts for it?"

"Why you little—"

"Mr. Salviti. Packy. How about if I call you 'Packy'? After all we've been through together."

"Yeah, call me Packy. Like 'No. no. Don't do it, Packy.' You little creep. I get my hands on you—"

"I have something else in mind. I've got something for you. You don't know it, but it's the most important thing in your life right now."

"Yeah, what is it? You got them stones? You bring 'em over here. Maybe you get to live another day."

"It's actually something you need more than the stones. You don't know it, but your life depends on it. And, Packy, hear this. It's not going to be that way. This time, we meet on my terms."

"What the hell you talkin' about, your terms? The hell I—"

"Packy, for once in your damn useless, pusillanimous life, listen. You've got a choice. And if you're going to keep that pampered, puckered ass of yours from being chopped up like stew beef, you better make the right choice. Are you tuned in?"

"Who the hell're you threatenin'?"

"Not me, Packy. Someone you're going to get to know really well if you make the wrong choice. Here it is. We meet on my terms. Both alone. Five o'clock tonight. I'll give it to you then."

"Just cuz I'm askin', you little punk. What's the other choice?"

"I'll spell it out. You show or you don't show. That's your choice. If you show, alone, I'll give you something that I guarantee is a matter of life or death. For you. You don't show, it goes directly to someone you don't want to meet on your best day."

"You got somethin' for me, you send it—"

"No, no, no, Packy. I give it to you in person or not at all. I don't give a damn either way. I have ten more seconds to waste on this crap. Decide. You're down to nine."

There was a break in the blustering from the other end. I could read his mind. *How do I show up with enough firepower to get what he has and then blow him to kingdom come?*

I had no problem with that thinking. I just needed him there. With what I had in mind, I figured I could handle the rest.

"Eight, seven, six. Reaching to hang up now, Packy. Five, four, three . . ."

"All right, all right. Where the hell you want this meeting?"

It was quarter of five when I climbed the marble steps to my favorite eating landmark in the golden city of Boston. I never enter the mahogany-paneled dining room of the Parker House on School Street without feeling the mantle of historic figures and events settle gently and humblingly on my shoulders.

My favorite table is the one at which Jack Kennedy proposed to Jacqueline, and it's my usual choice. But not today. Today I asked George, the maître d' and an old friend, for a table in a far, secluded corner.

I was reasonably certain that I could read Packy's predictable mind on the phone. As I'd guessed, at five minutes to five, George nodded to me when he escorted two unfamiliar ponderous apes, who could have been right out of the cast of the *The Sopranos*, to a particular table in the center of the room. I had actually prechosen that table in case it played out as I predicted. Good old Packy had never quite mastered the meaning of the word, "alone." My fervent hope was to enhance his education before the evening ended.

In less than thirty seconds, George escorted a trim, rangy Irish-looking gentleman, well turned out in a conservative suit and tie, to the table I chose directly behind the one occupied by the two Cro-Magnons who were now pawing through the Parker House rolls on their table. I was beginning to have a deep affinity for Seamus Burke.

Right on cue, at five o'clock, George ushered the king of the apes, my dinner date, Packy, to my table. I could see him puff up with smirking confidence when he gave a quick, reassuring glance over at his two-man army at the nearby table.

He gave me a sneering look and plunked his overstuffed sausage of a body into a chair with his back to the wall. I deliberately left that seat vacant to accommodate the life-securing habit of his paranoid existence.

"Mr. Salviti. Packy. How decent of you to favor me with your company for our little meeting. I trust the surroundings are to your taste."

I loved the irony. The "surroundings" of the room where historic pacts had been forged by statesmen since 1855, and where literary luminaries met for sessions of the renowned Saturday Club, could not have been more out of sync with the thuggish demeanor and mentality of my dining companion. If the ghosts of such members of the Saturday Club as Henry Wadsworth Longfellow, Ralph Waldo Emerson, Nathaniel Hawthorne, and the "Autocrat of the Breakfast Table," Dr. Oliver Wendell Holmes, father of the Supreme Court jurist, and the one for whom Arthur Conan Doyle named his illustrious detective, were taking note of what I dragged against his will into their hallowed confines, it would have rattled their chains.

"What the hell we doin' in this dump?"

"Thank you, Packy. You confirmed what I was just thinking. I'll tell you what we're doing."

I gave a signal to George, who was quick to appear table side to escort us to a small private dining room. Whatever combustion was about to occur from this unlikely meeting required a good dose of privacy. I rose and signaled the befuddled Packy to follow George.

"The hell is this?"

He looked over at his dynamic duo. He gave a curt whistle to get their attention out of the roll basket. A head jerk served as a command to follow us into the adjoining room.

With that order given, he followed George. The implication was clear that "alone" was not in his plans. I brought up the rear. When we reached the door, he stopped to look back at what he assumed was his accompanying fortress. It wasn't there. A flash of shock gripped his face when he saw his security force still glued to their seats at their table.

An instant later, he caught sight of the gun in the hand of my new traveling companion, Seamus Burke. It was barely visible under the fine white linen, but its purpose was perfectly clear to the two apes who remained table bound.

Packy was stuck on dead center in the doorway, until I opened my suit jacket to show the absence of a weapon and the presence of a sheet of paper. I whispered in his waiting ear. "Life or death rides on this paper, Packy. Yours. I can at least promise you'll leave this room alive. If we talk. Let's get on with it."

He must have seen the truth in my face. He moved into the room and took a seat at the table George had prepared for us, needless to say with his back to the wall.

There was a bottle of wine opened on the table with two glasses. It was an excellent Chianti. George poured a glass for each of us, withdrew, and closed the door.

I was as comfortable as if I were locked in a cage with King Kong, but I could see in his shifty eyes that he was equally out of his element without the armed retinue. We both sat and took the wine. There was no toast.

"So, what ya got? I ain't got all day. You got the stones?"

I took another sip of the liquid courage and looked him dead-on.

"I'll answer that in a minute. I told you I have something else."

I took the paper I had dictated to Julie out of my suit coat pocket, opened it, and placed it in front of him on the table. He looked at it as if it were a coiled snake. In a way it was.

"Read it. I take it you can read."

"Listen, smart-ass—"

"Just read it, Packy. If you still feel like playing a scene from *The Godfather*, you'll have plenty of time. I'll wait."

I took another sip of wine and picked up the bottle to read the label. I wanted to give him a semblance of privacy to focus on every word.

I'd kept it to three short paragraphs, but they had all the punch I could pack into them. If the proof of the pudding is in the eating, the proof of my writing was in his reaction. It proved out perfectly in the flush of pink that deepened to red and then to deep scarlet from his size twenty neck to the three strands of hair on his flat pate.

He was on his feet. His beady eyes were burning down on me across the table. "What the hell is this crap you're pullin' here, you little shyster?"

"Got your attention, right, Packy?"

"You ain't gonna live to leave this joint, ya bum."

"Sit down, Packy. It's your life that's in question. Sit down. And for one damn minute stop playing a caveman. Sit down and I'll tell you what you just read."

To my surprise, the blustering stopped. He slowly sat. His eyes never left mine.

"What you just read is a criminal complaint. It charges you with the felonies of kidnapping, attempted murder, assault, subornation of perjury, conspiracy. There's a collection of others, but those are the headlines. I'm sure you remember that despicable business you pulled with Finn Casey about Monsignor Ryan. Then there was the matter of the kidnapping, beating, and torturing of a man worth twenty times you on your best day, if you ever have one. That would be Lex Devlin. You understand, Packy? That paper's just a summation. The official charges are ready for filing in both state and federal courts."

That was oversimplified. There'd be the formalities of a grand jury hearing, indictments, and such. But I wasn't giving him a course in law.

His answer was just a silent, burning glare. But that was enough.

"There are witnesses who will be happy to nail your despicable carcass to the courthouse door. They're beyond your reach. You are going to be the poster child for full-scale criminal retribution. You'll also be a career maker for two blood-hungry prosecuting attorneys. You'll be arrested the instant these charges are filed. Maybe you noticed the tall gentleman outside keeping your two goons entertained."

I let the reference to Seamus Burke go at that to give his imagination some room to play. He was stone silent, but I fired one more salvo. "Take a look out that window, Packy. Look at that sunshine. The next time you'll see the sun outside of prison bars will be in approximately a hundred and twenty years. Except that probably won't happen. You know why, Packy?"

The silence hung on. The only change of expression was that his mouth was slightly ajar and a stream was trickling down at the corner. "I'll paint you a picture. How many mortal enemies you figure you have in the state prison in Walpole? How many in Danbury Federal Prison?"

I leaned over the table for unnecessary privacy. "And think of this. How many people have you ordered killed in prison, Packy? It's easy, isn't it. They're sitting ducks, right?"

He was just staring. He was stripped of the only kind of defenses he understood—a frontline of hoods with guns. His face had now gone the gamut from burning crimson to pasty white.

I refilled each of our glasses with wine and took a healthy swallow of mine. It was an unabashed dramatic pause. I needed the reality I'd hit him with to settle into the deepest pocket of his consciousness.

My next move was the springing of the trapdoor that I was counting on for leverage. I moved in slow motion to be sure it had full effect.

I reached across the table and picked up the paper that was sitting like a smoking gun in front of him. His eyes followed my hands as I made a grand flourish of tearing the paper into small pieces.

His mouth was now at half-mast. The whipsawing of the previous two minutes left his expression totally blank. He truly did not seem to know if he was afoot or on horseback. But again, the proof would come in the next two minutes.

I leaned in close. "Listen carefully, Packy. The copies of those complaints are in the hands of people who can file them with the court in a heartbeat. Your well-padded ass is well and truly an inch from the meat slicer."

I leaned back to give him room to breathe, but close enough to hear my every syllable. "Here's the deal. I want information. This time, no halfway. I want a complete answer to every question. And know this, Packy. I know enough of the truth to tell if you slip one half inch. One quarter inch off the mark, and I give the signal. If I do, those papers will be filed in both courts. If they are, nothing can call them back. Your life is gone. *Capisce*?"

He was still in shock. I handed him his glass. He took a mechanical sip. Then he finished the glass. I poured him another. He downed that one too. I set the bottle aside. I wanted him to have enough wine to recover from the numbing shock, but not enough to give him any liquid feeling of false confidence.

When he looked back up at me, I sensed that I had hit the balance. His eyes were clear, with just enough fear left inside to prime the pump.

I was primed too. I'd waited for this moment, it seemed, since the nightmare began. I finished the wine in my glass, hit the start button of the recorder in my pocket, and began the interrogation of my young life.

# CHAPTER TWENTY-SIX

So there we sat, Packy Salviti, a gangster practically from the time he left his mother's womb with a conscience as calloused as a longshoreman's fist, and a lawyer who, but for the grace of God, could have followed a parallel path with an equally thuggish gang in the Puerto Rican barrio on the other side of the city. And to crown the anomaly, we sat conversing in the very room in which Charles Dickens presented the Parker House Saturday Club with his first American reading of his immortal *A Christmas Carol*. God bless the twists of fate that keep life surprising.

We each took one more draught of George's excellent choice of Chianti. I was confident that the ground had been prepared for a fertile harvest, but there was still an urgency to seizing a moment that could pass in a blink of an eye.

"Let's start easy, Packy. While he was alive, you worked for Barone, right?"

There was a hesitation. "Maybe. Listen, I don't like usin' names. Ya know?"

"You listen, Packy. It's your ass that's in the meat grinder at the moment. Not Barone's or anyone else's. Let's not lose sight of the obvious. One more time. Did you work under Barone in the Mafia, *La Cosa Nostra*, whatever you people call yourselves?"

He mumbled something, and I wanted a clear recording.

"Speak up, Packy. You've never been shy before."

"Yeah. Yeah. I was number three in line."

"Good. Pesta's the godfather, to misuse an old word. Barone was next in line, and then you. Right?"

"Yeah."

He said it with what sounded like a spark of pride, and I loved it.

"Barone was killed. So now that makes you the second in line to Pesta. Right?"

"Yeah. You could say that."

"All right. We've got the cast straight. So, somehow Barone got involved with those damn diamonds that seem to be getting people killed. How did that happen?"

He stretched himself back in the chair. To get to the heart of this thing, I had to get out of the tooth-pulling mode. A sudden notion struck me. It was a serious gamble, but I took the recorder out of my pocket. I made a flourish of pretending to turn it on. It had actually been running for some time.

I watched him stare at that thing in the center of the table. It could have gone either way. It could have clammed him up, God forbid. Or it could have just the effect I wanted. I'd seen it happen with witnesses in a trial.

It went my way. He was suddenly on stage. This pitiable ape, who had never had anyone's attention that he didn't get without breaking a leg or having a henchman do it, was suddenly important enough to have someone recording his every word. His voice came up. He was no longer slumping.

"Them diamonds. Yeah. Sally Barone. He got into that. He was always talkin' about takin' over in them days. Takin' Pesta's place. That ain't so easy. Pesta was don of the family. The rule is you can't kill a don without the permission of the dons of the other families. The best way to get permission is to show the dons you can bring in more money. A lot more money. That's why he wanted to get into this diamond business. Not the legit ones. The ones they smuggle outta places like Sierra Leone. "

"Makes sense. But how? You need contacts in that business."

He took a breath and leaned back. Crazy as this sounds, he was beginning to enjoy his fifteen minutes of fame. He was an "expert" with something to say. And both the recorder and I were tuned in.

"He knew them Irish bums in Southie were into the business. They had the contacts. You might say he struck a deal with the devil."

"Why were the Irish willing to deal with the Italians? They've been shooting each other over border wars for years."

He rubbed his fingers and thumb together—the universal sign for money. "That bum, O'Byrne, tipped him off to a contact in Ireland. He heard of some guy from Africa who had some stones for sale. I think O'Byrne wanted to broaden his network, maybe open up some other kinds of deals with our organization. My guess, Sally offered to share his drug sources with O'Byrne in exchange for giving him the diamond contact. O'Byrne could up his profits in the drug end and they both make out. Why the hell not? The Irish work their parts of the city and stay out of ours.

"Anyway, Sally went for the deal. He flew over there and made a deal. He left a hundred grand in the bank over there and brought a bag of stones back. Twenty-two of 'em. He owed the guy from Africa another nine hundred grand. The deal was he'd sell 'em to O'Byrne for a hell of a lot more'n he paid for 'em. He'd pay off the African guy and still have enough to impress the other dons. Maybe get permission to knock off Pesta and take over. I don't know. Maybe share the take with the other dons. That was the plan."

"So what went wrong?"

He leaned back and looked at the ceiling. It was either to gather his thoughts or to stretch the enjoyment of his new professorial role. In a few seconds, he snapped forward. I was delighted that he was talking to the machine instead of me. Whatever worked.

"It's like this. Sally Barone had this 'soldier' we call him. He didn't like it when Sally was a traitor to Tony Pesta. He went to Pesta and spilled it."

"Who was the soldier?"

"Tommy Franzone. A good kid."

"Is he still alive?"

"Yeah. Why not? Anyway, Pesta exploded. He gave the contract to this kid, Franzone."

"Contract?"

He looked at me for the first time in minutes. "Yeah. To kill Sally Barone. What're you, born yesterday?"

I just waved him to go on.

"But the timing was funny. I was in Sally's office when he left word with O'Byrne's people to meet so's he could deliver the stones and get the cash. They had it set up for a place on them Irish bums' turf. Some beach in Southie."

He paused as if he were pulling it all back in his memory.

"And?"

"I'm gettin' there. Hold your horses. That's where it went screwy. The next thing I know, I'm having a few drinks in Collini's in the North End. This kid, Franzone, he drives up in Sally's Cadillac and Sally ain't nowhere in sight."

"Go ahead."

"Then it really gets nuts. Franzone comes in. He leaves the car runnin'. All of a sudden, the car's movin' down the street. Franzone runs out screamin', but it's gone. Next day the police find it some-wheres in Roxbury."

Now the pieces are going together. I had a flashback of the night I told O'Byrne to have his man drop the car off at the Community College lot in Roxbury.

"And do you know who stole the car?"

"I heard it was O'Byrne's kid. I think his name's Kevin."

"And now for the mother of all questions. Who has those damn diamonds now?"

He looked at me with his hands up. "The hell should I know? Franzone did the deed on Sally Barone. He brought him back to Collini's in the trunk of his Cadillac. No one had a chance to search Sally or his car for the diamonds before this O'Byrne kid boosts the car."

"Any ideas about where the diamonds are now?"

He shrugged. "I figure the O'Byrne kid found 'em in the car. I'll tell you this. I get my hands on that little crapper, I'll know where they are in five minutes."

"Have you ever talked to Frank O'Byrne about it? He was apparently working with Barone on the deal."

"Oh, yeah. I'm sure he'd be glad to help. Think about it. If they got the diamonds and never had to pay for them, what the hell're they gonna do with me I walk into O'Byrne's joint in Southie for a chat about him payin' up. Damn, I'll be on the menu for dinner. It'll be my ass on toast."

A thought came to mind. If I walked into O'Byrne's myself after the New Hampshire episode, I'd probably be the hors d'oeuvre.

I figured I'd gotten all of the gold out of that mine. I hit the stop button on the recorder and put it back in my pocket. If I could guess at the expression on Packy's face, I would have called it depleted, empty, now that his moment of importance had expired.

One more question occurred. I clicked on the recorder. "Where can I find this kid, Franzone?"

Packy gave a half grin. "You do have a death wish, don't ya?"

"No, Packy. No death wish. Just a few loose ends left. Does he hang around Collini's?"

"Hell, no. That's for the guys at the top. If you still want to get yourself whacked, he's most times around Maria's in East Boston."

We both stood up. I turned off the recorder and poured the last two glasses of Chianti.

"One last question, Packy. You don't have to answer this one. Where do you stand in all this? Are you with Pesta? Or are you in it for yourself like Barone? This'll go no further."

He looked up at me, and our eyes met for the first time like two human beings communicating with each other. "What do you think?"

"I think you play it as safe as you can. I don't see you leading any rebellions. I could be wrong."

He looked back down at the table. "I do whatever the hell I gotta do to stay alive. Right now that's finding them diamonds for Pesta."

I actually felt an emotion I never would have connected with Packy Salviti. Pity. This time I held out my glass of wine. He did the same. We touched the glasses before drinking.

I walked to the door first and opened it. I was about to walk out when his voice caught me. "Hey, lawyer. It ever comes to that. You know, in court. Would you represent me?"

"Packy, you are one of the saddest pieces of human flotsam I've ever met. I could drown in pity for you. But the day I get into bed with you as your lawyer is the day they build snowmen in hell."

I could have said that to him when we first began our conversation. But I couldn't bring myself to say it now. Given what I'd come to know of his life circumstances, it seemed unlikely he'd ever live to stand trial anyway.

I just said, "We'll see when the day comes. Take care of yourself, Mr. Salviti."

I walked out through the main dining area. Seamus Burke fell in step beside me. I paused at the table of Packy's crack team of body-guards. "Gentlemen. I hope you've enjoyed the ambiance and the fine cuisine. You must come back Thursday for the lobster thermi-dor. George will be delighted to handle your reservations."

The expressions said I could have been speaking Swahili.

Seamus and I stopped in the bar area before leaving. The best way to fill him in was to play the recording. He looked over when it clicked off. "What about this kid, Tommy Franzone? Anything there?"

"Maybe. Right now we've got a gap. Barone goes to meet Frank O'Byrne to do the diamond deal. Franzone goes about the same time to whack Barone in a very specific way. He does that and brings the body back in the trunk to Collini's, I assume that's to prove to Pesta that he's carried out the assignment. Then Kevin steals the car. I know that Kevin moved the body before he brought the car to Frank O'Byrne's. There was a gap in the bloodline."

"All right, so?"

"It's like a three-card monte game in Times Square. Which one of those clowns came out with the diamonds? Maybe this kid, Fran-zone, can give us that piece."

Burke just shook his head.

"What?"

"According to this recording, we can find Franzone at Maria's Bar in East Boston. That's another Italian Mafia fort like the North End. This Irish Catholic would get a better welcome on Shankill Road in Belfast."

"No problem, Seamus. Take the day off. I'll handle this one myself."

That was a hook in the water baited with a young, tender worm, and a prayer that he'd bite. Burke gave me a look.

"I'll be at your office at nine tomorrow morning. Be ready to move, lawyer."

"That's 'Michael.' Remember?"

# CHAPTER TWENTY-SEVEN

We were about to split up when I remembered the two thuggish members of Frank O'Byrne's mob who had tailed us when Terry and I left the Molly Waldo. I called the police station in Marblehead to see if they were still in custody. I was delighted to hear that they were still guests of the town. At my request, as an implied wealthy resident of their fair city, they agreed to hold them for another hour.

I drove to the Marblehead jail, passing the Molly Waldo, and basking in the memory of that brief respite of pure joy the previous evening. I logged a mental promise to make up for lost dates with Terry if this thing reached a conclusion during our lifetime.

Seamus had been kind enough to accept my invitation to follow in his rental car for a drive along the north shore. I had something in mind that could call for two cars if it worked out.

I approached the officer at the desk with a request to get an identifying look at the two thugs for purposes of future reference. In their continuing desire to please a propertied and voting local citizen, they hauled the two into a line-up room. I was able to fix a good image of each of them in my memory bank without being seen by them. The line-up also happily served to impress on the two goons that they could be up to their pink Irish ears in deep legal crap.

The next move was to declare to the Marblehead officers that I was clearly mistaken the night before. It was simply a case of mistaken identity. The two should be released immediately. After a bit of paperwork, the release was imminent. This is when I withdrew from the scene, and Seamus took the stage.

He accompanied the officer with the keys to the holding cell.

Needless to say, the two inmates were happily surprised to be sprung from their overnight accommodations.

Seamus did all the talking. His babble in his best Irish accent deliberately gave them the distinct impression that Seamus was sent by O'Byrne to bail them out. He implied full knowledge of the orders O'Byrne had given them to pick me up for whatever despicable purpose the night before. All of it, plus Seamus's commanding demeanor, put the two goons into Seamus's car with the firm belief that Seamus was carrying out Frank O'Byrne's orders, and that they were under his orders to assist in every way possible.

Seamus followed the directions I gave him directly to Maria's Bar on Chelsea Street in East Boston. Packy Salviti had been kind enough to tell me in our Parker House rendezvous that this was where Barone's killer, young Tommy Franzone, hung out. I figured that if I could talk to him alone, Tommy could fill in one of the gaps.

I followed and parked across the street out of sight. I saw Seamus tell his two new assistants to wait in his car. He walked into Maria's like any other customer. Thirty seconds later he walked out.

He casually walked up the street to where I was parked. I rolled down the window.

"What do you think, Seamus?"

"Typical bar. Couple of pool tables. There are six stout lads in there that look like they could be soldiers in Pesta's army."

"How about Tommy Franzone?"

"Bartender pointed him out. Asked why I wanted to know. I ordered a beer and told him I'd be right back. I don't want to keep him waiting."

"Wait a minute, Seamus. If there are six of them, to hell with it. We'll think of something else."

He stood back and straightened the tie he wore to the Parker House. "Listen, Michael. You brought me this far. The plan is you want a quiet word with Franzone without interruption from the other five. Simple enough. Having O'Byrne's goons along for help was your idea. I could have handled it alone. I'm not over the hill yet."

"At least take O'Byrne's guys with you. They'll help even the odds."

"They'll be a bloody nuisance. But I'll grant your wish. You stay out of there till I come to get you. I'll be busy enough without worrying about you."

"I don't like it, Seamus."

"Take a nap. Read a book. Just stay out of the way for two minutes."

He strode off before I could finish the argument. I saw him walk to his car and pick up O'Byrne's two goons. The three of them marched like a resolute army straight through the door of Maria's.

I was jumping out of my skin. I ran to a position outside the door of the bar. I knew my presence inside would just give Seamus one thing too many to think about.

The place went stone silent the minute the three walked through the door. I could hear Seamus just inside the door quietly parceling off targets to each of the soldiers with him. I heard him bark the command, "Now!" And all hell broke loose.

I heard furniture smashing against bodies to the tune of grunts and cries, and air being driven out of lungs. I could hear pool cues splintering in rhythm with bones snapping. The unmistakable sound of pool balls hitting soft objects and rolling across the barroom floor was followed by the sound of bodies dropping full weight to the floor. The splintering of beer bottles barely drowned out the concussive sound of glass on skulls.

And two minutes later, as suddenly as it began, there was dead silence. I held my breath and pushed through the door. Thank God, Seamus and his two Irish companions were the only ones standing, including the bartender.

The scene was right out of a western movie. There were horizontal bodies strewn across the floor, bent over pool tables, and hanging across the bar. The two Irish soldiers of O'Byrne were leaning over a table, panting from the exertion.

At the far end of the room, Seamus had lifted a tall, skinny man of about my age by the back of the neck and plunked him in a chair.

Seamus stood over him with his hand on his neck, holding him up-right in the chair.

"Michael, I thought I told you to wait in the car."

I was still gaping at the scene. Words failed me.

"No matter. Come over here. Let me introduce you to Tommy Franzone. I believe you wanted a word with him."

My legs carried me over to the seated man, but my mind was still in disbelieving shock.

Seamus said in a low voice, "I'll leave you two to chat while I get rid of those two." He nodded toward the two O'Byrne men. "I told you I didn't need them. Still, they gave a good account of them-selves."

Before he walked away, he lifted the chin of the man in the chair and leaned to speak directly into his face. "See that you speak nicely with this gentleman, Tommy. Don't make me come back over here again. Understood?"

Seamus released his grip to allow Franzone to nod in compliance.

My senses were slowly returning. I pulled a chair over next to Franzone. The trick was for me to assume the commanding stature Seamus had left for me.

"I'll make this brief if I get what I came for. Otherwise, it could be an extended discussion. Do you understand that?"

Actually, I had no clear idea of what I meant by it, but apparently he did. Seamus had left him in a frame of mind where he was quick to nod.

"Let's go back to that night when you were sent to do a job on Salvatore Barone."

I could see a spark of fear in his eyes. We were talking about a confession to murder, and apparently this kid had not become quite as hardened to the core as some in his adopted profession. That could be counterproductive. Tension was not what I wanted. I needed him loose and talkative.

"Listen to me, Tommy. You've got nothing to fear from me as far as the law's concerned. That's between you and your conscience, if you still have one. I only want one thing: information. Then, you and

I walk out of this place and never see each other again. I give you that on a stack of Bibles. You understand?"

He gave a tentative nod of the head. It was enough to press on.

"Go back to that night. You told Pesta about Barone's being a traitor, setting up a deal to sell diamonds to the Irish gang. Right so far?"

He was stuck on dead center. "Listen, Tommy. That much I know. Suppose you answer the question anyway. Just to show good faith, so we don't have to disturb that big gentleman over there again. You wouldn't want that, would you?"

This time his head moved readily side to side.

"Then let's move on. Am I right so far?"

He slowly gave me a nod.

"Let's make it verbal, Tommy. Am I right so far?"

"Yeah."

"And you got your orders from Pesta about Barone, right?"

"Yeah."

"All right. Your turn. What happened that night?"

He looked over at Seamus who was leaning on the bar looking on at our progress. "He sent me to do a job."

"Tell me about it."

"I told him what Barone said. He was meeting O'Byrne that night. Mr. Pesta told me to follow Barone. I followed him to Carson Beach in Southie. Barone parked his car. O'Byrne hadn't got there yet."

"And?"

"I did what Mr. Pesta told me to do."

"What?"

"You know."

"You killed him the way you were told. Like a traitor."

"Yeah."

Seamus waved a .38 handgun in front of him. "With this."

"Yeah."

Seamus had apparently taken it from him in the scuffle. He

tossed it back to him. I could bet my life that Seamus had removed the bullets.

"Then what?"

"I put him in the trunk of his car. I drove the car back to Collini's like Mr. Pesta told me. You know, to show him I did it."

"And that's when the car was stolen, right?"

"Yeah."

"Now listen to this, Tommy. Get this one right or you're in more trouble than you could imagine. Did you take anything off Barone's body or out of his car?"

"No. Nothing. Nobody told me to do that. Like what?"

"Like anything."

"No."

I leaned back out of his face. *I believe you didn't, Tommy.* I'd have bet my life on it.

I walked back through that bar that looked like it had been bombed by the IRA. Seamus fell in beside me. We walked to my car.

"Where are your two Irish sidekicks, Seamus?"

"I told them to take a cab. They're probably having an interesting conversation with your Frank O'Byrne about now. I think you should stay away from him for a while."

"It's my most fervent wish."

We reached my Corvette. I got in and lowered the window. "That was quite a performance you put on back there."

He looked at me with a smile. "It's good to keep in practice. What do you think about young Tommy?"

"He didn't take the diamonds. He had limited orders. Maybe Pesta was going to search Barone's body when Tommy brought him back to Collini's. He never got the chance, thanks to our juvenile delinquent, Kevin."

"That eliminates another one."

"And then there was one. I think we can be sure that Kevin has those damn diamonds. Kevin and Papa Frank."

We were both thinking about where that left us. One thing

seemed clear. At least for the time being, we were still on the same side.

The dawn brought a new day to face old problems. At least the issue was narrowed down to what might have been an oversimplification. Find Kevin, and you find the diamonds. Find the diamonds, and somehow the rest of the fine mess will resolve itself. And everyone will live happily ever after. An unlikely hope, but it helped put one foot and then the other over the side of the bed.

I started the morning at one of my most productive thinking places—the Dunkin' Donuts on Beacon Street. It had never failed me yet, and it was not about to start now. When I eliminated Frank O'Byrne as a possible source of information for the obvious reason, I could count the leads to finding the elusive Kevin on one finger. That finger stood for Chuck Dixon. He had been with Kevin the night Kevin most probably lifted the diamonds from the cold body of Sally Barone. The problem was locating Chuck Dixon.

When I placed my usual order for one old-fashioned, one jelly, and coffee, the waitress, who has known me as a regular for at least five years, responded, "*Gracias. Buenos días*, Michael."

When I responded, as I usually did, "*De nada. Buenos días, Emilita*," I was hit with an idea. I got everything to go, and sprinted out the door. I was into my faithful Corvette and wheeling toward the Northeastern University student affairs office in less than a minute.

I knew I'd be pushing it, but I had to draw from that well just one more time. I found Luisa, my previous Puerto Rican contact, working at her desk. There was again enough of a hum of human voices in the room to speak in confidence—in Spanish.

I explained that irregular as this would sound, lives literally hung on her slightly breaching the privacy rules for the last time. Any understandable incredulity seemed to be overcome by the affinity between two very minority Puerto Ricans—even though it was only half on my side.

Without tipping too much, I explained that Chuck Dixon, the same junior-year student I asked about before, was at the center of a murder investigation. Unless it were handled discreetly—my every intention—it could seriously reflect on the good name of Northeastern University.

That was enough to bring a most welcome, "What do you need?"

I told her that Chuck had gone missing two days before. That meant he wasn't in class, nor likely to be in class in the near future. The chances were excellent that he was covering his academic posterior by contacting the university with some kind of excuse. Could she see if that had happened?

Her fingers played a rapid rhythm on her computer keyboard for an interminable minute. It was worth the wait. She said it quietly and in Spanish. He had sent an e-mail to the college registrar, explaining his absence on the basis of family illness. He requested a leave of absence for the term.

That was interesting. I interpreted it to mean he was neck deep in whatever Kevin was doing with the diamonds and would be tied up in it for an unpredictable spell. It also convinced me that he was either with Kevin or at least in contact with him.

Now to the tricky part. The e-mail address from which he sent the message, and at which he expected a reply from the registrar—was it the same as his usual e-mail address on record with the university?

More clicking on the keyboard, and Luisa shook her head, no. That's what I was hoping. That meant he had set up a separate e-mail address for communication while he was into his new adventure. He must have been confident enough in the privacy-protecting protocol of the university to use his new e-mail address. Thank God.

I gave Luisa my most pleading-puppy look. She jotted some letters down on a Post-it note and slipped it under her desk blotter. She left her desk to walk to the coffee machine without actually giving me any compromising information. By the time she returned, neither I nor the Post-it note were in the building.

This had to be done as carefully as each step of a tightrope walker. I figured Chuck had entrusted the new e-mail address only to the university registrar and those few in Kevin's inner circle. That would give any message to that address a presumption of inner-circle confidentiality—if I didn't blow it with the message.

I set up a separate e-mail account for this message, only with no reference that would suggest my name. Then I agonized over every word before I typed the message. I read, reread, and re-reread it before I hit the send button.

"Plans gone haywire. Too much interference by you-know-who. Lost contact with K. Need phone number immediately."

My fervent wish was that Chuck would assume that the e-mail was from Papa Frank O'Byrne, and that "you-know-who" referred to the only fly in their ointment—me.

I barely made it back to my office when a check of the return e-mail on my new account produced gold. The answer was no more than a series of digits, but I thanked God that they were more than likely Kevin's phone number.

I asked Tom Burns to tap into his private sources to check the number. It confirmed the intuitive feeling I'd had for days that a flight to Ireland was in my immediate future. Tom got back to me in minutes to report that the number was the direct line to a room in the Shelbourne Hotel in Dublin.

With that, I figured I'd just be spinning my wheels on this side of the Atlantic. I was so sure of the answer I'd get when I briefed Seamus and asked if he was aboard, that I had already asked Julie to get two tickets on the next flight to the fair city of Dublin.

Her antenna for worries went up when I asked her to make them one-way. The fact was, I had as little idea of what I was about get involved in as I did about when—or whether—I'd be coming back.

# PART FOUR

# CHAPTER TWENTY-EIGHT

Sierra Leone, Africa. The present.

When the plane touched down at Lungi International Airport out-side of Freetown, Sierra Leone, Bantu felt a slight sense of comfort in slipping out of the name he had assumed in Ireland, Johnny Walker, and back into the name of his birth. From the airport, he called the cell phone of the single person he trusted in Freeport, his Mandingo friend, Jimbo. He caught him in the middle of an after-noon tankard of rum in Alex's Beach Bar.

"Bantu! You son of a gun. Howdabody?"

"I'm good. You?"

"Like always. Where you?"

"I'm back. I need to see you."

There was a pause. "I gotta see you too. When?"

"Right now. Can you meet me at Bunce's office?"

"Why not? Half hour."

Bantu waited for Jimbo to arrive at the building under the sign, "Morty Bunce. Diamonds Bought and Sold." They climbed the stairs together. This time Bantu was greeted with open arms by Bunce.

"You did me proud, Bantu. I couldn't have done better with those rascals in Ireland. I shouldn't tell you, but you made me a good profit. Can you do it again?"

Bantu half smiled and just shook his head at the thought. He had reported the good news of the result of his dealing with Declan O'Connor without going into detail about the gamut he had run.

"I mean it, Bantu. I got another shipment for you. You say when."

Jimbo went to Bunce's liquor shelf and poured three shots of rum. He handed them around while he waded in on Bantu's behalf.

"Let the boy rest, Morty. He just made you rich. He need time in his home. Right, Bantu?"

Bantu took the rum and spoke quietly. "I have no home here, Jimbo. I barely got out with my life last time. You should remember. You pulled me out."

Jimbo lifted his glass for a three-way toast. "I know. So what'll we drink to?"

Morty chimed in with "To good times for us all."

The glasses clinked. Bantu noticed that Jimbo was the last to drink the toast.

"What's the matter, Jimbo? You said you had to see me."

"Sit down, Bantu."

Jimbo pulled his chair up to face Bantu.

"I had to go out there two days ago. You know that little town where you found your brother?"

"I know it well. What about it?"

"I nosed around a little. Just a little. I don't mess around much with them RUF guys."

"Come on, Jimbo. What?"

"I'm sorry, Bantu. After you got out of there, you know, they couldn't find them stones you had. Someone must have overheard he was your brother. Anyway, they figured he let you go with the stones."

"And? Come on, Jimbo."

"They strip him down to search. They couldn't find them stones. They gave him some beatin'. But they keep him alive. He don't tell 'em nothin' 'bout you. That's what I hear."

"Where is he now?"

"They don't trust him. So they just use him. They got him workin' in a diamond pit like they had you all them years."

Bantu's mind was rocking. He had received a phone call on his cell from Declan O'Connor in Ireland before he left the Lungi Airport. He now knew that Salvatore Barone, who had purchased and taken his bag of diamonds on the promise to pay one million euros, was found dead in America. That meant that there was no chance of getting the money he had counted on to buy his father's freedom from the RUF. It was even less likely that he'd get back the diamonds.

His next thought was that it now almost ceased to matter. His only thread of contact for assurance that his father was still alive, and where he was being kept, had been his brother.

He set down the rum. He had to keep his head clear.

His first words were to Morty Bunce. "You have another shipment. When do you want me to leave?"

Morty was caught off guard. "Um, tomorrow. Today. As soon as you're ready. We'll do it the same way."

"I'll do it. But not tomorrow. I need a few days."

"All right. I'll set it up."

"There's something else, Mr. Bunce. This is part of the deal. I need money now. In advance."

Morty got a bit edgy. "Really. How much?"

"I need six hundred euros. Right now."

Morty's mouth dropped in semimock surprise.

Jimbo jumped in. "Get off your ass and get him the money, Morty. He just make you rich. Gonna do it again in a few days. Where you find the likes of him you can trust?"

Bantu stood as if to leave. "This is not open to debate, Mr. Bunce. In a week or two it may not do me any good. Maybe even not now. But I've got to try. Yes or no?"

Morty got up with a grin. "Sweet crap in the mornin'. I see how you deal with those Irish. So that's how you make me rich. All right. But it comes out of your commission next time. Yes?"

Morty went into the next room to his safe, being careful to close the door behind him. Jimbo walked up close to Bantu and whispered. "Whachu gonna do, Bantu?"

"Not me. We. You've got to help me."

"Me? What the hell. You gonna get me killed?"

"I hope not. You want to sit around the Beach Bar wasting away in a jug of rum? Or you want to do something heroic?"

"Between those two, a jug of rum looks good."

"The hell it does. Besides, you'll just be backup. It'll be a piece of cake."

"Piece of cake, eh? You gettin' to sound like them Irish now. Okay. Keep talkin'."

Bantu whispered directly into his ear. "There could be some good stones in this for you too."

Jimbo smiled. "If I do this, I do it for my friend. But them stones don't sound too bad either."

Bunce came back and counted out six hundred euros on the desk. Bantu picked them up and shook hands with Bunce.

"Thank you, Mr. Bunce. I'll be back in a few days. You want a receipt?"

"Why do I need a receipt? I got eyes and ears all over this jungle. I can find you if I have to. Besides, I never use this word, but I think I trust you."

Bantu rode with Jimbo in his Jeep to the Mammy Yoko Hotel on Lumley Beach outside the city. He was still in European clothes when he checked in. He and Jimbo found seats in a deserted section of the bar.

"So, tell me. Whachu got in mind for Jimbo's tired old body?"

"Tell me this first. Do you know which diamond pit they have my brother working?"

"Yeah. 'Bout four, five mile from that town you just barely got out of last time."

"Can you find it?"

"I can find every ant mound in Sierra Leone."

"Is there a road for a small truck?"

"If you got a good driver. Like me."

"Good. Can you have a small truck at the front door here at eight tomorrow morning?"

"I guess."

"All right. That's the easy part. I want you to arrange a meeting for me. Tonight. Not here. Alex's Bar on the beach."

"Who you want?"

Bantu told him. Jimbo broke into a grin. "Hot flyin' monkey shit. This gonna be interestin'."

Bantu was sitting at the bar in Alex's when he saw Jimbo walk in with a white man in a dirty white Panama suit with no shirt. Between the shaggy gray hair and the full scruffy beard, only the beady eyes gave a clue to his expression.

Jimbo led him to a far end table. Bantu got a bottle of good rum and three glasses from the bartender. He noticed that when he approached the table, the suited man got edgy. The bottle Bantu set on the table took his attention and seemed to distract some of the edginess.

Jimbo did the honors. "My friend. This here the man you was askin' to see. I'd introduce you, but you ain't neither gonna use your right names anyway. So, what the hell. Besides, we talkin' cash deal here, right?"

Bantu sat. He addressed the man directly. "Cash it is. This is what I need. And I need it in one hour. Are you ready to deal?"

The little man's eyes narrowed. He squinted as he peered into Bantu's eyes. His high-pitched voice had a nondescript, vaguely Middle Eastern accent. "What's the big hurry? I don't know you."

Bantu leaned over. "I don't know you either. And I don't want to. We do this deal for cash to be paid tonight. Or not. Your choice. Then we part company. Forever. I want four items. You know what they are. One hundred euros each. Cash on delivery in one hour. Yes or no?"

The man's eyes shifted from Bantu to Jimbo and back. Bantu gripped his arm. "You're dealing with me. I'm the one with the cash. It's a simple proposition."

His beady eyes narrowed. "One hundred and fifty."

"One hundred. If you had another cash customer for more than that tonight, you wouldn't be at this table. I'll throw in another

twenty euros for four large wooden crates. I don't have playtime.
You're not the only dealer in town. Again, yes or no?"

The man looked at Jimbo. "Hey, Jimbo. Your friend here. He's
not too friendly, is he? Like he's got a cockroach up his ass or something. He doesn't make me comfortable."

Jimbo just raised his arms as if to say, "He is what he is."

Bantu's patience was being assaulted from many directions. He
got the man's attention with a tap on the arm. "Listen. And don't let
this affect your business decision. I detest every minute of this conversation. You deal in death and pain and misery for people who
never harmed you. And you do it for money. If I seem less than af-
fectionate, it's because I find you a lower species than that cockroach
you thought I had up my ass. But that's all irrelevant. Let's not make
this more than it is. Do you want to make four hundred and twenty
euros in the next hour for that crap you sell or don't you? Just answer
the question."

The man's mouth was hanging slightly open when he looked back
at Jimbo. Jimbo stood. He reached over and gently lifted the man
out of his seat by his elbow.

"Don't waste my friend's time. You know sure's hell you gonna
do it. Come on. I drive. We pick up the merchandise, and I give you
the money."

Jimbo held out his hand, and Bantu gave him a roll of bills.

When Bantu was alone, he scanned the bar for a likely prospect for
one last essential ingredient. There was a table of rowdy RUF boy
soldiers at one of the tables, but they were not what he was looking
for. He noticed a pair of slightly older teenage RUF soldiers in uniforms that indicated that they were high-ranking officers. They were
sitting alone at one section of the bar. He had his target.

It was nearly midnight. Bantu noticed that while the two were
both drunk, one was more deeply into intoxication than the other.
Bantu approached the bartender and whispered a message while his
hand slipped a bill under a napkin on the bar. The bartender picked
up the napkin and approached the two officers at the other end of

the bar. He spoke quietly to the less-intoxicated officer. The officer looked aggravated. He slipped unsteadily off the bar stool and made his way out into the street in search of his car.

Bantu moved fast. He slid in next to the officer left at the bar. He used a bit of small talk to get as much of the officer's attention as had not been drowned in alcohol. He went on the hopeful assumption that if the RUF officer had been on guard at the diamond pits, there was a good chance he had palmed a stone or two from the daily take for his personal enrichment.

Bantu held the soldier's glassy-eyed attention with an exorbitant offer for rough stones. He quietly flashed the corner of the roll of euros he had left.

The officer was drunk enough to lose caution, but not too drunk to show a glint of greed. The officer fumbled inside his shirt to take out a small pouch. Bantu put his hand over the pouch and whispered, "Not here. Outside. Come on."

Bantu had to help the officer navigate the path across the floor to the back door and out into the darkness. When the hot humid air hit the officer, he tumbled off the small landing and rolled across the flat ground. He came to rest in a total state of alcoholic unconsciousness against a garbage bin.

The stage was set. The props and wardrobe were in place. Bantu forced a few hours of restless sleep by trying to banish from his mind every thought of how much of what mattered in his life depended on what would happen in the next twelve hours.

# CHAPTER TWENTY-NINE

It was barely past dawn when Jimbo was wheeling a medium-size canvas-covered truck around the ruts and washouts of a road that was all but recaptured by jungle overgrowth. Each glance at the passenger to his right gave him the shivers.

"You know you creepin' me out, don't ya?"

The uniform of the RUF officer was ill fitting on Bantu. The build of the officer in the beach bar the previous night had been shorter, and more evident of an appetite seldom left unsatisfied than Bantu's taller, trimmer frame. On short notice, it was the best he could do. He thought if he stayed in the shadows, it might pass.

"Just keep your eyes on the road, Jimbo. When we get there—if we get there—you'll thank God for this uniform."

It was dusk, and the shadows were long when the truck approached the guards at the perimeter of a slime pit about the size of the one to which Bantu had given nine unimaginable years of his youth.

Three human forms in RUF soldier's uniforms who had been lounging under banana trees at the perimeter of the pit snapped to their feet. Bantu estimated their age at about fifteen years, given the aging effects of drugs and atrocities.

One stood flat-footed in front of the truck. A second walked up to the passenger side beside Bantu. The third approached the driver's window. The AK-47s in their hands were all steadied on the human targets in the truck.

Jimbo tightened his grip on the wheel with his left hand and rapped Bantu's leg with his right fist. "Oh shit, oh dear. What the hell we got here?"

Bantu whispered without changing his expression or his focus straight ahead. "Don't say a word. Keep your hands on the wheel. Don't obey their orders. I do the talking. No matter what."

The man at the driver's side gave the window frame a sharp rap with the barrel of the rifle. "You! Get out of the truck! Now!"

"Don't move an inch. Look straight ahead." The words hissed through Bantu's locked teeth. His whisper froze Jimbo in place.

Jimbo whispered without moving his lips. "Yeah, sure. While this bastard shoots my ass off. Do you mind if I shit my pants?"

"I'd rather you didn't. We have a long ride back." The calm tone partly settled the panic in Jimbo's stomach. He started to say, "Can you come up with—?"

He got that far, when Bantu threw open the passenger door. It caught the boy beside him square in the midsection and knocked him back a few steps. By the time he recovered and leveled the rifle, Bantu was out of the car. He walked straight at the boy who was now gawking at the officer's insignia on his uniform.

Bantu slapped the rifle away. He grabbed the boy by the front of his shirt. He threw him sprawling in the direction of the wooden bar across the road to the pit. "Open it!"

The boy scrambled to his feet. "Open it! Now!"

The boy stared for a second without moving. Bantu turned to the other two guards. "Take him! Throw him into the pit. Let him work with the slaves till he learns to respect an officer."

The tone was steady and commanding. The other two jumped out of fear of a similar punishment. They grabbed the boy by the arms, pushed open the gate, and dragged his struggling body to the edge of the pit.

Bantu signaled Jimbo to drive through. Bantu walked to the edge of the pit and barked out the order, "Wait. Hold him right there."

The attention of every guard and slave in the pit was on the boy soldier to see whether he would be broken from master to slave for one mistake.

When Jimbo had driven through the gate, Bantu signaled him to turn the truck to face out. Jimbo wheeled the truck to a position twenty feet from the pit, facing out toward the jungle.

Bantu walked slowly, deliberately to the back of the truck. He whispered back in the direction of Jimbo in the cab, "Keep the engine running."

Bantu threw off the canvas covering the rear end of the truck. He climbed onto the truck's back platform and barked an order to the two soldiers who were still holding the third soldier by the arms. "Drop him. Stand over here." Bantu pointed to a spot fifteen feet from the back of the truck.

He turned and yelled a command at the two armed soldiers who were stationed at the rim of the pit, standing guard over the six slaves who were sifting gravel in the slimy mud. He ordered the two soldiers to come up to the line of the first two soldiers.

Bantu slowly scanned the four guards with a cold expression that gave no clue as to whether they'd be shot or rewarded. He held them in that posture for what seemed to Jimbo like an eternal minute.

Bantu let his eyes roam from the guards to the pathetic faces of the barely living scraps of enslaved humanity in the pit. He fought to keep the pain from showing in his face when his eyes fell on one slave in particular. The seminaked body showed the welts and scars of the familiar beatings enjoyed by the drugged-out guards. The protruding ribs and the arched backbone brought back in painful consciousness the ceaseless hours of back-bending labor far beyond the bounds of exhaustion.

Bantu's heart nearly cracked when he saw the familiar look of total despair in the eyes of his brother, Sinda.

Bantu struggled to control his bursting emotions. His face remained etched in stone. He reached into the back of the truck and took out one of the gleaming new AK-47 rifles he had bought in Freetown the previous evening.

He barked an order to the four guards who stood rigidly waiting in line for a clue to their fate. "Throw down those rifles! Throw them into the pit!"

One of the guards began to plead. Another fell on his knees. They had Bantu outnumbered, but they knew from experience what happened to any soldier who resisted an officer.

Bantu barked again. "Now! If you want to live, throw those rifles into the pit! I won't say it again."

The one on his knees was first to obey. The one pleading was the second. Bantu screamed, "Get on your feet! Stop sniveling. What do you look like in front of the slaves?"

The one guard struggled to his feet, while the other muzzled his whimpering. The other two guards followed. They obeyed the command by throwing their rifles into the pit.

Bantu ordered the line of now unarmed guards to approach the truck. They moved slowly forward. They were completely sobered with fear of what he intended to do to them.

When the line was ten feet from the edge of the truck, Bantu barked, "Halt!"

They froze in position. The slightest smile began to cross Bantu's face. He looked each man in the eye as he spoke.

"Your work has been recognized. Production is up. You have done your jobs well. You are to be rewarded."

With a suddenness that shocked all four, Bantu thrust the gleaming, new rifle he was holding forward in an arc into the hands of the guard on the left. The guard caught it and held it fast. His face was alive with relief for his life and, when he recovered enough to think of it, the pleasure of the new weapon.

Bantu reached into the back of the truck three more times. Each time, he produced a new rifle that he threw to one of the waiting guards. He gave them five seconds to inspect with delight their new toys. They first checked to see that each rifle was fully loaded with ammunition. They were.

Bantu caught their attention again with his next command. "There are cases of ammunition to be unloaded. Get me three of those slaves. I want that one, and that one, and that one. Get them up here. Now!"

The guards were quick to hustle the three indicated out of the pit to the back of the truck. They moved as fast as their cadaverous bodies could be made to step.

When the first one approached, Bantu took a wooden box from

the back of the truck and laid it on his shoulders. He called to the four guards. "You four. Stack this ammunition in the shed over there."

It broke Bantu's heart to place an extra ounce of labor on what, but for the grace of God, could have been his own back. For the moment it was necessary. He told himself, *Not forever. Just for now.*

When the second slave approached the truck, he laid another box on his shoulders. The slave moved off slowly in the direction of the first.

Bantu softly pounded the roof of the truck to get Jimbo's attention. "Be ready," he hissed.

When the third slave came up to the back of the truck, Bantu looked over to see the four soldiers gathered around the first two ammunition boxes. One of them was prying the first box open. Just as he got the lid open enough to see that what the box held, the guard shouted to the others, "They're rocks! They're just rocks!"

The four spun back in Bantu's direction. Bantu knew it was now life or death. He reached down and grabbed the third slave by a fistful of his pants and swung him up into the back of the truck. He screamed, "Go!"

Jimbo hit the gas pedal with a thrust that almost put his foot through the firewall of the truck. The tires spun gravel and mud in the direction of the four soldiers as it picked up speed.

Each of the four soldiers brought a bright new AK-47 to his shoulder. They all aimed at the moving, sweat-soaked back of Bantu and squeezed the trigger. They squeezed again and again, and what filled the air was silence. Bantu thanked God that he had remembered to remove the firing mechanism from the rifles the night before.

The soldiers squeezed harder, with no greater effect. They ran to catch the back of the truck, but it was hopeless. Within five seconds, Jimbo had wheeled the truck through the open gate and onto the jungle path. Another five seconds, and the jungle had swallowed the truck completely.

Bantu could now bend over the prone body of his brother, Sinda.

He studied the glazed, disbelieving eyes that looked sunken and distant. It brought back to Bantu's mind what a week in the pit could do to both body and soul. Again, he marveled and thanked God that he had survived nine years of that inhumanity.

The flash of an idea had flooded his mind for a brief instant barely minutes previously when he was looking at the shriveled bodies of the slaves in that pit. With the immediate crisis passed, it surged again in his mind. And he made a vow.

The drive back to Freetown took longer because darkness had set in. On the other hand, the darkness was an ally against being waylaid by RUF on the lookout for the truck.

On the way, Bantu just held the exhausted body of his brother in his arms. There would be time later for talk. Sinda had fallen almost instantly into a sleep that had been denied him since the day he was taken to the pit.

When they reached the Mammy Yoko Hotel, Bantu had Jimbo drive around back to the servants' entrance. Freetown was crawling with RUF, and Bantu had no idea how soon the word of the rescue of Sinda would reach the west coast.

When the way was clear, Bantu half carried his brother up to his room and laid him on the bed. He filled the bathtub with warm water.

Bantu stripped off the shredded bit of muddy clothing that had survived the week in the pit and lifted Sinda into the warm, clean, soothing water. He helped Sinda wash away the scum and slime encrusting every inch of his body. He drained the fouled water and ran a completely fresh tubful to let his brother just soak the crippling pain out of his limbs.

While Sinda was resting in the water, Bantu stripped off of his own body the detested RUF officer's uniform. He took it to the alley below and burned it.

An hour later, he helped Sinda dress in some of his own clothing, which hung loosely on Sinda's diminished body, but nevertheless served the purpose.

Bantu went down to the bar where he could order mild food to begin nourishing his brother's body. Sinda was barely through taking in what his shrunken stomach could hold, when he fell back on the bed into a deep fitful sleep.

It took three days of rest and increasingly solid nourishment to bring Sinda back to a functioning state. The demons at night now plagued his sleep with the pain of conscience for what he had done to the victims of the lust for blood diamonds when he was an officer in the RUF.

During those three days, Bantu had long conversations with Sinda in which loose plans were woven around the vow Bantu had made back at the pit. As often as not, Jimbo joined in the talks.

When Bantu felt confident that his brother was able to fend for himself, he left him with enough money to pay for the room and buy food and clothing until Bantu returned. They agreed that it was absolutely necessary that Sinda stay out of sight of the eyes of any roving RUF or their snitches.

Bantu said his good-byes and met that afternoon with Morty Bunce as agreed. By that evening, Bantu was on a boat bound for the west coast of Ireland with a bag in his inside belt that carried Bunce's next cache of the bloodied stones.

Once again Bantu put on the suit of the business class of Ireland. Once more "Bantu" was left on the shore, and once more "Johnny Walker" entered another world.

# PART FIVE

# CHAPTER THIRTY

Dublin, Ireland

It was a soft Irish morning when Seamus and I landed on his native turf. Since his apartment was somewhere in the boondocks outside of Dublin, we both checked into the Gresham Hotel on O'Connell Street.

One shower and shave later, we were in a taxi heading directly to the office of the man whose name had surfaced when diamonds were mentioned, Declan O'Connor.

Seamus and Declan greeted each other with a warmth that I attributed to comradeship in arms during times and circumstances that neither of those warriors would be likely to open to me.

Seamus introduced me to Declan in a way that indicated more respect for this out-of-the-loop Yankee than I would have anticipated. It apparently served as all the credentials I'd need to gain the initial trust, perhaps confidence, of Declan.

That tentative bond being formed, and with a great deal of information to exchange, we adjourned to Declan's preferred place of business, the Brazen Head Pub on Bridge Street Lower—a hefty walk to me, but to the Irish, a mere stretch of the legs.

I asked Declan why the name of the pub was ringing bells.

"And well it should, Michael. Have you read James Joyce's *Ulysses*, or has your education been neglected altogether?"

"I have." I didn't add that it was under compulsion for a college course at an age when Lee Child was more to my taste.

"Then you'll know that Joyce said 'You got a decent enough do in the Brazen Head.' And you will. It's only been pouring the good stuff since 1198."

That quashed any thought of bragging to a Dubliner on the fine historical elegance of my 1855 Parker House in Boston.

The hour of the morning was early enough to get us a secluded table in a private room, particularly since we were in the company of Declan O'Connor. The proprietor apparently had a penchant for those inclined to "talk a little treason with their friends." The time of day was not, however, premature for the drawing of three fine draughts of creamy Guinness dark, and three more after that.

I sipped and listened while Seamus brought Declan through the events from my engagement as counsel by the O'Byrnes to our recent unpleasantness in New Hampshire. Declan took in every word with equanimity and without interruption. But I saw something flash in his eyes when Seamus mentioned the murder of Salvatore Barone and the disappearance of the diamonds he had bought on credit, as it were, from someone in Ireland.

Seamus detailed our unsuccessful efforts to locate the diamonds. He wrapped it up with the notion shared by both of us that they were now in the hands of the younger of the two O'Byrnes.

Declan, between servings of the Guinness, filled us in on a few missing pieces that made Seamus's presence in America more understandable to me.

"I've been dealing with your Frank O'Byrne for some years. I get supplies of the rough diamonds that come from some hellhole in Sierra Leone. There's a Morty Bunce in Freetown. He buys them from a ragtag rebel group in the diamond pits in the east. Morty sells them to me, and I sell them to O'Byrne. He has the contacts to trade them off to a middleman in America who sells them to a diamond merchant in Antwerp, Belgium. It's brought a good profit to all of us in the chain. Not enough to catch the attention of the ones that police that black market, but enough to make it worthwhile. "

I got in a word while Declan took a sip of the Guinness. "And that's where these diamonds that we're chasing came into the picture?"

"No. Not at all. There's a man I met here. He came from Sierra

Leone. He delivered Bunce's last shipment. Calls himself Johnny Walker, like the whiskey. But—"

"But what?"

"There's something about this man. I took to him. He has a hell of a story. He was one of the slave workers in those damn diamond pits. Somehow he escaped with a bag of rough diamonds. He wanted to sell them for all he could get."

"I don't blame him."

"No. This is different. He needs the cash to buy his father out of the hands of those pissant rebels that captured some of the diamond pits. Anyway, there's this thug in the Italian Mafia in your home town, Michael. Salvatore Barone."

"This *former* thug."

"Correction noted. I heard that he came to an unfortunate end, you might say. Anyway, this Barone wanted into the 'blood diamond business,' as some call it. He wanted to buy some of these diamonds from Sierra Leone. He was looking to deal at a level higher than anything I wanted to handle. He'd apparently already made contact to sell diamonds to this Frank O'Byrne, for the love of all the saints. A more unlikely pairing of two badass gangsters you'd be hard put to find. I guess he had little choice. There's not much market for the blood diamonds these days except on the black market."

What he said made sense. Barone was driven by his ambition to use the diamond profits to stage a coup and take over the New England family. I figured that was what drove him to get into bed with his Irish archenemy, O'Byrne. I didn't interrupt.

"Anyway, O'Byrne put Barone onto me as a source for the diamonds. Like I said, it was too rich for my blood. I wanted no part of a deal that was big enough to attract the attention of the authorities on three continents. But I was willing to pair Barone up with this Johnny Walker. They did the deal for Johnny's diamonds, and Barone took them back to America to sell them to O'Byrne."

Declan raised his glass to Seamus. "And that's when I sent my best man here to see that Johnny Walker gets his money."

Seamus said quietly, "And with Barone dead, it got complicated.

I've been on the scramble ever since to come up with those damn diamonds. Which is what brings us back to Dublin."

"Tell me about it. What've you got?"

Seamus looked over at me, and I picked up the telling.

"Your man, Seamus, and I have had a busy week. We've got it narrowed down. I'll bet the next round of drinks that Kevin O'Byrne, Frank's son, has them with him right now. I'll bet the round after that that he's in Dublin at the Shelbourne Hotel."

The lines in Declan's forehead deepened as I spoke. "That explains a lot. This kid, Kevin O'Byrne, he called me yesterday morning. He must be in it with his old man. He wanted the name and address of an upper-level diamond merchant. He said they wanted to bypass their American connection and go right to the man in Antwerp. Cut out the middleman. I thought what the hell. It's no dip into my profits. I thought he was talking about the diamonds I've been selling to Frank O'Byrne. I didn't know he had Johnny Walker's diamonds. I gave him the name of a man I'd heard of in Antwerp."

Declan slammed the table hard enough to make the glasses jump. "Damn! I wish to hell I'd known it was Walker's stones he was talking about. I'd have wrung his bloody neck to get 'em back for Walker."

Seamus put down his glass. He straightened up. I could tell he was ready for business. "Where's the little punk now, Declan?"

"Hell if I know. You said you thought he was staying at the Shelbourne. Maybe he's still there. He'd probably want to make contact with the man in Antwerp. Then he'd have to arrange a flight. That'd take some doing. There may be time."

Seamus was on his feet, and I was one step behind him. Declan caught us in mid-motion. "Hold it, Seamus. It's more complicated. Johnny Walker's back in Dublin. He came to see me yesterday. He was asking me for any lead I could give him to anyone who could have any information about his diamonds. I figured you had no information or you'd have contacted me right away like you always do. I gave him Kevin O'Byrne's cell phone number. I didn't know what you just told me. I just figured since the O'Byrnes were involved in the business, it could be a lead."

I looked at Seamus. "It could be a dangerous lead. I haven't trusted that little punk since I met him."

"Then we better get our asses on horseback."

Seamus and I caught the first cab from the Brazen Head. I dropped a twenty euro note onto the passenger seat. "What's your best time to the Shelbourne Hotel?"

The driver looked at the note beside him. "Twenty minutes, traffic as it is."

"There'll be another to match that one, plus the fare, if you make it in ten. And to hell with the traffic."

He smiled. "Buckle your seatbelt, Yank."

We pulled up to the front of the stately Shelbourne in ten minutes flat. I made good on my promise of another twenty euro note plus fare to the smiling gratitude of our cabbie. I figured we could throttle back on the speed now, since we were in position to spot the elusive Kevin if he decided to leave the hotel.

This time the lead was mine. Seamus took a seat with a view of anyone checking out or passing through the lobby. I gave him a full description of Kevin.

I stopped at the reception desk for the purpose of asking the clerk to ring Mr. O'Byrne's room to announce my presence.

"And your name would be, sir?"

"Bieber. Justin Bieber."

The clerk smiled. "Indeed, sir. Perhaps related to *the* Justin Bieber?"

I returned the smile. "Cousin, on my father's side." Now I had his full attention. "Would you tell Mr. O'Byrne that I have a package for him here in the lobby?"

"I'd be delighted. Do you see him frequently?"

"Mr. O'Byrne?"

"No. Justin Bieber. You know, the other one."

"Only at family gatherings. Christmas. Fourth of July. Groundhog Day."

"Really, sir? My daughter absolutely—"

"Not to rush, but do you suppose you could make that call?"

"Of course, sir."

The clerk pressed a short series of numbers. That told me that the little punk was indeed registered there and, more to the point, had not yet checked out.

The clerk gave me a mime signal that there was no answer. "Shall I leave a message, sir?"

"No. I'll check back."

I moved in closer for a quiet word. "Could you do one more thing? This is a bit of a surprise for Mr. O'Byrne. Could you give me a ring at this number if you see him come in? I'll drop back with the package."

He took my cell number. "I'd be delighted, sir."

I started to move away. He caught me in midstep.

"I say, sir. You don't suppose, possibly, an autograph for my daughter, Niamh?"

"More than possible. Probably around the family gathering on the Fourth of July." I figured by that time he'd have forgotten, and his daughter would have outgrown the infatuation.

My limited experience has taught me that a gracious reception clerk will grant favors if asked with a bit of finesse. But the chances of having the rules really bent out of shape improve if you deal quietly with a concierge. They are the civilian equivalents of Air Force sergeants. They combine a code of ethics unique to their position with an uncanny talent for accomplishing the impossible if they're properly motivated.

I stopped a bellboy for a whispered inquiry as to the full name of the concierge. He complied.

As I approached the concierge's station, I took the measure of the stately, debonair figure of approximately forty years attending charmingly to the requests of an elderly female guest. I waited. When the moment of privacy occurred, I walked up with the most ingratiating smile I could manage.

I could have addressed him as "Bernard." My quick-draw psychology told me that familiarity at this stage would be counterproductive.

"Mr. Phelan, might I have a word with you?"

"Of course, sir."

The ingenuous smile told me that although I was certain he knew I was not a guest of his fine hotel, he would deny me nothing within reason. The trick was to keep it within reason, and to show no sign of a tip until we were on closer terms.

"This is a bit awkward, Mr. Phelan."

"In what sense, sir?"

"I'm going to be completely honest with you." That was a fact. My rule of thumb is simply, when stuck for another approach, try the truth. Sometimes it works.

"There's a dangerous situation developing. You have a guest. An American. About nineteen, twenty years old. Blond, curly hair. About five feet ten."

"We do indeed, sir."

"To be brutally frank, in spite of his boyish appearance, he's an American gangster. I have good reason to believe he intends to do serious physical harm to a gentleman who deserves my protection. You have nothing to go on but my word. I'm counting on your intuition to believe me."

"Interesting, sir. And what did you want of me?"

"I believe he'll set up a meeting with the man he intends to harm. I need to know where it's going to be. He'll probably take a cab. It could well be this evening. I need to know where the cabbie is taking him before it's too late. Is that within the realm of possibility?"

His expression remained unchanged, except that, perhaps out of wishful thinking, I noticed a slyness creep into his professional smile. I wondered if he fancied a bit more excitement than filled his usual tour of duty.

He excused himself to answer a brief question from an elderly gentleman. He turned back when we again had privacy.

"It's an unusual request, sir."

Timing is everything. I took a hundred euro note out of my

breast pocket where I had it ready with the numbers clearly showing. I quietly placed it inside a brochure I had picked up at the front desk. I placed the brochure on the surface in front of him. We both appeared to ignore it.

"It's an unusual situation, Mr. Phelan."

"It is indeed. Shall we see what can be done, sir?"

I took that as an unqualified yes. I gave him my cell number, and started to walk away. I got ten feet, when he called me.

"Sir, I believe you forgot your brochure."

He handed it to me, and I walked to where I had left Seamus. The brochure seemed thicker than I expected. I opened it and was surprised to see the hundred euro note there untouched.

# CHAPTER THIRTY-ONE

I picked up Seamus at a jog. We left the hotel as quickly and unobtrusively as possible. If Kevin was returning to the roost, I had no desire to be spotted at that point. For the sake of the safety of Declan's friend, Johnny Walker, which was apparently of serious concern to Declan, we had to let the drama play out before we made a move.

We walked a few blocks to Doyle's Pub on College Street. We settled in at a table against a window for a wait of undetermined length. Lunch passed the first hour for us. For the rest of the afternoon, we spelled each other for walks outside by one while the other held the table.

The day drew on into evening. We had dinner around eight. Through the entire waiting period, we rationed ourselves on the tempting Guinness to be ready for an alert scramble at a moment's notice.

Around eleven thirty, when I was about to suggest we cash in our chips for the night, my cell phone jarred me upright. It was Bernard Phelan, my trusty concierge. He was speaking in a hush.

"What you wanted to know, sir. He just left in a cab with another American gentleman about the same age."

That could only be the equally elusive Chuck Dixon.

"Thank you, Mr. Phelan. Any idea where?"

"Ah, that's the beauty of having a symbiotic relationship with the cabbies. They're heading to the Ha'penny Bridge over the Liffey River. It's just off the Temple Bar area. Do you know it, sir?"

"I do. You're a gem, Mr. Phelan. You'll hear from me."

◆ ◆ ◆

We were out of Doyle's and going from a jog to a full run down the sidewalk. Seamus was in the lead. "Keep up, Michael. This'll be faster than a cab this time of night."

We arrived at the pedestrian bridge across the river that cuts Dublin in half called the Ha'penny Bridge. When it was built in 1816, the price of half a penny was well spent to get from the south to the north side of the river.

At close to midnight on an early week night in the chill of winter, there were not even stragglers on the bridge. We had apparently beaten Kevin's cab to the spot.

Seamus took command. He found me a bench on the south side of the river where a light pole hid me from the view of anyone on the bridge. He gave me the "Sit. Stay." sign. I did.

An occasional glimpse around the pole was all I needed to see Seamus stagger like a sot in his cups, his coat flapping in the wind, to a point a third of the way across the bridge. He swayed precariously by the side rail of the bridge, and dropped to the floor. It was the perfect performance of a drunk passed out cold.

He had an audience of three. When he was nearly at the passing out point, a cab pulled up on the south side. There were two passengers. I couldn't make them out in the dark. One of them got out of the cab. They exchanged a few words, and the cab drove off with the other.

The man on foot began moving slowly across the bridge. When he passed the drunk, he glanced down, but he scarcely bothered to interrupt his pace.

At about the same time, another solitary figure began the crossing from the other side. The second man walked with a more deliberate step to the center of the bridge. He stopped and leaned against the rail. In the dim light, the only thing I could tell about him was that he was a man of color.

He pulled the lapels of his coat up around his neck against the river wind that had blown up. I could see his head rotate from side to side inside of the collar, scanning both sides of the bridge. When he could make out the features of the man approaching from the south, he turned to face him full. I heard him call out a name. I couldn't make it out. The first man made no response.

They were now thirty feet apart. They appeared to be looking into each others' faces. There was nothing but silence between them. When they were twenty feet apart, I heard the man of color call out a name. This time I heard it. "O'Byrne!"

There was no response. They were fifteen feet apart. Another call. The white man was walking at that same deliberate pace directly at him. Still no response.

My heart began to pound. I began running toward the center of the bridge. Apparently Seamus sensed an internal alarm at that same moment. In a flash, the drunk was on his feet. He ran like a cat. There was not a sound.

The two men facing each other were now two feet apart. I saw a brief glint of reflected light. The mouth of the black man suddenly sprang open in a look of terror.

I saw Seamus at full speed leave his feet. He sprang straight out in a flying tackle that sent him and the white man tumbling one over the other across the floor of the bridge.

They rolled to a full stop against the wall. An instant later, Seamus broke his grip. He got to his knees. I could see a knife in the hand of the white man thrusting toward Seamus's midsection. I thought it struck solid flesh, but it seemed to have no effect.

Seamus jumped to his feet. He grabbed with both hands. Each hand clamped like a vise onto a clump of the white man's clothing. In a burst of power born of violence, Seamus hoisted the flailing body of the white man above the rail of the bridge and cast him headlong into the river below.

I was close enough at that point to see one last thing. As the body hurtled end over end toward the black rushing water, an instant before submersion, I saw the face. It was not the face of Kevin O'Byrne. It was the face of his classmate, Chuck Dixon.

I didn't know which wounded man to go to first. Seamus was leaning over, supporting himself on the bridge rail, panting for breath. He nodded to the other. The black man was down on his back, clutching his shoulder. I went to him first.

"Mr. Walker, I'm a friend. Where are you hurt?"

He looked up into my face in disbelief. He looked over at the man who had rescued him. He must have assumed we were together and believed me. He pulled opened his coat. I could see blood streaming from an open wound in his left shoulder.

I ripped open his shirt. There was a handkerchief in my pocket that I used to cover the wound. I took his right hand and put it on top of the handkerchief and told him to press hard. He did.

I ran to where Seamus was beginning to sway back and forth. This was no feigned drunkenness. I grabbed him under the shoulders and slowly lowered him to the ground.

"Where is it, Seamus?"

He pointed to the side of his abdomen. A flow of blood made the point of entry of the knife certain. I ripped off a piece of my shirt and pressed it against the wound. Seamus knew what to do from there.

I dialed the emergency number for an ambulance on my cell. While we waited, I could hear Seamus mumbling. "Damn. I am losing it. When that little pissant juvenile delinquent can stick me, it's time to retire."

I relayed the information to the emergency phone worker. While I waited for the ambulance, I passed from one to the other to tell them to keep the pressure on.

Seamus never heard me. I could hear him mumbling. "I'll retire. I'll buy a farm in Kerry. Maybe I'll raise some damn sheep."

It was two thirty a.m. by the time the two wounded had been treated in St. James's Hospital. Mr. Walker was the more serious. The report was that he'd need a few days in the hospital before release.

I suspect that Seamus was worse off than he let on. He insisted on settling for a stitching of the open wound in his lower abdomen. The two of us dropped in on Mr. Walker before leaving.

We briefly exchanged and melded the information we had on the location of the diamonds. Mr. Walker shared with us in more personal detail why he needed the diamonds and the cash they'd bring. It was easy to see how he'd won the allegiance of Declan O'Connor.

As Seamus and I walked to the front door of the hospital, we shared our conclusion that the diamonds were with Kevin O'Byrne. It was equally clear that he was on his way to make a deal for their sale with the diamond merchant in Antwerp that Declan O'Connor had given him.

"What's your plan, Michael?"

"Who says I have a plan?"

"That look in your eye. The pace you're movin'. I know more about you than you think. I didn't stay alive this long without learnin' what makes the likes of you tick."

"The 'likes of me'?"

"Aye."

I stopped and looked at him. "Okay, Doctor Freud, if you can see into the mind of 'the likes of me,' what's my plan?"

He looked me dead on. "You're going to be on the next plane to Antwerp. You'll hunt down this pissant O'Byrne. You'll pull off some whacky-ass stunt to get the diamonds from him. Then you'll fly back here and give them to that poor wretch up there in the hospital bed. All of that, I suppose, if you don't get your bleedin'-heart ass shot off in the meantime."

"If you knew all that, Mr. Burke, why the hell did you ask?"

"I don't know. Just to hear you say it."

He started walking toward the door. I caught his arm. "And just what are your plans for the immediate future?"

"You should know. It's damn little choice I have, isn't it?"

"The hell. You can go back to Dublin and drink Guinness. I thought you were going to raise sheep."

"Ah, damn the sheep. I'd die of boredom."

"Then what?"

"Antwerp. What else?"

"Why you? This isn't your fight."

"Why me? Because who else is going to be there to wipe your ass for you when you get yourself into another fine mess, as you like to say?"

I grinned at him. "You're a phony, Seamus Burke. You like to sound like a flippin' Irish tough guy, but in here, you're soft as a mushroom."

I walked off toward the door. He caught up. We hailed a cab and rode back to the hotel in silence. We planned to meet at breakfast in the dining room the following morning at seven for what could be a busy day. As we walked through the lobby toward the elevator, I heard him mumble in my direction. I could just make out the words.

"The hell I am."

"The hell you are what?"

"The hell I am soft as a mushroom."

He started me laughing. Maybe it was the tiredness, but I couldn't stop. By the time we reached the elevator, he couldn't stop laughing himself, even as he was grabbing at the fresh stitches.

"Have it your way, Seamus. Tomorrow, seven a.m. sharp."

It was shortly before seven in the morning when we were both wading into a full Irish breakfast. It left us just time to catch a ten o'clock plane to Antwerp.

Before checking out, I called Declan O'Connor. He was pleased to give me the name and address of the diamond merchant he had mentioned to Kevin O'Byrne. He was pleased, I think, because it meant to him that some slim hope was still alive that the diamonds would get into the right hands.

Kevin had also asked him for a hotel recommendation. If he followed it, we had another advantage. We needed every break we could get.

The last thing I did before leaving was to take the first step in what Seamus would tell me more than once was, as he predicted, a "whacky-ass" plan.

I called a number I knew by heart from previous adventures. I was, as usual in these circumstances, delighted and relieved to hear on the other end the sleepy voice of my Harvard classmate—Harry Wong.

# CHAPTER THIRTY-TWO

Harry Wong and I go way back. I got my first good look at that six-foot-plus Chinese beanpole from an odd angle. He was my freshman teammate on our house wrestling team at Harvard College. Since we were both from a more irregular lineage than the ultrawhites who made up the rest of the team—Harry being originally from China, and my mother being a purebred Puerto Rican—the coach avoided unnecessary disharmonies and looks askance by pairing the two of us for practice bouts. My first real look at Harry was a squinting side view from flat on my stomach with him pinning me to the mat.

We became close friends through those four years of college. The friendship has only deepened through the years, in spite of the fact that we seldom see each other more than twice a year. One of those happy times is annually at the Thanksgiving table of my mother. She prepares her Puritan specialty of arroz con pollo, and Harry brings that old Pilgrim favorite, wonton soup.

I'd forgotten the time differential when I called Harry. Consequently, I pulled him out of a deep sleep in his bachelor apartment at MIT. The effect was favorable. Being unable at that hour to fathom what all the babbling about diamonds and gangsters meant, he simply said yes to my request.

Seamus and I flew into Antwerp to coincide with the arrival of Harry's plane. The three of us checked into the Leopold Hotel in the center of the city, across from Central Park. The Leopold had three golden features. It was an outstanding hotel; it was a short walk from the concentrated triangular diamond district bounded by Schupstraat, Hoveniersstraat, and Rijfstraat, and it was a fair distance separated from the Astoria Hotel where, according to Declan O'Connor, our target, Kevin, had taken up residence.

Harry, Seamus, and I met in my room immediately. I brought Harry up to speed on what had brought us there. He had his usual reticence about his part in one of my plans that could, in his words, get his Chinese neck wrung like a chicken by people he didn't want to know. As usual, I salted the conversation with a subtle, demur implication that if he were doing the asking, I'd be the first one in the starting blocks. That always brought him around. He was gracious enough never to mention that, given the difference in our lifestyles, it was highly predictable that he'd never have occasion to ask.

It was showtime. Declan O'Connor had given me the name of the diamond merchant he had recommended to Kevin. He was in the phone book under "Ralph Schlichternlein, diamond merchant." I put the phone on speaker and slipped into my best deep-throated State Street Boston accent.

"Hello, Mr. Schlichternlein. Andrew Carnegie here. Firm of Bailey, Banks, and Bogdanof. I trust you're well."

"Yes. Yes, Mr. Carnegie. Thank you. Have we met?"

"Haven't had the pleasure. I seldom get out of Boston. We do have a mutual client. Mr. Frank O'Byrne."

I held my breath and prayed that the pause was reluctance to breach a confidence instead of a total blank on the name.

"What is your interest in Mr. O'Byrne?"

Thank God. First base. Trying for second.

"It's a delicate matter. I'm sure you understand. We're setting up a trust fund through his son, Kevin, to be funded by the purchase price he expects to receive for certain objects. Well, good heavens, no secret between us on that score. It's rough diamonds, isn't it?"

"I don't understand what you're asking."

"Of course. Let me be perfectly forthcoming with you. I'd prefer to be circumspect, but you're entitled to full disclosure. On the understanding that this will go no further. I think we understand each other?"

"Yes. Of course."

"Mr. O'Byrne would not under any circumstances want this made public. There's a certain humility to his beneficence. I just wouldn't want to offend. Nonetheless. Mr. O'Byrne is planning to build a home for disadvantaged children coming through the courts after a brush with the law. Introduce them to a new life. Complete with a top-grade college prep school, basketball courts, pool, complete medical facilities. Fast track from a gang to a profession. Do you understand the concept?"

Again a pause.

"Actually, plans are in the formative stage, but immediate funding is essential. And that brings us to your part in this worthy enterprise."

"My part?"

"The initial funding is seed money. It will be the springboard for other wealthy donors to jump into the deep end of the pool, as it were."

"I see. And this involves me how?"

I loved his defensive tone. He thought I was going to hit him up as a donor. His relief when I didn't put the bite on him could score some crucial points.

"Mr. O'Byrne has given us to believe that he has, or has at least discussed, an arrangement with you for your purchase of certain rough diamonds. That will be the seed money. We simply have to know, within parameters, the amount of this initial funding."

Again a pause. "May I ask, Mr. Schlichternlein, if I may be direct, have you considered even a tentative figure?"

"Why don't you ask Mr. O'Byrne himself?"

"I would. I've been unable to reach him at his hotel. Even as we speak, I have two gentlemen whose names would be immediately recognizable to you on the other line. They simply need a figure before they are willing to commit to a sizable donation. On the basis of their immediate commitment, I have construction contractors ready to break ground this afternoon."

"This is very unusual."

"I agree. I want you to feel comfortable with this. I believe it was

Mr. Declan O'Connor of Dublin who introduced you to Mr. O'Byrne. You've done business with Mr. O'Connor for some years. Might I hold the line while you check this out with him?"

"I'll do that. Shall I get back to you?"

"I'll be happy to hold the wire."

While I was dreaming all this crap up, my fingers were doing the walking around my cell phone, texting a heads-up to Declan in Dublin.

Apparently, Declan came through like a trooper. Mr. Schlichternlein was back within minutes.

"What did you want to know, Mr. Carnegie?"

"I assume Mr. O'Byrne had an asking price. I also assume that you need to do an appraisal of the stones, if you haven't already, before committing to a purchase."

"Yes. That will be necessary."

That was interesting. I wondered why he hadn't already appraised the diamonds.

"Assume for the moment that the diamonds live up to Mr. O'Byrne's claims, would you be willing to meet his price?"

"His claims for the gems are quite formidable. However, if they are as he claims, his price is not unreasonable."

"And for the sake of our contractors, may I ask if the price exceeds one million euros?"

"By a small amount."

"Would I be safe in representing it as between one and one and a quarter million euros?"

Again, some trepidation. I was getting my own twinges of conscience for the deception. I heard from Declan that in Antwerp the diamond trade is done mostly in cash on a strong basis of trust. Much as I hated to play games with that, I had a higher motive. I gave him time. It paid off.

"I believe you could say that."

"Thank you profusely, Mr. Schlichternlein. I could kiss you on the top of your round little head. You little rascal, you are the cornerstone of my whole plan. I could offer you my season tickets to the Bruins out of sheer gratitude. I won't, but I could."

I didn't actually say any of that, though I felt it to the core of my soul. I bid Mr. Schlichternlein a marvelous afternoon and turned to my comrades in arms.

"Gentlemen, we're in business."

Seamus, who'd been listening, was shaking his head with a slight grin. Harry was just shaking his head. "Michael, what the hell are you talking about? Convicts, basketball courts, pools? Have you been smoking something since Thanksgiving? Your mother's going to be pissed."

"Nothing of the kind, Harry. That brings us to your part in all this."

I prepared Harry for the scene he was about to play as completely as if I were Martin Scorsese. I dialed the number of Kevin's hotel and asked to be connected to him. When I heard him pick up, I handed the phone to Harry.

It may be like getting a horse to plunge into a raging river to get Harry to sign on in the beginning, but once aboard, my only fear is at the opposite end. Not to be critical, but Harry's acting can sometimes flow over the top.

I sat next to him to moderate the put-on Chinese accent with hand signals. He had to keep it intelligible.

"Mr. O'Byrne. We have not met yet. I hope to rectify that."

The speakerphone gave us both sides of the conversation.

"Really. Why?"

"I have heard from a mutual acquaintance that you have a certain product that you wish to sell."

"And who would that be?"

"Mr. O'Connor of Dublin sends his regards."

"Uh-huh. So?"

"I hope for your sake you have not already made a foolish deal."

"For my sake. What the hell are you talking about?"

"This is not the way to do business. I am prepared to offer you twice the price you get from any merchant in this country. I do that for a very good reason."

"How do you know what my price is?"

"Why you insist on all this talk on the telephone? This is offensive. We'll meet like two respectful businessmen. I shall be there at eleven a.m."

"Wait a minute. I don't know you."

"And do I know you? No. Yet here I am presenting an offer that will double your profit. Eleven o'clock. Be punctual. I don't wait."

Harry hung up with a self-satisfied grin. "How was that, Michael. He's eating out of my hand."

"Great, Harry. Where're you going to meet him?"

"Oh shit. I forgot."

I wrote a name on the phone pad. I dialed the number and put Harry back on.

"Mr. O'Byrne. I forget. TapaBar. Pelgrimstraat. Don't be late."

He hung up before he got an answer. "How was that, Michael?"

"I don't know, Harry. We'll find out at eleven."


I had my doubts. If I were on the other end of that phone conversation, would I respond to Harry's gracious invitation or just chalk it up to a Chinese lunatic? It could go either way. My best asset was Kevin's greed. I wondered how Martin Scorsese keeps his sanity.

At quarter of eleven, our threesome found the TapaBar. I spoke to the headwaiter about a small private room toward the back. With the quiet exchange of some euros, he set us up nicely.

Final instruction time. It was obviously useless to pick Harry's words for him. I gave him the gist of what I wanted him to get across.

"Let me have your cell phone, Harry."

I dialed my own number so that we'd be connected through the next half hour. "Keep the phone on, Harry. I want to hear every word."

"Why? I can tell you about it later."

"Actually, you're about to do some risky business with a kid who will kill you on a whim if he gets the faintest whiff of a phony deal. We could easily be shipping your body back to Boston in parts for reassembly for the funeral. I like you too much to have that happen. Keep me connected."

That was the thought. Those very words would have had Harry on the next thing smoking back to the United States of America. I just said, "I want to be sure you don't forget anything. Be careful, Harry."

"Piece of cake, Mike."

Seamus and I took seats as far removed from the path to Harry's private room in the TapaBar as possible. Two large menus were good camouflage. I checked the phone contact. All systems go.

In about ten minutes, I got the first glimpse of my former client since that fateful night at the Slainte Bar. The headwaiter took him directly back to the private room. He closed the door behind him. And I prayed.

Seamus and I moved to the table closest to Harry's private room to be ready to spring in case things got testy. I put my phone between us. We huddled close to it and tuned in.

"You on time. That is good, Mr. O'Byrne. Two more minutes and you'd be here alone. Sit down."

There was no sound of Kevin sitting.

"What the hell is it with you? You give orders like someone made you king. To hell with you. I can sell my product without you and your damn orders."

"Not at my price. Sit down. Now we be properly introduced. My name is Huang Liu. You are Kevin O'Byrne. There. Now we acquaintances. Soon we be business associates. Both make more money than you think. For the love of crap, sit down."

He apparently got away with the Americanized "love of crap." I heard a chair pulled out.

"Now we talk business. No need to 'beat the bush' as you Americans say. You have rough diamonds. They blood diamonds. I don't give a crap. In my country, I sell them for many times what you get here. How much you get for them here?"

There was a small gap during which Kevin was, I'm sure, calculating how much of a chump he had with him at the table. "I have an offer of two million euros."

I thought to myself, *You lying little phony. Go get him, Harry.*

Without a tick of the clock, Harry came back, "Four million euros. Paid in cash. No need to tell your Uncle Sam, right?"

I think it took Kevin's breath away.

"When would I get the cash?"

"As soon as I get the diamonds. But hold onto your horses. First, you show me the diamonds. I check 'em out. If they as good as Declan O'Connor say, you gonna be rich man right away."

I could hear Kevin push back in his chair. "How long are you going to be in Antwerp?"

"Why? You get diamonds. Show me. I check 'em out. We go to my bank here. We get the cash. Do it now."

"There's a problem. I need two days. I'll meet you here in two days."

"Why you wanna wait? Do it now. I go home."

I'm listening to all this and thinking, *Don't press it, Harry. Give him the two days.* I knew why he needed the time sure as hell. He didn't have the diamonds with him. He had to fly back to the United States.

I had a sudden flash. I slapped Seamus on the arm and whispered with my hand over the phone. "Crap, Seamus. I just got it. I know where those damn diamonds are. I'd bet my life on it."

Harry must have found himself up an alley. He had to concede. "Okay. I wait two days. I meet you right here. Two days. Eleven a.m. Just to show you I serious, I pay for travel wherever you have to go. How you like that?"

I whispered to Seamus, "Will you get Harry the hell out of there before he ad-libs us into bankruptcy."

I scooted to the other end of the restaurant. Seamus, who had never met Kevin, knocked on the door and told "Mr. Liu" that he had a phone call at the bar. Kevin rose and walked past both of them with a determined step.

Harry couldn't resist firing off one last line. "Eleven a.m. You five minutes late, I gone."

Harry watched Kevin leave. Then he walked proudly to my table across the room. He took a bow as if he were Kenneth Branagh after a triumphant *Macbeth*.

I thanked God it was over and gave him a nice round of applause.

# CHAPTER THIRTY-THREE

Time was definitely of the essence. Our little band of musketeers—Harry, Seamus, and I—caught the earliest direct flight back to Boston. I put together a plan based on the weak assumption that I was right about where Kevin stashed the diamonds.

When we landed, Harry and Seamus went their way. I rented a car at the first agency I came to. I was on Route 93 heading to New Hampshire fifteen minutes after the immigration officer squinted at my passport photo and admitted me into the country.

At ten p.m., it was pitch-black on the dirt road that led deep into the pine woods to the O'Byrneses' decimated cottage. The moon, thank God, chose somewhere else to shine. I was fairly sure that I was the first one there. Whether I was right about that or not, I needed the headlights to find the dirt ruts that led to the cottage.

I ran inside through the back door behind the lowest beam of a flashlight. Maneuvering between piles of rubble, smashed shelves, and dismantled cabinets required a higher level of beam. Five minutes later, I ran out and drove the car a short distance to a blind pull-off. With all lights doused, the car was completely hidden from sight. I made my way back on foot through the woods to a point where I could lurk behind a tree and see through the appropriate window of the cottage.

It was shortly after midnight when a bobbing set of headlights signaled a car bouncing over the washboard road. I practically willed the car to turn into the car-width path to the cottage. It did. I could see the now recognizable figure of Kevin go inside through the back door.

Timing was still the key to success. I called Harry at his Cambridge apartment as prearranged. I had him dial up Kevin's cell phone number and sit tight without hitting the call button.

Within five minutes, I could just make out the form of Kevin, flashlight in one hand and a small sack in the other, moving around in the cottage. I gave Harry the signal. True to his MIT graduate engineering training, Harry hit the "call" button right on cue. I could see Kevin put down the flashlight and flip open his cell phone.

I could tell by Kevin's body language that he was reacting to the change of plan I had asked Harry to relay. The new plan was for Kevin to bring the diamonds and meet Huang Liu (Harry) in room 228 of the Parker House at noon the following morning to consummate the deal. Harry was to bait the hook by saying that he would have the cash on hand and Kevin had better have those diamonds. The Lord only knows how Harry delivered that message.

I could see Kevin erupting into some mild histrionics at the change of plan. I suspected that Frank's pampered son could go ballistic over a change of breakfast cereal. I was confident that much of the bluster was to keep what he considered a dominant hand in the negotiation. Since the net result was to be a cash windfall for him and his father, I figured the squall would pass. It did.

I watched a relatively cool, collected Kevin walk back to his car and drive off down the dirt road. There was no point in following closely. The hook had been set.


The next morning, I caught Mr. Devlin as he stepped off the elevator at our Franklin Street offices. Julie told me that it was his first day of coming in for a few hours. She told me that the doctor's orders were to keep the excitement down. Given our line of work, I assumed that was a relative thing.

He may not have been ready for the Olympics, but I could see in his eyes that the fire was back just being in the old digs. That did more for me than my morning's Dunkin' Donuts.

I brought him up to speed quickly because I needed him to work some of that Devlin charm on the district attorney's office. There was still a major piece of the puzzle that needed placement before anything significant was going to happen.

Mr. D. carefully bypassed Angela Lamb, the Dark Queen of that particular realm. He knew she'd say no to whatever he proposed if only to avoid making a tactical blunder. He talked the very under- standing receptionist, Mary Cornelius, into giving him Billy Coyne's private line without sending any flares in her majesty's direction. Billy was on in three seconds.

"Lex. You've just changed my career plans. When I heard you might be out of the wars, I seriously considered retiring. There'd be no fun in it. How're you feeling?"

"Like a first-year associate. More fire and brimstone every day, Billy. Thank you for the compliment."

"I meant it. And now that we're through being nice to each other, what unfair advantage do you want to take of me this time?"

"Why, Billy! When have I—"

"There was the Huntington case, there was the Scheer case, there—"

"Ah, but those are bygones. I'm a new man. Nothing but straight arrow from here on."

"If I believed that, I would retire. Come on. Skip the warm-up. Straight out. What do you want from this poor humble servant of the people?"

"Nothing that can do you any harm, Billy. I take it you still have an indictment out for Kevin O'Byrne."

"What do you care? I heard you people withdrew as defense counsel."

"That we did. But we didn't withdraw from our interest in seeing justice done."

"Oh my, Lex. I'm lifting my feet, and the bullshit is still up to my knees. A simple question. What do you want?"

"How would you like both O'Byrnes right in your lap?"

"What the hell, Lex? Are you on my side now?"

"I think in a way all these years, we've always been on the same side."

"We'll talk about that over a Scotch some night. Assuming what you said could happen, what's the price?"

"A look at the autopsy report on Salvatore Barone."

"I can't do that, Lex. You're out of the case now. Among other things, there are privacy laws."

"Yes, there are, Billy. There are such things. And there are other things. There's a blaze that could go up like tinder between the two biggest organized crime gangs in this city. The North End Italians and that plague on our mutual heritage, the South Boston Irish. They could exchange more than words if this thing isn't doused. How does that stack up against your so-called privacy laws?"

"You haven't lost a step, have you? You can still play my emotions like a harp."

"An appropriate reference, Mr. Coyne. So?"

There was a pause. I could hear footsteps going and then coming back with the sounds of a door opening and closing in between. We both figured Billy was checking for lurking ears.

"I take it your interest is the cause of death, Lex."

"None other."

"Well, I suppose it could have been that rope around his neck."

"It could."

"But it wasn't. It could have been that knife in his back."

"True."

"Nope."

"Which leaves?"

"Without divulging anything contrary to my oath of office, I suppose it could have been that hollow-nose .22 that splintered in every direction inside his brain."

"And your conclusion?"

"I conclude that I'll not step any farther outside of the bounds of discretion."

"Billy, you're a gem. What would the Commonwealth do without you?"

"The day you retire, I'm afraid they'll have to find out."

◆  ◆  ◆

Now I was armed with something better than firepower. The information Billy gave, without actually giving it, could well provide the leverage I needed. The trick was to parlay it with a realization that had been growing for some time. Packy's comment the last time we were together confirmed in my mind the fact that you could take all of the self-sacrificing loyalty to the corps among the current generation of mobsters and put it in a peanut shell and still have room for three M&M's. That meant that with a little finesse, they could be played off against each other. At least in theory.

I arrived at the Parker House at quarter of noon. I met Harry as planned in Room 228. We went over the scene he was about to play. Rehearsals with Harry only called to mind the number of ways he could grab the bit in his teeth and run in a direction that could cause us both physical harm. Still, there's no one I'd rather have as my front man.

At noon on the dot, there was a knock on the door. I scooted through the adjoining door to Room 230. Harry dialed up my cell number on his cell phone to let me hear the discussion. As he opened the door, I heard him start babbling Chinese in a high-pitched voice into the phone. It sounded as if he were threatening some poor imaginary soul with the wrath of God.

I opened the adjoining door just a crack. I could see Harry wave Kevin into the room. Between Chinese outbursts into the phone, he gave a firm "stay" signal at the door to the bulked-up bodyguard Kevin brought with him.

When Kevin could get a word in, it was to insist that his giant shadow be admitted with him. That sent Harry into the contortions of a one-man band. He continued to pour vitriolic Chinese into the phone to no one, while he continued to wave off and start to shut the door in the face of the totally stymied bodyguard. At the same time, he glared at Kevin and waved his arm theatrically around the room with a wild expression on his face that seemed to be asking why he needed a bodyguard when there was no one else in the room. It was one hell of a performance.

I was watching through a tiny opening of the door. I didn't know whether to laugh or applaud. Kevin was equally stunned. Eventually, if only to calm the maniacal Chinese typhoon, he conceded the logic of Harry's position. He told the bodyguard to stand outside the door. I noticed that Harry closed the door and slipped on the bolt lock.

Harry returned to relative normalcy, but not before a final invective into the phone, which he appeared to slam shut without really disconnecting it.

Harry was now all business. According to the script, he pulled out of his pocket a jeweler's eyepiece and took a seat at the desk. He turned on the light and gave Kevin a look that demanded production of the subject of the meeting.

There must have been some hesitancy, because Harry pounded the desktop. I hardly needed the phone to hear, "Come! Come! What am I here for? Produce them! Now!"

Kevin made a vain attempt at controlling his end. "Suppose you show me the money first."

"Suppose you get the hell out of the room!"

Harry was up and pacing now. "Who you think I am? Nobody told you who I am? I leaving now. You pay for room. That teach you some respect for your betters." Each phrase was interspersed with Chinese I wouldn't want to hear translated.

Harry grabbed his large briefcase from beside the desk and headed under a full head of steam for the door.

Kevin caught him by the arm. "Please, Mr. Liu. Wait. No offense intended. Damn, you're touchy."

Harry let that last phrase pass, but not the hand on his arm. He jerked his arm away and faced Kevin straight on. Harry dropped his voice to a whisper that hissed through clenched teeth. "You ever touch my person again, you be in more pieces than jigsaw puzzle."

Kevin did his best backing-off move. "I'm sorry, Mr. Liu. Really, no offense. Let's calm down. We have business to do. I'll show you the diamonds. Just calm down, will you?"

I was thinking the same thing. *Calm down, Harry. You've got a scene to play before you run out of steam.*

Harry acceded to both of our wishes. He strode back to the desk like a clerk at Tiffany's. How he could turn the hysterics on and off was awesome.

From the doorway, I could see him pop in the eyepiece. He had a demanding way of simply holding out his hand. I could see Kevin reach into his inside sport coat pocket. He produced a small leather pouch with a drawstring.

Harry waved the fingers of his outstretched hand to speed up the process. Kevin pulled loose the drawstring and dropped several small objects into Harry's open hand.

Harry felt the rough stones between his fingers. He took one and set the others down on the desk. He held it up to his free eye. He gave a withering look at Kevin who probably took it as business posturing.

Harry held the little item between his fingers and pretended to study it through the jeweler's eyepiece for several seconds. He suddenly dropped his hand to the desk. There was a blank look on his face that had Kevin staring at him.

In one sudden motion, Harry used his free hand to slap the eyepiece out of his eye. He rose to his feet almost in slow motion. He held the stone in his left fist while he grabbed the edge of he desk with his right.

I could see it coming. I almost bolted into the room to stop him. Instead I just whispered to myself. "Crap, oh crap, Harry. Don't go over the top."

But he did. In one synchronized move, he overturned the desk and screamed something in Chinese they must have heard on Tremont Street. He turned a slow look toward Kevin that said he could eat him alive.

Kevin backed off practically to the wall. His mouth fell open and he started to cringe. Harry was, after all, over six feet tall.

With his back to the wall, Kevin started screaming, I think more out of fear than anger. "What the hell is wrong with you?"

Harry screamed back at him. "With me? With me? What wrong with you? You think you do this to me? To me?"

They were face-to-face and screaming. Harry was acting, but Kevin was practically in hysterics. "Those diamonds are good. What are you yelling about?"

Harry held the fist with the diamond up into Kevin's face. "You still lie. I catch you, and you still lie. I show you your good diamond!"

Harry hauled back. He threw the diamond against the wall with all of his force. Kevin gaped at the sight of his diamond shattering into a million pieces against the wall and sprinkling crystal dust over the rug.

Harry grabbed the leather bag out of Kevin's hand. He opened it, took another stone out of the bag, and threw it with the same force against another wall. It shattered in a spray the same as the first.

Kevin's mouth just hung open as he edged his way along the wall toward the door. I could hear the goon Kevin brought with him pounding on the other side of the heavy door.

Harry followed him along the wall screaming. "You cheat me! Glass! You think you cheat me! You not see the sun tomorrow!"

Kevin reached the door. He fumbled for the knob, unlocked the door, and pulled it open. When the door flew in, the goon on the other side came tumbling off balance into Kevin. In one panicky struggle, Kevin fought to get out past him, while the goon fought to get in. For a few seconds, they were locked in the grip of each other. Neither of them was going anywhere.

In the uproar, neither of them could tell, but at some point, Harry stopped screaming Chinese and started laughing himself helpless at the scene. He broke totally out of character. He was doubled over in uncontrollable laughter. Thank God, before they noticed, the two got their act together and beat the hastiest retreat they could manage.

When he could just about straighten up, Harry pushed the door closed. By then, I was in the room, catching Harry's fits of laughter that kept us speechless for the next two minutes.

I bolted the door in case they came back for the other pieces of glass, unlikely as that seemed.

The two of us finally fell on the sofa in sheer exhaustion. Harry said in unaccented English, "I don't think that kid's got a career in crime." That set us off again.

"Harry, you are more than a piece of work. You are an Olympic thespian."

The smile still hadn't left his face. "Most fun I've had since Chinese New Year."

# CHAPTER THIRTY-FOUR

Before Harry and I left the Parker House, I called Seamus's cell phone. He had been working on another piece of the puzzle. His chosen assignment was to pick up and hold for a bit of private conversation Tommy Franzone, whose belt had been notched with the murder and trunk stuffing of Salvatore Barone.

"What luck, Seamus?"

"No luck to it. Either you know what you're doing, or you don't."

"Does that little piece of modesty mean what I think it does?"

"It means that Mr. Franzone has accepted our gracious invitation to chat."

"How gracious was the invitation?"

"Under RSVP, there was just one choice. How'd it go there?"

"Perfect. Harry pulled it off like a Chinese Clint Eastwood."

"Meaning?"

"Young Mr. O'Byrne is now thoroughly convinced that the diamonds have magically slipped out of his possession. When he catches his breath, he's going to run through the cast and figure out who has them. He won't know how it happened, but eventually he'll figure it out that I found them. When he gets that far, he'll know that I switched them for the twenty-two pieces of rough glass I picked up in Antwerp before we left."

"Awesome."

"God willing, that'll set up the next two acts of our little drama."

"Where are you now?"

"Parker House. Harry and I are just leaving. Where do I meet you?"

"Cabin 6. East Coast Motel. It's on Route 1 in Saugus. I thought neutral territory would be best for all parties. Mr. Franzone has graciously agreed to await your arrival."

"I won't keep him waiting. See you in twenty minutes."

"Whoa there! You don't leave that phone till you tell me how the hell you figured out where he hid the diamonds."

"Remember after we saw that cottage torn apart, we both thought there was something peculiar about it? I finally figured out what it was. It was too thorough. There was not a single possible hiding place for the diamonds that wasn't not only torn apart but laid open for anyone like us to see. It was like the stage was set."

"Set for what, Michael?"

"For you and me—most probably me—to look at it and say those diamonds are definitely not here. Then we'd write it off and go chasing wild geese somewhere else. In fact that was my first thought. It was a perfect hiding place."

"So, what brought you back?"

"When we heard that Kevin didn't have the diamonds with him in Antwerp, I knew he needed someplace to stash them till he could make a deal with that diamond dealer he'd never met before. As he told Mr. Schlichternlein, it was someplace he needed two days to get to and then back to Antwerp. His father was clearly in on it too. He was so confident we'd take one look at that cottage and walk away, he even gave me the location in New Hampshire."

"So where were they?"

"The only logical place."

"You're draggin' this out, Michael. Where the hell were they?"

"You remember I told you Frank arranged a signal to contact Kevin on the cottage phone? And you remember after we ducked the shotgun blast, I went back in and hit redial and got Frank? It finally hit me that the only thing in the whole place that wasn't cracked and laid open was that big old-fashioned wall phone. Why did they leave the phone intact?"

"To hide the diamonds. You're a damn genius, Michael. It's a pleasure to be riskin' my neck with you. I've not said that to many."

"I appreciate the honor, Seamus. I've never taken great pleasure in neck risking with anyone, but I'll say this. You come the closest."

Within twenty minutes I knocked on the door of cabin 6. Seamus opened the door.

"Tommy boy awaits your pleasure."

"Good. Let's not keep him waiting."

I was surprised to walk in on a very disconsolate Tommy Franzone, tied to a chair like a standing rib roast. His expression was halfway between highly pissed and frantically counting the number of minutes he had left on this earth. If I could have ordered up a state of mind for him, that would have been it.

"Tommy, we meet again. It always seems to be under unpleasant circumstances. Especially for you."

Now I had his full attention. "What the hell you want from me?"

"That will become clear almost immediately. But, to put first things first, I actually have hopes that you'll walk out of here in good health, not much the worse for wear. Do we share that wish?"

He just stared. I saw a glimmer of hope in his eyes. I played on it.

"I'd like to hear you join in the conversation, Tommy. You probably guessed there's a condition. Would you like to hear it?" I saw the look of hope diminish, but still glimmer faintly.

"What do you want?"

"Now we're conversing. You probably guessed. I want the truth, the whole truth, and nothing but the truth. They say that in court. You may be in court one day soon. You see, you are smack in the middle of two powerful entities. One or the other is absolutely going to be a threat to your life. You have to decide which. If you pick the right one, I may be able to improve the chances you'll go on living. What do you think of that?"

His panicked expression almost made the words unnecessary. "I don't know what the hell you're talking about."

"I know you don't, Tommy. So let me lay it out as clearly as I can. Then, you get to choose. Are you listening carefully?"

His open-mouthed stare answered that one.

"Let's look at it this way. Either you killed Salvatore Barone and stowed him in his trunk or you didn't."

"I told you once. I did it. What the hell you want from me?"

I held up a silencing hand. "Let's pretend that question is still open. Now here's the split. Kevin O'Byrne is already indicted for that murder. If you stick to your story that you killed Barone, Kevin will certainly know it. You can bet your life, literally, that he'll be happy to lay the whole rap on you. That means the Commonwealth of Massachusetts will be looking to lock you up in a maximum-security prison for the rest of your life. And that may not last too long. The boys in your club all the way up to Antonio Pesta will have a personal interest in clamming you up just in case you decide to go for a lighter sentence by flipping on the bigger fish. You'll be a sitting duck in prison. Are we on the same page for that half?"

"You told me before I wouldn't have any legal problems."

"From me, Tommy. And you won't. The O'Byrnes will be frying your legal ass without any help from me to get Kevin off. Are we ready for part two?"

Again the slack-open jaw said yes.

"Okay. On the other side we have the man who demands all your loyalty, the same Don Antonio Pesta. If it turns out that you didn't kill Barone, that would mean Kevin killed him and you made some kind of deal with Kevin and the Irish mob that night at the beach in South Boston. Maybe it's just me being oversensitive, but that could sound like rank treason to Mr. Pesta. He seems to expect unconditional loyalty to his Italian organization. Once again, I don't think I'd write any insurance policies on your life. Are we clear on that half?"

His breathing was becoming more shallow and rapid. "I did kill him. Just like Mr. Pesta told me."

"You took that gun you've been carrying, and you shot him right in the back of the head, right?"

"That's right."

"Then I'd like to hear you explain to Mr. Pesta how you shot him with your .38-caliber handgun, and he died of a .22-caliber hollow-nose bullet to the brain. The only bullet in him. So says the autopsy."

I let the silence hang to give him time to absorb his dilemma. I walked over to Seamus. "Have you got a cigarette?"

His eyebrows went up. "Has all this crap driven you to smoke?"

I winked. He pulled out a Marlboro.

"How about a light, Seamus?"

Again the eyebrows. "Right. How you fixed for socks and under-wear?"

"I'm good. Just a light."

He fired me up. I took one deep, dramatic drag that would have done Al Pacino proud, and nearly coughed up my shoelaces. I resolved to stick to other dramatic devices.

In spite of my antics, Tommy was still on the verge of panic.

"So, we have two choices here, Tommy. It's decision time. We can simply cut you loose and open the door. You can walk out into a world that has one death or another waiting no matter where you turn. That's one choice. There's another."

He was able to manage one word. "What?"

"Right now. You tell us the absolute truth about what happened that night with Barone. I mean not one whisker out of line. I'll know the truth when I hear it."

He just breathed for five seconds. "What if I do?"

"You get to start life all over again. You cut loose all the baggage of a life of mistakes. I think you got yourself sucked into this rathole with a couple of wrong moves and couldn't get out. I could be wrong. I don't think you're really part of that gang of murdering miscreants. If I'm right, this is your absolutely last chance to get clean."

He looked me full in the eyes for the first time. "How?"

"I get you into the witness protection program. A totally new life, courtesy of the federal government. No one can touch you. I can do it."

Another few seconds. The sweat beads on his forehead were growing. He finally said it in one exhaled breath. "Yeah."

"Yeah what?"

"I want it."

"Then buy the ticket right now. What really happened that night? Complete truth."

He licked his lips while he was thinking back.

"I was with Mr. Barone. He was my capo. You know what that is?"

"Yes."

"He just got back from someplace in Ireland. He was showing us these diamonds he bought from some guy over there. He was gonna sell 'em to O'Byrne, the Irish guy. He was braggin' about makin' enough to take over the family from Mr. Pesta. Anyway, he makes a call to O'Byrne. The father. He's not there. He's out of state somewhere. His kid takes the call. The kid says he wants into the father's business. Wants to show his father he can handle things. He sets up the meet with Barone at Carson Beach in Southie."

"Where was Kevin going to get the money to pay Barone for the diamonds?"

"I don't think he ever intended to pay for them. I think he was going to show Daddy he was ready by popping Barone and stealing the diamonds."

"So what happened?"

"I went to Mr. Pesta. I told him about Barone and him takin' over. Mr. Pesta liked that I told him. He said he'd give me a chance to make my bones. He told me to kill Barone like the traitor he was and bring him back in his own trunk. Then he'd get the diamonds off his body."

"And?"

"I went to where O'Byrne and Barone were meeting at the beach. When I got there, Barone was dead. He was slumped over the steering wheel of his Cadillac. Kevin O'Byrne was searching his pockets. I came up behind him. I had my gun on him. He turned around. He had a gun on me too."

"So what'd you do?"

"I was scared crap out of my mind. I knew if I went back without killing Barone and the Irish guy got the diamonds, Mr. Pesta'd kill me."

"So?"

"O'Byrne didn't want a bullet either. We made a deal. We'd say I killed Barone. I fixed him up like a traitor like Mr. Pesta told me. O'Byrne said he'd go along with the story if I let him get the diamonds. It had to look right. I had to get back to Pesta quick. I told O'Byrne I'd put Barone in the trunk. I'd drive the Cadillac back to Collini's like I was supposed to. I'd leave the keys in the car while I went in, like I was going to come back and search Barone for the diamonds later. The O'Byrne kid could steal the Cadillac. Then he could search the body himself for the diamonds. I guess that's what he did. Then he drove the car back to his father's place."

"And that's when Frank O'Byrne called me in to make the peace for his poor, sweet, innocent son."

"That's the truth."

"I know it is, Tommy. It sounds right."

I looked over at Seamus. He gave me an agreeing nod.

I walked outside the building and dialed the private number of Billy Coyne.

"You remember that promise I made you about the O'Byrnes? I'm one step closer, but I need your help. I'm going to give you the mother lode. I need to have you work some of that witness protection magic. Can you do it?"

"Who is it?"

"Tommy Franzone. He can give you testimony on everyone up to Antonio Pesta. He can also lay the murder of Barone on Kevin O'Byrne."

"How about the father?"

"That's a little tricky. I've got to stay clear of anything I learned when I was representing Kevin. That was before he tried to kill me. I'm working on that. If it works out, you should be able to get him at least for accessory after the fact to Barone's murder."

There was a pause. "Okay, kid. Franzone's good for a starter against Kevin O'Byrne. I'll need more. Defense counsel will tear Franzone apart as a witness. He's a thug himself with a rival gang. You know what you'd do to him on the stand."

"I know. At least give me credit for a good start. I'm working on the wrap-up. What'll I tell Franzone?"

"I'll set it up with the U. S. Attorney. He'll want a piece of this too. Where's Franzone now?"

I told him.

"Stay with him. I'll send someone."

"I'll babysit, but make it fast. These days I don't feel good about being in one place too long."

# CHAPTER THIRTY-FIVE

The stage was set for what I prayed would be the final scene that lay between me and a life of title searching. As nearly as I could figure, each member of the cast was primed and motivated according to plan. It was now up to me to bring them together and let the sparks fly.

In one corner, we had Kevin and Frank O'Byrne. Fortunately for my wishes, Kevin had interjected himself prematurely into Frank's plans for a deal in blood diamonds—and he had blown it monumentally. His blundering efforts had left the two of them with no diamonds, no profits, and a murder rap hanging over their heads. I figured that any option to get back in the game would sound appealing—even if it came from me.

In the other corner, we had Packy Salviti, the heir to Salvatore Barone's ambition to make enough profit on the sale of diamonds to the Irish to take command of the family out of the hands of Antonio Pesta. Packy had also blown it. He, too, had neither diamonds nor profits. And unless he came by an immediate windfall of cash and the power that came with it, he could find himself on Pesta's short list of disposable soldiers. That could motivate him to accept the invitation I had in mind.

My first approach was to the O'Byrnes. I figured Kevin had had time to bring Frank up to date on his latest fiasco as a big-time mobster. They had also had time to attribute the switch of the glass for diamonds to me. I had no intention of taking my vulnerable body into that hornets' nest. I reached them by phone. Frank answered.

"You damn little shyster, you! You think you pull this crap on me and live? I have men looking for you in every rathole in this city. I'll tell you what I'm gonna do to you. I get you, I'm gonna—"

I figured it was best to let him spew it out. I held the phone down to avoid taking in images that could cause sleepless nights. When the rant seemed to have petered out in what sounded like, "You hear me, you damn shyster?" I chimed in.

"Good morning, Frank. Say, with all we've been through together, may I call you 'Frank'?"

That seemed to have rewound his rubber band. He ripped on for another minute. I jumped in at the first silence for fear of a slamming of the phone on his end that would leave nothing accomplished.

"Hear this, Frank. I have a deal that could put you right back where you want to be in the diamond business. There's money to be made. A lot of it. If you're through with the temper tantrum, let's talk business."

That seemed to cut through Frank's Irish temper to the part of his brain that told him it's all about business. There was a welcome silence and no hang up.

"What the hell you talkin' about?"

"I'm talking about a deal that puts you at the table with Packy Salviti. He has the diamonds. He's ready to sell. Same price as before Junior decided to get his feet wet in the big pool. You bring the cash. Packy brings the diamonds. We sit down like businessmen. We do the deal and leave. No gunplay. No cheating. Nice and clean. Are you in or out?"

Again, a pause. I think the sudden turn had him off balance. Not for long. At the center of Frank's alleged heart was a cool, hard core of greed.

"Hey, lawyer. What the hell do you get out of this? Why should I trust you?"

"Because if you have half the sense people say you have, you can see that all the shooting and knifing and gangster shenanigans has left everyone holding the crap end of the stick. If we do it my way, you make out. Packy makes out. And I get a good commission from

Packy. Plus, I get to go on with my life and forget about the both of you. That's what's in it for me. Again, and for the last time, are you in or out?"

I could hear talking through a hand over the phone with someone in the room—probably Kevin. It took thirty seconds, but he was back.

"So, how do we do it?"

I laid down the ground rules that I had thought out in advance. Frank agreed, for whatever the word of a lifelong thug was worth. I didn't care. The trick was to get them to the table. Whatever fireworks went off after that was out of my control anyway.

The next call went to Packy Salviti. This promised to be easier. At least at our last meeting, he hadn't tried to blow me into numerous pieces. That was a plus.

"Packy, I bet you never expected to hear from me again."

"Yeah. Broke my heart. What the hell is this? An invitation to lunch at the Four Seasons?"

"Not quite. Although we might wind up there for a celebration dinner."

"Celebratin' what?"

"The completion of a successful business deal. I'm giving you the chance to sell those diamonds you've been looking for for one hell of a profit to the original buyer, Frank O'Byrne. He still wants to do business with you and your organization."

"What the hell?"

"That's right. O'Byrne agreed to get the deal back on track. This time like businessmen, not—forgive the indelicacy—two gangs of imbecilic thugs. What do you think?"

"I think you got your head up your ass. Where I always thought it was. There's one problem."

"Which is?"

"You gotta have the damn diamonds to sell 'em. I don't. You might remember."

"Not a problem, Packy. Frank O'Byrne will bring the cash. You'll bring yourself. And I'll bring the diamonds."

"The hell. You got 'em?"

"Would I lie to you, Packy?"

"Yeah. Every time you open your damn mouth. Hey, listen, lawyer, what do you get out of this if I get the cash?"

"I keep getting that question. I'm beginning to think you people don't trust me. I'm sensitive about that, Packy."

"Cut the crap. Answer the question."

"If I can get you the price originally agreed on, I'm sure you wouldn't mind cutting me in for, say, fifteen percent."

Packy rebounded faster than I gave him credit for. "Ten percent."

If it panned out the way I hoped, the percentage would be irrelevant, but I had to make a show. "Thirteen percent."

"Twelve percent."

"Done."

I laid out the ground rules as I had for the O'Byrnes. Packy was edgy on a point or two, but the prospect of a good cash flow won out.

I set the time of the meeting for the following day to give me time to get a few details in line—details that I chose not to share with my prospective meeting mates. The place of the meeting was to be a small private meeting room in the Hilton Hotel on Dalton Street in the Back Bay. I wanted privacy in a public place, but not my dear old Parker House. When I put nitro and glycerin together, there could be an explosion to which I would not subject that grande dame of hotels.

Seamus and I showed up first. We arranged the table to accommodate Packy on one end, Frank and Kevin on the other, and me in the middle. Seamus would stand at the door to prevent unexpected intruders. We could trust either one of the attendees as far as we could throw the hotel.

Packy was the first to arrive. He had two Italian bodyguards with him as provided for in my house rules. Kevin and Frank were hard on their heels, followed closely by their two Irish bodyguards.

The glaring and staring of daggers that went on could have ignited an inferno. This was the touchy part. If we got as far as having everyone seated, I figured it would be a victory no matter what happened next.

That being the priority, I did all the talking. One hot word by anyone else in the room could have touched off heaven knows what. According to the rules, Seamus ran a search of each of the four bodyguards in turn for weapons. He indicated that they passed.

I had suggested, and it was mutually agreed, that as a token of trust the principal parties would not be searched. That was pure posturing on my part to pretend that a microgram of trust existed in that room. In fact, I would have bet my Bruins tickets that the O'Byrnes and Packy were all armed to the teeth. I also could not have cared less. I was betting that no bullets would fly before the business portion of the meeting was concluded. At that point, Seamus and I would be out of there, possibly leaving skid marks.

At last, all the players were in position. I proposed that on my signal, the O'Byrnes place their suitcase of cash on the table in front of them and Packy place the bag of diamonds, which I had slipped to him when he came in, on the table in front of him. Nods from both sides.

"Good. On three. One. Two. Three."

So far so good. Each performed like a trained pony.

"And now, gentlemen. We make the switch. On three."

"Hold it right there!"

That came from Frank, and it was just what I was counting on him to say.

"Is there a problem, Mr. O'Byrne?"

"Yeah. I'd say there's a problem. With all the shuckin' and jivin' that's been goin' on, how do we know they're real? Could be another one of your little glass tricks."

I couldn't have written the script for him better.

"Then let's test it. Mr. Salviti, the diamonds, please."

Packy passed the leather bag to me. I carefully poured the diamonds out of the bag onto the table in front of me and spread them out.

"Mr. O'Byrne, point to any one of the diamonds."

He squinted at me with a piercingly suspicious look.

"No trick. Any one you want."

He pointed to one of the diamonds. I made a graceful gesture that would have done Harry Wong proud in picking up the indicated diamond. I held it between open fingers to show I was not pulling a switch. I walked directly to a magnificent mirror over a false fireplace on the wall behind me. With a bit of a flare that I couldn't help enjoying, I carved my initials smoothly and fluidly with a sharp edge of the diamond deeply into the thick glass of the mirror. I figured I could pay for the mirror later.

I turned back to the table. "Gentlemen, is there anything further to say?"

There was a silence that I took to mean that the stone had passed the test. I walked back to my seat at the table. I caught Frank's eye and with a gesture invited him to watch carefully as I replaced the diamonds carefully one by one in the leather bag. That completed I sat down. Now going for the gold.

"Gentlemen, I have just two requests to make before we complete the deal. We're alone in this room. Every one of us is party to this and everything that's led up to this moment. That means that if one of us goes to prison, we could all go to prison for any part of it, including murder."

I looked into each face. Every eye was glued on me, and no one knew enough law to disagree.

"That being the case, before we conclude this transaction, since each of us is in equal legal jeopardy, for the sake of us all, I'd like to know what happened the night this all began."

There were some side-glances between the O'Byrnes, but no one spoke.

"In other words, if I'm going to benefit from the murder of Salvatore Barone, I'd like to know who takes the credit for it."

Packy and Frank, as I'd imagined, knew enough to keep their mouths shut. Kevin, on the other hand, was like the kid in class who can't wait to get his hand in the air.

"That was me."

Kevin said it with a look at his father as if he were expecting Frank to rejoice that his son had, as the Italians say, made his bones like a man. Frank instantaneously snapped a look at Kevin that left Kevin's mouth hanging. "Shut up, Kevin. Damn it."

I jumped in to keep the train from derailing just yet. "No harm done, Mr. O'Byrne. As I say, we're all in this together. If one of us falls, we all fall. I think that insures our mutual discretion."

Frank was still glaring at Kevin, but anything worse than a look had been averted. I retreated to less sensitive ground.

"Then, gentlemen, there's just one last bit of business. It's personal. This case has been one to remember. I'd simply like as a memento to have that leather bag that's carried those rocks all the way from Africa. Any objection, Mr. O'Byrne?"

I think he was still evaluating any danger from Kevin's last outburst. He just shook his head.

"Then watch carefully. Please hold out your hand and count them, Mr. O'Byrne."

I poured the diamonds slowly out of the bag to allow him to count each one up to twenty-two. The count was right, but O'Byrne was still giving me a suspicious look.

"I want you to be satisfied, Mr. O'Byrne."

I reached over and between two fingers took one of the stones from his hand. I went back to the mirror and elaborately etched his initials in the smooth deep glass. That seemed to satisfy him to the point where I felt comfortable in handing him back the diamond and sliding the open briefcase with the cash across the table to Packy.

That done, I stood. "Gentlemen, we've all done well here today. Let's do it again soon."

I gave Seamus the signal that this was probably a choice moment to get the hell out of Dodge. He held the door, and I was through it as fast as order and decorum would allow.

I whispered to Seamus, "Close the door behind us." He did. I figured that this was when nitro and glycerin would merge, and I would have no control whatsoever. On the other hand, I grabbed Seamus's arm and stopped him a short distance down the corridor.

I had no way of actually knowing what would happen, but I'd have bet my life on my prediction. It was less than a count of five before four gunshots came from the room and echoed down the corridor. Seamus and I gave it another fifteen seconds. We ran back to the room and knocked. One of the Italian bodyguards opened the door.

The first glimpse we had was of Kevin and Frank O'Byrne both splayed across the floor behind their chairs. Each had a gun in his hand. Neither was moving. My second look was at the two Italian bodyguards. Each had a service revolver in his hand with a trickle of smoke coming out of the barrel. It was about ten seconds later that Packy crawled out from under the table.

I looked at the Italian who'd opened the door. "What happened, Marty?"

"It was like you said, Mr. Knight. The O'Byrnes both pulled guns. They were going to open fire on us and Salviti. They wanted to take both the diamonds and the money. Pete and I got shots off first. It's a good thing you told us what might happen."

Seamus was squinting question marks in my direction. I hadn't let him in on the whole plan on the need-to-know theory.

"I forgot to tell you, Seamus. The two bodyguards for Packy are cops. They're Italian so it would look right. That's why I told you to overlook the guns strapped to their legs when you frisked them. I wanted them here to listen for Kevin's confession to the murder. I guess it doesn't make much difference now."

Packy was still shaking. I picked up the twenty-two diamonds that Frank was still clutching. "Packy, I'm going to do this deal with you in reverse."

I opened Packy's hand and put the diamonds into it. He could barely hold them, he was shaking so badly. His eyes popped. It was like a personal gift from Santa Claus. I picked up the briefcase of money. "Since Frank gave this to you, I'll take it in payment for the diamonds. Square?"

Packy was so delighted to come out of it with his life, let alone diamonds, he just nodded. Seamus and I went out the door with a last word to the Italian cops. "You did well, boys. If you need a statement for your report about the shooting, you know where to find me."

Seamus and I walked the streets of Boston until my blood pressure came back down to something that was within measurement. The end of our trek was an Irish pub on Beacon Street for about four Guinnesses.

When we were well into the second, Seamus gave me a funny look. "I'm surprised at ya, Michael."

I looked back at him. "Oh?"

"After we've chased those damn diamonds all over hell and back, what in the world possessed ya to give them to that scumbag Salviti?"

"Well, Seamus, it's this way. My heart began to ache for him. He's had a hard life. His father was a poor but honest bootlegger. His mother had to sell spaghetti on the corner to make ends meet. The lad never had a pony growing up. All of his friends—"

"Oh, cut the bullshit. I mean it, Michael. You could have slipped a few of them to me for the effort."

"You mean these, Seamus?"

I took twenty-two diamonds out of my pocket and held them under his nose.

"What the hell?"

"I'm not as daft as you think. You know this leather bag I wanted for a keepsake? I'd put another leather bag inside of it with a small hole in it before I came to the meeting. When I made a big show of putting the diamonds back into the bag, I was slipping them through the little hole in the inside bag. That's why I wanted to keep the bag. When Frank had no objections to me keeping the bag, I just poured into his hand twenty-two other diamonds I had stashed in the small inside bag. I kept the bag with the original twenty-two diamonds in the bottom."

He leaned back and looked at me. "You *are* a bloody genius." He took a few sips and then snapped back. "But why the hell did you give those other diamonds to Packy?"

"Let him keep 'em. They're low-grade industrial diamonds. I

bought the whole bunch for two thousand dollars. As you say, something for his effort."

A grin crept across Seamus's face. "I'm getting' to know you better every day, Yank. You scammed old Packy. You figure stealin' from a thief is not stealin' at all."

I took a deep breath for this one. I put a hand on his shoulder. He caught my seriousness. The smile was gone. "It's not over, Seamus. I didn't do this for you or me. Your man, Declan O'Connor, told me about the African who brought these cursed diamonds from some hellhole in Africa. He's got a need deeper than anything in our lives. He's with Declan now. My friend, you and I are going to take a flight to Ireland. What do you think of that?"

# PART SIX

# CHAPTER THIRTY-SIX

Seamus and I landed at the Dublin Airport and walked out into a brisk early morning drizzle. I couldn't sleep on the flight. Every time I'd start to doze, I'd be jabbed awake by a shot of adrenalin at the thought of what lay ahead. Seamus slept like a baby. I hadn't told him what I'd be getting him involved in over the next couple of weeks.

We didn't even check into the Gresham Hotel. That could wait, but I couldn't. I'd called Declan O'Connor the night before and asked him to have his African friend—the one he knew as Johnny Walker—in his office at ten a.m. I gave him no clue as to why.

I may have been guilty of relishing to excess the drama of what was about to happen, as Seamus has occasionally reminded me. I figured I'd paid for the moment in close calls and near misses on my life over the previous couple of weeks.

Declan reintroduced us to Johnny Walker, who had met us only briefly in the Dublin hospital. He was courteous but totally clueless about why he was meeting with this Irishman and Yank again. Declan suggested an adjournment to the Brazen Head for a pint or three while we chatted. I rejected the idea out of hand. I was chomping at the bit to get to it, and I felt we needed a totally private time with Mr. Walker.

By the time we settled into four chairs in Declan's private office, we were all on a first-name basis. My flare for dramatic timing had the other three, including Seamus, over the top on the curiosity scale. I could feel every nerve in my body jumping, and the others sensed it.

It was my show. I opened by asking Johnny what he had planned on doing with the diamonds or the cash they might have brought. I kept a somber face, but it couldn't match that of Johnny. He was dredging deep inside to talk about a driving personal goal that now had not a chance in hell of being accomplished because of the loss of the diamonds.

I kept it all inside, while I let him talk about the lost dream of ransoming his father. He even mentioned the utopian thought of his father, his brother, and him escaping to a life anywhere on earth except Sierra Leone. He finished close to tears, and I couldn't stand it one more second.

I pulled my chair over to look him directly face-to-face. He had to see in my eyes that what I would say was not a lie or a dream.

"Johnny, I have no idea how you'll do what you planned. But it won't be the lack of money that'll keep you from doing it."

I reached into my pocket and took out the now-worn leather bag that he had carried from Freetown to Dublin and had put into the hands of Salvatore Barone in that very office. His eyes told me he still didn't believe it.

I handed it to him. He felt it tentatively to see if there was anything in it. His eyes began to widen when he felt the tiny solid lumps. I could see his fingers shaking when he pulled open the strings and took out the rough stones one by one.

He looked up at the three of us with an expression that asked if they were real. I just nodded, and he knew. And the knowledge overwhelmed him. The tears flowed. I could see in his face the desperation being smothered in a slowly rising surge of hope. It was almost too much for him to take in at that moment.

He just looked at me with one word. "How?"

I looked at Seamus. He had the third grin I'd seen cross his face since I'd known him. I looked back at Johnny because he'd only heard half of the story. When I thought he could absorb it, I finished the telling.

"Johnny, those diamonds are extremely high quality. I have an offer for them from a chap in Antwerp for something around a million and a quarter euros. I'm sure Declan can get him up to that full amount."

Declan's eyes showed surprise at being drawn into the group as an actor. I looked at him with an expression that asked for a commitment. He held up his hands in a "why not?" gesture.

"The buyer made the offer to a young man we followed to Antwerp. He's out of the picture now. I'm sure the buyer doesn't care who's selling them. Declan can probably do the deal tomorrow. Yes?"

Declan chimed in with, "Quite possibly."

"Good. Johnny, we'll have the money put in an account at your disposal."

The tears had stopped, but he just sat there looking at the stones and shaking his head. I figured I'd better lay it all open so he could adjust his world to the entirely new reality.

"Johnny, there's more. Listen to me."

I briefly sketched in the last meeting we'd had with Frank and Kevin O'Byrne and Packy Salviti. Without too many specifics, I intimated that Packy Salviti had given me a briefcase full of cash in payment for certain other diamonds. The total amount in the briefcase was equal to one million euros. I didn't mention that the profit on the hasty deal with Packy was enormous since I had bought those particular cheap industrial diamonds in Antwerp for a couple of thousand dollars. Packy lost a bundle of money on the deal. There may be hell to pay later. That's his business. All things considered, he was lucky to walk out of that hotel room with his life.

"Here's the bottom line, Johnny. In addition to those diamonds you started with, Seamus and I will set up an account in your name for the additional million euros. They'll be at your disposal. That should cover whatever you have in mind."

Johnny was frozen to the chair as if he could not move a muscle. He just looked from one of us to the other. No words could get around what he was feeling, so nothing was coming out. For some reason, it started the rest of us laughing. It was just a letting out of the best feeling we'd had, perhaps in a lifetime. At some point, Johnny joined in the senseless laughter and the waterworks started all over again.

It was about eleven that morning when we did adjourn to the Brazen Head and took a quiet booth in the back of the pub. On the walk there, Johnny was slowly able to get his mind around the reality that his dream, his plan, was now full steam ahead. It was like watching a virtual cadaver come bounding back to life. It was hard to get him to stop pouring out his gratitude and focus on what he intended to do. Once he did, he got down to details. The more he talked, the more details he laid out for us, and the more the details gelled into a plan.

It was a wild plan. It was like nothing I'd ever imagined being a part of in my life, but I wanted very much to be a part of it. It was right up Seamus's alley. I could see him signing on almost from the beginning of the telling.

It was dark outside when we left the Brazen Head with a solid Irish dinner under our belts and a fairly concrete idea of what the four of us would be jumping into when the next sun came up.

The following morning, Johnny, Seamus, and I were at the airport to board a flight for Freeport, Sierra Leone. Johnny had telephoned his brother, Sinda, at the Mammy Yoko Hotel the previous evening. They had apparently shared the first moment of the sheer joy of optimism they had experienced since they were children together in their village.

Johnny filled us in on Sinda's previous life with the RUF. His familiarity with the lay of the land in Sierra Leone made him the right choice for the piece of the plan that Johnny placed completely in his hands.

When the plane landed at the Lungi Airport, I could see a subtle change come over Johnny. Before we passed through customs, he reintroduced himself to Seamus and myself in his real identity and in his real name, Bantu.

The cab ride from the airport into Freetown was a wrenching shock in a number of ways. The blast of over one-hundred-degree heat and sky-high humidity was the least jarring. The most unnerving jolt was the hammering realization that such extreme poverty could exist in any country, let alone one salted with the potential wealth of Sierra Leone's diamonds. The blatantly clear misfortune was that rampant greed and corruption had turned that wealth into the curse of constant fighting and deprivation for its people. I had read about a United Nations report that ranked Sierra Leone at about the bottom of its list of poverty-plagued countries. That was just words on a page. This was numbing reality.

The dregs of beggars of all stripes, including amputees who had fallen victim to the rebel RUF boy soldiers, littered more than populated the streets on that first drive through the heart of the city. By the time we reached the address Bantu gave the driver, I was deep in doubt that any amount of money or effort by us could lift any part of the squalor surrounding us to anything tolerable for human beings. I marveled at Bantu's optimism.

The three of us checked into a nondescript hotel in the center of Freetown. When we left the taxi, Bantu directed the driver to pick up another passenger staying at the Mammy Yoko Hotel and bring him to us. Bantu used no names, but I knew it was his brother, Sinda.

Our little group, now four, gathered at Bantu's room within half an hour. Bantu waved us in. He was on the phone. I could hear his side of the conversation with someone named Jimbo. He was apparently someone Bantu trusted who had contacts like an army master sergeant to acquire anything manufactured on this planet for a price.

I could hear Bantu relaying a shopping list that had my mind spinning even though I had a fair idea of the plan. The last words of the conversation were to set up a meeting between Jimbo and Bantu that evening in the bar of the hotel.

Bantu introduced us to Sinda, and the talk got serious. I realized that Sinda had taken on a part of the operation that was totally separate from ours, and time was crucial. He needed access to the funds in the account we had set up in both his and Bantu's name. We gave him the necessary information, and after some heartfelt wishes of success, he left and blended into the night.

Bantu relayed to Seamus and me what he had learned from Sinda. Apparently, the government forces had been successful in driving the RUF rebels back and retaking many of the diamond pits in the eastern part of the country. The RUF still held a few pits in the northeast, including one large one where they now concentrated their boy-soldier force. This was where they kept the bulk of their store of weapons, and to our particular interest, where they held most of the slaves as pit workers and mules to smuggle the diamonds across the Liberian border.

I asked Bantu if that was where his father was being held. The best answer Sinda had been able to give him was "most likely."

Sinda could, however, give with assurance the one piece of information we needed immediately. The RUF general in charge of acquiring the two most basic needs of the RUF—weapons and drugs—had his headquarters in a bar in Freetown exclusively occupied by RUF troops.

Bantu huddled with Seamus and me to lay out strategy for the opening move. "We need to make a deal with this general. We need to sell him a large supply of new AK-47s and cases of ammunition. We'll make the price attractive. Delivery on-site for payment in three days. That'll give Jimbo a chance to contact the arms dealers in town and put a shipment together."

"Good. When do you see this general?"

He put his hand on my shoulder and for the first time looked tentative. "I don't. You and Seamus may not like this. You can always say no. It has to be done by a white man. The big arms dealers in Sierra Leone are generally white. I can't ask you to do it. But if you volunteer? I can only promise it will be dangerous."

He looked at me, and I looked at my Irish freedom fighter. There was no hesitation written on his face. I had no desire to die in Sierra Leone, but I had to match his grit.

"When and where?"

"Tonight. There's a bar in town. Get some rest. I'll send word to the general you'll be there at ten to do business."

Seamus and I picked up a couple of white cotton, prewrinkled suits. By the time we wore them through the day in hundred-degree heat, they were flavored like any other dealer in scurrilous merchandise in that community. I figured our accents may be out of sync with the trade, but at least our wardrobe would blend.

At about ten fifteen that evening, just late enough to show a confident contempt for the general's time, Seamus and I strode slowly into the bar. As predicted, it looked like a biker's bar for a band of degenerates. I was prepared for that, but not for the teen and subteen ages of the inhabitants.

There wasn't an eye in the bar that wasn't glued to these white creatures from the cast of *Star Wars*. I noticed some of them hoisting their ubiquitous AK-47s from the tables to a ready position. As I'd learned in the past, and as Seamus was born knowing, we never made eye contact with any of them.

The second protocol was to take a direct route to the man with the information, the bartender, and walk at a slow, unconcerned pace. It also helped not to move my lips while I prayed.

Thank God, practically everyone in Sierra Leone speaks some form of English, that being the official national language. I told the bartender the general was expecting us. He looked doubtful, but he knocked on the door behind him and said something unintelligible. There was some small outburst from the room behind him. When it subsided, he waved us in.

We walked in. The door closed behind us. The first thing I saw across the room against the wall was a massive couch that looked like a Goodwill reject. Seated pompously in the center with a barely teenage girl on either side was the smoldering figure of what I assumed was the general.

My second awareness once inside was of four boy soldiers, none of them over fifteen years from the look of it. Each of them had a weapon slung over his shoulder. One was beside the couch and the other three were lined up behind us.

More than all the rest of it, what had my nerves strung tight were the two girls. I knew the whole dynamic would be askew if the general was playing tough for the benefit of the girls. That could double the unpredictability. The second assault on rationality was that the eyes of the four boy soldiers showed the intense agitation of drugs.

"You late!"

The general's bark jolted the soldiers around us. I expected it, and so did Seamus. We just cruised on. I stopped about five feet in front of the general. Seamus stood between me and the boys behind us with his hand on the back of a wooden chair.

"We were detained. Shall we do business?"

"You got guns to sell? New guns?"

"Dozens of them. Cases of ammunition to go with them."

The general grinned with a side-glance at the girl on his right. "Then, we do business. We do business my way."

"Meaning?"

The grin broadened. "Meaning you my prisoners." He pointed to a phone on the wall. "You call now. You have guns brought here. When I see guns, I may be generous. You get to leave with your lives. You hear me?"

The words, *Up shit's creek*, and many like it rolled like subtitles across my mind. Over it all, I kept saying to myself *Hold it together!*

I dropped my voice out of the soprano that would have come out. "Seamus, we have a situation. What shall we do about these people?"

Seamus appeared as cool as if he were watching a rugby match in Dublin. He looked at the juveniles glaring at us. "Oh, for the love of all the saints, Michael, what's your pleasure? Do you want me to blow their noses or wipe their little arses?"

That did it. The soldier beside the general grabbed the rifle strap and swung the weapon into firing position. The hyped-up look in his eyes meant business.

The gun barely rose to shoulder level. Seamus's massive fist clenched on the wooden chair beside him. He moved faster than my eyes could see. He hurled the chair from the floor in a direct line at the soldier beside the general. One leg caught him square on the forehead. Another doubled him up in the stomach. The gun flew in the air, and the boy was on the ground out cold as a mackerel.

It was a ballet. In the instant Seamus's hand was jetting the chair forward, a thrust of his left foot caught the soldier behind him in a doubling-up crunch to the groin. The other two against the wall pulled their rifles into position, but the shock of it all caused them to lose a critical fraction of a second. In that instant, Seamus pulled a pistol from inside his jacket and fired two rounds into the legs of each of them that sent them sprawling and cursing.

The general was on his feet and just gaping. The girls were on the floor covering their heads. My most immediate concern now was a rush into the room, guns blazing, by the dozen soldiers in the bar. I just froze. At first, I could only hear the groaning of the two with leg wounds. The seconds passed. No one came through the door.

Then I heard it. Roars of laughter from the bar. I thanked God when I realized that they must have thought it was the two white dudes who were getting their asses mauled by the brave RUF troops. So be it.

If ever a situation needed immediate seizing, it was then—the next step of Bantu's plan needed accomplishing.

"Sit down, General. I came to do business. Guns. Bullets. Remember? Now we do it my way. The price is ten thousand euros. No bargaining. You can pay in diamonds on delivery. Yes or no. I don't give a damn. I already have an offer from the Kamajors."

The boy general was still recovering from the small massacre around him. What pulled him back to the conversation was the mention of the tribal force that had always fought the RUF with just machetes and spears. AK-47s could change the balance.

"I'll have an answer, General. While we're still young."

He looked at me, but nothing came out. I turned and started toward the door.

"Come on, Seamus. No one home here."

A voice that was ineffectively trying to regain steam stopped me. "Wait. When?"

"Delivery in three days. By my trucks. You pay me then. Yes or no?"

"All right. We do business."

"Where do we deliver them?"

"Never mind where. I send man to meet you here. He go with you. Show you where."

"Done. One last item, General. Look around you." I nodded at the strewn bodies. "Don't disappoint me. Now get your ass off that couch and walk us out of here. You go first. Remember, Rambo here'll be right behind you."

Seamus and I hit the still-sweltering air outside and kept walking. We covered a few streets in several different directions to lose any would-be followers on the way back to the hotel.

Bantu was waiting at the door. I could see the anxiety in his eyes. "How did it go?"

I was about to elaborate, but Seamus summed it up.

"Piece of cake."

# CHAPTER THIRTY-SEVEN

It was all hands on deck on the morning of the third day. The sun was hardly up when Seamus and I hopped into Bantu's rented Jeep. We drove to the general's bar. His man was ready to climb aboard to show us where the rifles were to be delivered. He was about fourteen, trying to act thirty in the unaccustomed company of a couple of white copassengers. His bravado came off as surliness, but who cared. We needed directions, not conversation.

We drove out of the city and picked up a slightly paved road into the thick of the jungle. It was banana trees, dense vegetation, and animal sounds until we rounded a bend into a sizeable clearing. All of a sudden, we were reminded of what we'd taken on.

The road was clogged with two massive, armylike trucks with camouflage canvas covering the cargo section. A man jumped down from the cab of the lead truck and introduced himself simply as Jimbo. He and Bantu just smiled and nodded to each other as if all the preparations had been talked out before.

There was no time for sipping tea and idle chat. Jimbo got up into the cab of the second truck in line. I took a seat beside him. Bantu took the wheel of the lead truck and Seamus rode shotgun for him. Our surly navigator squeezed in beside Seamus.

The convoy rumbled on over the rutted jungle road, whacking branches when it got narrow and baking in the sun when the clearing for the road expanded.

We rolled on without stopping until the sun was just beginning to drop below the level of the treetops. The first inkling that it was zero hour came with a blast of the horn of the lead truck. Bantu pulled to a stop in front of a roughly constructed fence of barbed wire. The horn brought two soldiers with rifles out of the woods. They trained the rifles in our direction until our guide in his RUF camouflage T-shirt, shorts, and flip-flops hopped down and announced the arrival of weapons.

One of the guards pulled the poles holding the barbed wire across the road to let us pass. I noticed they replaced the fencing behind us.

We drove on until we approached a massive clearing. There was a shallow, muddy pond twice the size of the pond in Boston's Public Garden. At least three dozen black bodies were bent over double in the smelling, fetid water working with large sifters. Eight guards with AK-47s over their shoulders kept an eye on every movement of the slaves in the pit.

The real beehive of activity was around a wooden barnlike structure. Twenty or so RUF soldiers were milling around the large open entrance. The AK-47s over their shoulders were as much a part of their uniforms as the camouflage T-shirts and flip-flops.

As planned, Bantu stayed in the cab of the truck. It was possible one of the guards could recognize him from the days of his own captivity. Jimbo jumped down and approached the boy with the ranking insignia on his shirt who came forward.

Jimbo was his usual smiling, jovial self. The boy officer was, as expected, officious and demanding. I could hear him command that the boxes of rifles be unloaded to the ground and opened before there'd be any talk of diamonds in return.

Some of the slaves were dragged out of the pit to do the heavy lifting, two men to a case. When that wasn't fast enough for the men at the barn, some of them joined in the effort. The hum now was centered on the cases of new rifles and ammunition.

The boy soldiers became as impatient as spoiled kids attacking Christmas loot. They began prying open cases. When the first gleaming new rifles emerged, the impatience doubled, and the activity around the cases became all-absorbing.

I could see Bantu now venture down from the cab of the truck. He stayed as well out of view as he could while scanning the faces of the slaves lifting cases and the ones in the pit. I could see frustration building as he looked from face to face without a shred of recognition.

It was just about then that I heard activity coming from the road we'd come in on. From the cab, I could see two RUF soldiers leading a straggling line of what looked like black bodies, at or beyond the point of exhaustion, laden with heavy sacks.

I jumped down and got close to Jimbo. "Who're they, Jimbo?"

He looked over at the new arrivals. "They mules. They slaves like these guys. They use'm to smuggle stones into Liberia. Carry weapons and drugs back. Looks of it, they probably walked all the way from the border."

The buzz continued around the cases we brought being cracked open and rifles being pulled out and handed around. I used the diversion to slip over to the edge of the pit where Bantu was scanning pathetic faces. I tapped him on the shoulder and tilted my head toward the line of staggering walkers who were now approaching the barn.

He looked over at the line. I could see him straining to match what he remembered from the time he was nine years old against the gaunt faces of the slaves in line.

I watched his eyes. I had a flashback to all of the crap Mr. Devlin and I had gone through with the O'Byrnes, Salviti, Barone—and all the crap Bantu must have gone through to bring us to this moment of what looked like a crushing defeat. As I looked at the condition of the slaves, it would have been another miracle if his father had survived it. I was sharing his heartbreak when I went to put my hand on his shoulder.

I got just that far when I heard him whisper through unmoving lips. "My God! My God! I don't believe it. Michael, is it possible?"

I looked where he was staring. A man who looked a hundred years old was staggering under a sack that bent him nearly double. Bantu and I both had the overwhelming urge to run to him, free him of the load, and carry his worn body out of that hellhole.

Bantu wiped away tears and straightened up. I could hear him mumble to himself. "Stick to the plan. Stick to the plan." He made his way back to the cab of the first truck and climbed in.

The excitement of the newness of the rifles was beginning to wear off. All of the wooden cases had been pried open to reveal no loads of rocks. I figured Jimbo had found a successful black market source among the scurvy lot of humanity in Freetown that dealt in that product. He must have used the money now in Bantu's account to buy them.

Now the attention was on unloading and cracking open the cases of ammunition. There, too, there was no deception. The commander was no dummy. He ordered a few of his soldiers to pick out a rifle, load it, and fire it. I remembered Bantu's tale of the rescue of his brother and the missing firing mechanism. If he was pulling that trick now, I knew I'd never live to see 77 Franklin Street again.

Thank God, the firing was a noisy, earsplitting success. The general now gave the command to have the slaves carry all of the cases into the barn. This was the moment I dreaded. It was time to collect the price from the commander. I didn't give a rat's ass if they paid ten cents for them. But the show had to go on, and it had to be convincing or we'd never pass through that gate again.

Jimbo did the bargaining. The commander produced a bag of rough stones, which I came to realize was the usual trading tender in those deals. Jimbo looked them over with what he pretended was a discerning eye. He expected to be cheated. The question was how much cheating he could accept and be believable.

I listened to the haggling for a full five minutes. I could hear Jimbo threaten to cut off any future supplies of these excellent, fresh-from-the-factory weapons. Eventually, and with great reluctance, the commander reached into his shirt and pulled out another small bag of stones. Jimbo was clever. He took the bag from the disgruntled commander, poured out half of the stones, and with his back to the other men, handed the bag with the rest back to the commander. He had made a friend, of sorts.

That was it. Deal concluded. Our little band, except for our soldier-guide, climbed back into the trucks. It must have broken Bantu's

heart, but he started the truck and drove slowly away from the pit.
Jimbo drove the second, now empty, truck close behind.

With one eye on the road and one on the rearview mirror, we
edged our way along the path. We watched as the soldiers, even those
at the pit, now gave full vent to their impatience to each grab a piece
of the gift Santa had brought. They ran to the barn and began
pulling rifles out of the boxes and stuffing ammunition into their
shirts.

I could see Bantu watching the line of slave mules come out of
the barn and amble to the filthy pit to splash water on their faces.
When they were all out, he stopped the truck and got out. He took a
small black box with push buttons on it from under the front seat of
the truck. I saw him hold it in his hand and stare back at the scene
behind him.

I could hear Bantu's words clear as day. "God help us. God help
us all."

He held the box in one hand and pushed one of the buttons with
one finger of the other. I thought the world was coming to an end. It
started with a crack like not-too-distant thunder. Then another,
louder. Then another, much louder. Then a rapid chain of explosions
that sounded like all of the deafening thunderclaps of all eternity.
Masses of fire burst through every opening in the blown roof and
out the splintered sides of the building. Pieces of wood and metal
were flying everywhere, carrying flames a hundred feet in the air.

At the first explosion, the boy soldiers dropped the loot they were
carrying. By the second they were in full-panic flight into the jungle.
They must have thought they were under attack by every United Nations force in Africa.

I looked back at the slaves in the pit and the mules beside it. They
were dumbstruck and frozen where they were. But Bantu was not,
and neither was Jimbo. They threw the trucks in reverse and backed
to the area of the pit. We all were out of the trucks and diving into
the furious business of helping the weakened bodies of the slaves—
now former slaves—into the back of the trucks. Some we supported,
some we outright carried. We started with the mules, because they

were closest. Bantu ran first with tears flowing to his father. His father didn't recognize him, but Bantu swept him up in his arms and carried him to the back of the truck. He gently placed him in the truck on a soft straw mat.

We ran back and forth dozens of times, until every one of those souls was out of that living hell and into one of the trucks. We were hitting high gear when we passed the gate guards running back to see if there was anything left of their camp.

When we reached the gate, it was full ramming speed. We shattered the wire fence, probably dragging some of it with us, but who cared?

We rode all night, heading west, picking up jungle roads that only Jimbo could have known. Our passengers needed food and water, but there was time for that when we reached safety.

I was riding with Bantu at that point. When we were nearing Freetown, I heard him use his cell phone to call his brother, Sinda. "Where do we take them, Sinda? What have you got for us?"

That was when I realized what part Sinda was playing in this epoch. I saw a grin spread from Bantu's ear to ear. He was practically yelling into the phone. "A village! You bought a village!"

Bantu turned to me with a face that could light up Africa. "My God! He bought a whole village!"

# CHAPTER THIRTY-EIGHT

I could see the glowing red ball of the sun rising on the rim of the eastern horizon when Jimbo drove the lead truck of our little convoy into the cleared outskirts of what looked like a village of huts. It was totally deserted, except for the waving and grinning figure of Sinda running to meet the first truck.

He waved Jimbo to pull directly into the large clearing in what looked like the center of the village, and Bantu followed. With the trucks stopped, we all got to work at a fever pitch to carry our depleted passengers out of the truck and into the protective shade of the huts. Sinda started to do the directing. With each weak body we lifted out of a truck, he'd point to a hut.

The first body Bantu carefully lifted out of the lead truck, he brought, running, to Sinda. Sinda looked down at the face of the man Bantu was holding. "My God, Bantu! It's him! I can't—"

Sinda reached out and took the nearly unconscious body into his arms. He carried his father to the nearest hut and laid him on a mat. Bantu took over the directing.

Sinda had apparently gathered some local help. I saw men and women of about our age come running from the river beside the village with fresh drinking water for each person once he was put in the hut that was to be his new home. Once the fear of dehydration was taken care of, the helpers began bathing the crusted, clinging slime from the bodies of those who had been in the pits.

When the relocation was complete, we all shifted our focus to distributing bowls of thick soup Sinda had brewed over a cooking fire in the area that would later be used for meals. For some, it was the first thing resembling a meal in their memory.

Jimbo, who was a man of many talents, put to use his early Mandingo training in curative leaves and poultices for those who had lesions and open sores.

The running never slackened through the day. We all ran from job to job at a furious pace. There was always something more we could do. But I was not too occupied to see Sinda and Bantu in the hut of their father. They bathed his stench-encrusted body and provided him the first of the clean clothes Sinda had purchased in Freetown and brought to the village for all the new arrivals.

In the evening, when the activity settled, the two brothers had a long hour to spend with their father. I think it took most of the hour to convince him that he was free, and that his sons and he were on the threshold of a new life.

I helped with the preparation and distribution of the evening stew and then finally collapsed beside Seamus in the eating area. We were well into a bowl of what was actually a very good concoction before we could really talk. Bantu and Sinda dropped down beside us. They, too, ate for the first time in two days.

The first words I could get out to Sinda were simply, "How did you do this?" One wave of the hand indicated that I meant the empty and waiting village. We all had the same question.

"I knew this village was here. During the conflict, it was raided by rebels. They killed most of the people. Took the rest as slaves. I knew it was deserted."

Jimbo had the follow-up. "Does anyone know we're here?"

"Some. Not many. I went to the right people in the government. I have a paper that says this village is ours."

"How did you do it?"

"The easy way. I bribed the right people. Very generously, thanks to what you brought us, Michael."

"Do we worry about them?"

"No. I told them the bribes would keep on coming as long as they gave us protection. And stayed the hell out of our village."

I looked at Seamus and nodded at Sinda. "There's the damn genius. Not me."

I lay back against a box of medical supplies and drew a deep breath for the first time since the plane touched down in Sierra Leone. I could see the bright yellow-red orb of the sun half hidden by the horizon. It reminded me of Benjamin Franklin's question when he looked at the painting of the half sun on the back of John Hancock's chair at the moment they were signing the Declaration of Independence. Was that sun rising or setting?

I looked around at "our" village. The evening meal had been served, and the people who could scarcely walk when we picked them up were now coming out of the huts and gathering together in groups. For the first time, they dared to speak to each other. I knew then that that sun was definitely rising.

We lit a large fire in the center of the village and sat around it talking until I thought the sun would be coming up for a new day. The ideas and plans were flying. Sinda had given it a lot of thought. He said a larger tent would be arriving to be used for a dining hall, looking to the day when all the now invalids would be able to walk to meals.

"We'll put another tent over there for medical supplies. I can't believe it. Some nurses from the city want to come out to work with us. Even a couple of doctors. There'll be more."

There was talk of a school, because Sinda said some women from other villages wanted to come here and get involved in the work. That meant that eventually there would be marriages and children.

I could see Bantu looking at a large clearing on the edge of the village. "What are you thinking, Bantu?"

"Right over there. We build a church. It'll have a roof for the rainy season, but no walls. We're going to grow. That way it'll hold as many as come to us and want to thank God."

"Amen."

The following morning, the hum started all over again. I pitched in for the meal distribution, but then it was time. I felt a real part of this new life, but I had another one that included a senior partner, a practice, and, most importantly, a fiancée.

Seamus and I got together for a ride in the Jeep to the airport. Sinda and Jimbo said their good-byes between running from one tent to another with fresh bandages and whatever help was needed.

Bantu walked us to the Jeep. There was nothing to say that wasn't completely expressed in one long hug. Even for my warrior friend, Seamus.

"Bantu, you said once that you and your brother and your father would find a home anywhere but in Sierra Leone. Are you coming with us?"

He just smiled and shook his head. "I'm home now, Michael."

Just then we heard Sinda calling. "Bantu, we need help over here!"

Bantu grinned from within. "You see?"

My last view of Bantu was seeing him run to help his father walk to the dining tent. He was still grinning.

I slept through the entire flight home. Reverse culture shock hit me with a vengeance when I walked down Franklin Street the next morning. The streets of Boston never looked so good.

My plans for a career of title searching dissolved in my first two-hour chat with Mr. Devlin. After a long monologue to fill him in on the Sierra Leone adventure, which was to end with my declaration of a new career path of nothing more adventurous than title searches, he jumped in to mention that one of my favorite jockeys at Suffolk Downs had been indicted for murder in a case that smacked of Mafia doings. The jockey was expecting a call from his choice of defense counsel—me. *Sic transit pax.*

About two weeks later, I got a letter with the return address of Free-town, Sierra Leone. The note inside from Bantu brought moisture to my eyes and a watermelon in my throat. It seems that more and more of the victims of the years of conflict were hearing of what was now being called Resurrection Village. New arrivals were coming in every day. Sinda had had to rebribe the governmental authorities to get the rights to two other nearby abandoned villages.

That was good news. Even better was the news that most of our original settlers we brought back from the pit, including his father, had bounced back to the point where they were working their hearts out to serve the new arrivals.

And so it grew. I guess you can't stop the Lord when he has good people in his corner.

When I picked up the envelope to replace the letter, something dropped out of it. It was wrapped in a banana leaf for luck. The note attached said, "May God bless you and your bride as you have blessed us. Bantu."

Inside the leaf was a sparkling diamond. It will be worn on Terry's finger as our engagement ring forever.

And one last thought. I'm delighted to announce that Terry and I have set the date. The wedding will be next spring.

Needless to say, Father Matt Ryan will perform the ceremony in the Sacred Heart Church in Charlestown.

In view of the passing of Terry's parents some years ago, she will be escorted down the aisle and given away by another father figure, Lex Devlin.

I'm sure it's no surprise that my best man will be my friend and adventure mate these many years, Harry Wong. I can't wait to hear the toast.

Sadly, John Kiley, our chosen organist, is now playing for the Lord, but his beautiful musical spirit will be there for sure.

The reception will be—where else?—the Parker House.

YOU ARE ALL INVITED.

# AUTHOR'S NOTE

The centerpiece of all the fuss, the diamond, is a unique piece of geology. Particular carbon atoms that, by a happenstance of nature, have been subjected to extreme pressures and temperatures up to 2,300 degrees Fahrenheit for millions of years at a level of 125 miles below the earth's surface are transmuted into a rough, milky stone, 1,000 times harder than rubies or sapphires.

Diamonds are then blasted through the earth's layers during volcanic eruptions in discrete channels called "pipes." They emerge to lie on or just under the surface of the earth to be mined, usually by some method of sifting, by whoever controls the small plot of the land at the top of the pipe.

Thanks to the hundred-year-old monopolistic trick pulled off by the De Beers Group in capturing most sources of rough diamonds, whetting the appetite of the world's consumers with the hypnotic slogan, "Diamonds are Forever," and releasing the supply of diamonds in a trickle, the impression has been indelibly created that diamonds are a rarity and therefore legitimately expensive.

Sierra Leone has been uniquely blessed with an abundance of pipes that have left quality diamonds strewn on or just under the surface for the taking. What could have been a natural endowment sufficient to turn the country into a paradise devoid of hunger, poverty, ignorance, and preventable disease has been turned into an unimaginable curse that has placed Sierra Leone at or near the bottom of the United Nations's list of 170 nations in degree of poverty.

The recipe for this curse is a government that has been a poster child for greed, graft, and corruption, combined with a rebel force, the Revolutionary United Front (RUF), that has massacred and terrorized the population in the diamond-rich areas of eastern Sierra Leone in order to control the mining, smuggling, and sale of the diamonds that finance the RUF's war on innocent humanity.

To be clear, the inhuman atrocities—and that is too mild a phrase by any measure—committed by the RUF and its captive child soldiers on many thousands of innocent villagers and townspeople of Sierra Leone are so far beyond anything I would have thought to be within the capability of human beings, that I have scarcely touched on them in the course of this novel. It is not overly dramatic to say that I have tried to convey some sense of the situation without being specific or comprehensive enough to subject the reader to the nightmares I've actually experienced in researching this book.

The diamonds, mined by slave labor, are smuggled by the RUF across the easy compliant border of Liberia. They buy rifles (primarily Kalashnikov AK-47s), ammunition, and rocket-propelled grenade launchers. They also buy the drugs fed to the child soldiers to enable them to commit acts under orders that no human being in control of their faculties could bring themselves to commit.

Lest we think that that this war on humanity affects only victims in a small country 4,300 miles from New York, consider this: In 2001, it is reported that representatives of Osama bin Laden's Al Qaeda network were in the Kono diamond district of Sierra Leone to oversee operations and arrange a purchase of millions of dollars' worth of diamonds from the RUF. Time was of the essence. It was only two months to September 11, 2001. Production in the diamond pits by the RUF was reported to be doubled.

The first retaliatory move of the United States after 9/11 was to freeze the financial accounts of bin Laden. If, however, as appears likely from reports, bin Laden was successful in converting millions of dollars in cash to easily stashed and saleable blood diamonds, the funding of Al Qaeda continued.

In March 2000, Robert Fowler, Canada's ambassador to the United Nations, released a commissioned report revealing in detail the link between the smuggling trade in "blood" or "conflict" diamonds and the hellish conflicts it finances. Global Witness conducted a campaign to pressure the United Nations, diamond-producing nations, and the legitimate diamond industry to produce a plan to stem the flow of illicit blood diamonds into the channel of legitimate diamonds that ultimately make their way into the shops of jewelry retailers that you and I patronize.

The result was the Kimberley Process Certification Scheme (KPCS), endorsed and established by the United Nations in 2003. The plan requires participating governments to provide documents certifying the legitimacy of source of all sealed packages of rough diamonds leaving their countries. These certificates are to accompany the rough diamonds through the channels to the diamond cutters and polishers in, e.g., Antwerp, and on to the retailers. Under the plan, participant countries are only allowed to trade their gems with other participant countries. Since 2012, fifty-four participants representing eighty countries have signed on to the Kimberley Process.

It's a step, but how effective is it? Reports indicate that it has had some effect in at least increasing the income from the legitimate diamond trade to the governments of countries that have been most victimized by diamond-fueled conflicts. However, an evil this entrenched and this profitable to smugglers, gunrunners, and mid-level dealers dies hard, if at all. Diamonds are the most easily transported valuable asset in the world. A person can carry enough diamonds undetectably on his/her naked body to finance a lifetime of opulence.

The result is that ineffective monitoring, weak enforcement against violations, bribery and corruption along the way, and a shifting of concern for the issue to the back burner has led to the weakening of KPCS effectiveness. Global Witness and others have noted that trading in blood diamonds unfortunately continues to fuel violence and human rights atrocities. In fact, the documentation of the Kimberley Process not only will not stop the dealing in blood diamonds, it might make detection of the dealing more difficult.

If you're up to a full exposition of the hellish world of blood diamonds, brace yourself, and read the excellent and gut-wrenching *Blood Diamonds* by Greg Campbell.